Hal Spacejock
Baker's Dough

Book Five in the Hal Spacejock series

www.spacejock.com.au

Cover images copyright depositphotos.com

Stay in touch!

Author's newsletter:
spacejock.com.au/ML.html

facebook.com/halspacejock
twitter.com/spacejock

Works by Simon Haynes

All of Simon's novels* are self-contained, with a beginning, a middle and a proper ending. They're not sequels, they don't end on a cliffhanger, and you can start or end your journey with any book in the series.
Robot vs Dragons series excepted!

The Hal Spacejock series for teens/adults

Set in the distant future, where humanity spans the galaxy and robots are second-class citizens. Includes a large dose of humour!

Hal Spacejock 1: A robot named Clunk
Hal Spacejock 2: Second Course
Hal Spacejock 3: Just Desserts
Hal Spacejock 4: No Free Lunch
Hal Spacejock 5: Baker's Dough
Hal Spacejock 6: Safe Art
Hal Spacejock 7: Big Bang
Hal Spacejock 8: Double Trouble
Hal Spacejock 9: Max Damage
Hal Spacejock 10: Cold Boots (2019)

Also available:
Omnibus One, containing Hal books 1-3
Omnibus Two, containing Hal books 4-6
Omnibus Three, containing Hal books 7-9
Hal Spacejock: Visit, a short story
Hal Spacejock: Framed, a short story
Hal Spacejock: Albion, a novella

The Robot vs Dragons Trilogy.
High fantasy meets low humour!
Each set of three books should be read in order.

1. A Portion of Dragon and Chips
2. A Butt of Heads
3. A Pair of Nuts on the Throne
4. TBA (2019)

The Harriet Walsh series.

Set in the same universe as Hal Spacejock. Good clean fun, written with wry humour. No cliffhangers between novels!

Harriet Walsh 1: Peace Force
Harriet Walsh 2: Alpha Minor
Harriet Walsh 3: Sierra Bravo
Harriet Walsh 4: Storm Force (2019)
Also Available:
Omnibus One, containing books 1-3

The Hal Junior series

Written for all ages, these books are set aboard a space station in the Hal Spacejock universe, only ten years later.

1. Hal Junior: The Secret Signal
2. Hal Junior: The Missing Case
3. Hal Junior: The Gyris Mission
4. Hal Junior: The Comet Caper

Also Available:
Omnibus One, containing books 1-3

The Secret War series.
Gritty space opera for adult readers.

1. Raiders (2019)
2. Frontier (2019)
3. Deadlock (2019)

Collect One-Two - a collection of shorts by Simon Haynes

All titles available in ebook and paperback. Visit spacejock.com.au for details.

HAL SPACEJOCK

BAKER'S DOUGH

SIMON HAYNES

Bowman Press

v 1.05

Published 2012 by Bowman Press

Text © Simon Haynes 2012
Jacket design © Bowman Press 2012

ISBN 978-1-877034-19-0 (Ebook)
ISBN 978-1-877034-13-8 (Paperback)

National Library of Australia Cataloguing-in-Publication entry

Author: Haynes, Simon, 1967-

Title: Hal Spacejock baker's dough / Simon Haynes.

ISBN: 9781877034138 (pbk.)

Dewey Number: A823.4

Dedicated to my family

The *Volante's* flight console held a vast array of controls, laid out in easy reach of the comfortable pilot's chair. This arrangement allowed the huge interstellar freighter to be flown by a single, competent human. With her left hand, a well-trained pilot could work the engines and thrusters, communicate with passing traffic and handle docking manoeuvres. With her right, she could activate the hyperspace motor, control the airlock and toggle the little sign telling passengers to fasten their seat belts.

Unfortunately, the *Volante's* well-trained pilot had departed two weeks earlier, leaving Hal Spacejock at the controls of the 200-tonne ship. Hal didn't know a thrust lever from a cigar lighter, and his version of 'piloting' involved sitting at the console picking holes in the navigation computer's efforts. 'My grandpa could fly faster than this,' he grumbled as the *Volante* rocketed through the atmosphere. 'In fact, if we go any slower we'll fall out of the sky.'

'This is our optimum cruising speed,' said the ship's computer, in a neutral female voice. 'The age and skill of your elderly relatives is irrelevant.'

Hal snorted. 'How long until we land again? Was it ten days or ten weeks?'

'Three minutes and forty-four seconds.' The Navcom hesitated. 'Incidentally, 'again' is inaccurate, since this planet is new to us.'

'How's Clunk doing with the cargo? Has he finished yet?'

'There are still two dozen crates to move to the rear doors.'

'What a waste of time. Why didn't he stack them there in the first place?'

'He did, and they remained there until you applied full reverse thrust.'

Hal touched a lever on the console. 'I thought this stick thing was the cigar lighter?'

'Obviously not. And why would you want the cigar lighter? You don't even smoke.'

'I was going to twizzle the hot end in my coffee to warm it up a bit.' Hal hesitated. 'So, the cargo. Any breakages?'

'Not this time,' said the Navcom, with a note of surprise. 'Incidentally, our landing zone is in visual range.'

'Show me.'

A broad swathe of countryside flashed up on the main screen, complete with lush green fields, narrow country lanes ... and gigantic wind turbines. The *Volante* jinked to the left, narrowly avoiding one set of whirling blades, then blasted right to skim the next. 'Shouldn't we ... you know, fly a bit higher?'

'If we do, ground control will ping you for speeding.'

'If we don't they'll have to bury me in slices.'

Zoom! Another turbine whipped by, the blades so close Hal could have reached out and touched them. His grip tightened on the arms of his chair, and a bead of sweat ran down his face.

0:47

A marquee appeared in the distance, and Hal could see

rows of tables and a big crowd of people. A column of luxury vehicles, decked with white ribbons and bows, was making its way along the narrow lane. The wedding party was arriving!

0:37

Hal swallowed. The job had seemed easy when he signed up for it: deliver fifty crates of party supplies in time for an open-air wedding. Crockery, cutlery, glasses of the finest quality ...brands so exclusive they were rented by the minute. Then there was the food ...delicate pastries, thinly sliced meats, aperitifs and a wedding cake so big you could hollow it out, cut a few windows in the icing and move in. The deadline had been achievable, just, but time had disappeared at an alarming rate. First Hal was convinced they'd be late, but now, with only seconds on the clock, it looked like the wild gamble had paid off.

'ETA thirty seconds,' said the Navcom.

They were going to make it! Elated, Hal pumped his fist. He'd shown them! No, he *would* show them! 'Give me manual control.'

'That is ...inadvisable.'

'Advise all you like. It's an order.' Hal took hold of the stick. 'I'm going to deliver this stuff in style.'

'Pull that lever and you'll deliver it on the guests,' remarked the Navcom.

'I don't understand. This was the flight stick last time.'

'A recent upgrade reconfigured my controls.' The Navcom hesitated. 'Would you like to enable tool tips?'

'Sure, if it'll help.'

'Tool tips enabled.'

Hal stretched his hand out and pointed to a large red button. 'Console,' said the Navcom.

Hal moved his hand to the left, hovering over a small screen.

'Console,' said the Navcom again.

Hal waved his hand over a bank of switches.

'Console. Console. Console.'

'This tool tip business . . . it's not very precise, is it?'

'It's a basic aide-memoire for inexperienced pilots.'

Hal sat back and folded his arms.

'Chair,' said the Navcom.

Hal moved his hand to the right.

'Floor,' said the Navcom helpfully. 'Armrest. Leg. Inner thigh. Scro–'

Hal moved his hand away.

'Knee.'

'I know you're winding me up.' Hal tapped the side of his head. 'I can sense it.'

'Blank media detected,' said the Navcom.

Hal's eyes narrowed.

'The flight stick is third from the left,' said the Navcom quickly.

Hal reached for it.

'Console,' said the Navcom.

'Switch that nonsense off.'

'Tool tips disabled. Would you like to submit user experience feedback to the manufacturer?'

'How's this for feedback?' Hal shoved the throttle forward and slammed the stick to one side, using far more force than he intended. The engines roared, the deck creaked, and the *Volante* flipped over and over in a series of tight barrel rolls. Hal's eyes felt like they were spinning on stalks, and the marquee, the cars and all the upturned faces blurred as the ship spun along its axis. 'A-auto land,' he shouted desperately, and the Navcom took over. The spinning stopped, and the ship came round in a rivet-straining turn, plonking down on a vacant patch of grass. The engines cut out, and in the sudden silence Hal could just hear the faint tinkle-tinkle-tinkle as they cooled down.

'Landing successful,' said the Navcom. 'Welcome to planet Greil.'

On the console, the clock showed 0:01.

◆

Hal staggered to the airlock and activated the passenger ramp, which unfurled towards the ground. Down below, in the *Volante's* shadow, a line of catering staff were standing to attention with anti-gravity trolleys at the ready. Their heads tilted further and further back as the ramp descended towards them, and they scattered as it came down like an oversized fly swatter.

Hal jogged down the ramp, which bounced and swayed under his heavy tread. 'Round the back,' he called to the staff, who were still trying to retrieve the skittish trolleys. Hal made for the nearest landing leg and flipped open the cover, revealing a control panel. He pressed the lower button, and there was a loud *hiss!* as the cargo ramp extended. By now, the staff had sorted themselves out, and they'd just assembled at the rear of the ship when they saw the huge cargo ramp bearing down on them. They scattered again, hover-trolleys zooming off in all directions.

Once the ramp thudded down, Hal switched to the door controls. He was a bit surprised Clunk hadn't got there first, then realised the robot was probably shifting boxes around.

Groan!

The doors shivered but refused to open. Hal frowned. The *Volante* was a new ship, not prone to failures. What was the matter with the things? Puzzled, he tried again.

Grooooaaan! Creeaak!

Hal noticed the dishevelled catering staff were looking to him for reassurance, so he wiped the worried look from his face and gave them a confident wave. Then he mashed his thumb on the button.

Click, click, CLICK! WHOOSH!

The doors sprang open, and a torrent of glass, wood fragments and pottery shards flooded out, slithering down the ramp and spreading across the grass in a crystal avalanche. The slithering finally ceased, and Hal gaped at the mess in shock. The implications had barely registered when a battered bronze robot staggered from the hold. Actually, 'bronze' was no longer accurate, since Clunk was covered from head to toe in sparkling fragments, and he looked more like an arthritic vampire than a nimble robot. Still, Hal was happy to see him whatever his chosen disguise. Clunk was calm, capable and wise, and he'd know exactly what to do in this situation.

'What blithering *human* took the controls while I was shifting cargo?' shouted Clunk, using maximum amplification. Birds fled, catering staff cowered, and several hundred metres away the wedding guests winced and pressed gloved hands to their ears.

Still cursing at full volume, Clunk stomped down the ramp, shedding pottery and glass. Super-heated air shimmered around his cooling vents, and underneath the sparkly layer his expression was a mix of rage and exasperation. Hal took one look and raced up the passenger ramp to the flight deck. He was halfway there when the airlock door slammed, cutting him off. He turned to run back down again, but Clunk was already at the foot of the ramp.

'Hi, Clunk!' said Hal, feigning surprise. 'Bit of a bumpy landing, wasn't it? I was just going to speak to the Navcom about it.'

'Mr Spacejock, not only have you ruined the cargo and destroyed this couple's wedding, you have also made a laughing stock of your already shaky reputation.' Clunk advanced up the ramp. 'Furthermore, thanks to your woeful flying skills, I just endured a spin cycle with fifty crates of fragile goods.'

'Woeful?' Hal frowned. 'Skilful, you mean. Six barrel rolls and a one-eighty, handled like a pro.'

'You pulled that stunt on *purpose*?' hissed Clunk.

'I just wanted to arrive in style!' They were face to face now, and Hal could only stare in fascination. The robot's entire head was coated in glittering fragments, held in place by a layer of sticky jam. His eyes burned through the frosting like heated coals, and there was a chocolate truffle stuck to the end of his nose. It fell off with a 'plop', and Hal made his second mistake of the day: he laughed.

Clunk's eyes narrowed, and his fists bunched with a creak. He stepped forward, and Hal realised it was all over: He was about to be flattened by a two-legged wedding cake. 'No, wait! Look on the bright side. We met the deadline!'

'Yes, with a ruined cargo!'

'It might need a bit of assembly, but we got it here on the dot.'

Clunk snorted in disbelief, blowing glass fragments out of his nostrils. 'You can't possibly claim *this* as a successful delivery.'

'Oh no? They said it had to be here on time. Nobody said anything about the condition.'

'But –'

Hal wagged his finger. 'You're always telling me to read the contract, right? Check for yourself.'

'But –'

'Come on, let's go.' Hal jerked his thumb towards the rear of the ship. 'Leave the doors open. The rest will drop out when we take off.'

◆

Hal sat in the flight deck, arms firmly crossed and feet firmly planted on the floor. Clunk had just left to clean himself up, and his warnings were still ringing in Hal's ears. Don't speak and don't touch anything. Don't even think about it. Just ... don't do anything.

The ship cruised towards the spaceport with the Navcom firmly in control. Everything was calm and peaceful.

After a couple of minutes Hal cleared his throat.

'I wouldn't,' said the Navcom.

'I was just going to ask the time!'

'Time to keep quiet.'

Hal frowned, then ... 'Show me a list of cargo jobs.'

'Unable to comply. Controls are locked.'

'I don't want the controls. I want information.'

'Information is locked. Everything is locked. I'm not allowed to listen to you.'

'Oh, go on! It's just a list of cargo jobs. Where's the harm in that?'

'I don't know, but I'm sure you'll find it.' The Navcom relented. 'Monitor three.'

'Thanks.' Hal leant forward to study the display, putting his elbows on the console. 'That wasn't me!' he said, in the sudden darkness.

'You're lucky it wasn't the hyperdrive,' said the Navcom.

The lights came back on, and Hal leant forward awkwardly, keeping well clear of the console. He studied the screen, and his mood brightened when he saw the impressive list of cargo jobs. 'Just wait until Clunk sees that lot.'

The lift pinged, and Hal cleared the screen and sat back in his chair, carefully folding his arms. Clunk entered, freshly scrubbed, and strode to the console. 'What did you touch?'

'Nothing,' said Hal.

Clunk sniffed. 'Navcom, show me a list of cargo jobs.'

'I bet there are loads,' said Hal. 'In fact, I bet you a hundred credits.'

'You're on.'

Hal grinned, and when the screen filled with data, he allowed himself a big smile. 'I told you this planet would be good for us.'

'Look closer,' said Clunk shortly.

Hal eyed the first few jobs, then stared. Under 'conditions' every one of them said 'No Spacejock'. 'What does that mean?'

'It means you owe me a hundred credits.'

'How did they ... '

'The wedding party are connected. And there's more. The groom is an executive with Garmit and Hash. I believe you've heard of them?'

Hal groaned. He'd bought his first ship with a G&H loan, still unpaid, and the only reason debt collectors weren't kicking down the *Volante's* airlock door was because the company thought he was dead. 'Aren't there any jobs we can do?'

Clunk relaxed the search filters, and two lines of data appeared.

'That'll do,' said Hal. 'How many jobs do we need, anyway?'

'The first is a search-and-retrieve mission. We're to locate a deposed dictator, fight our way through thousands of heavily-armed fanatics, and bring her back unharmed.'

'Could be tricky.'

'It's not really our thing, is it?' Clunk glanced at him. 'Unless, of course, we soften up her troops with a dusting of broken glass.'

Hal winced. 'What about the other one?'

'It involves transportation to planet Barwenna,' began Clunk cautiously. 'It seems a passenger –'

'No,' said Hal immediately. Deep inside, an old scar ached.

'There's nothing else, Mr Spacejock.'

'I don't care. No passengers.'

Clunk sighed. 'In that case, it seems we're on vacation.'

'Good, because I need a drink.'

'Are you sure that's wise? Drowning your sorrows –'

Hal frowned. 'For your information, I'm going to the pub to pick up some work.'

'Knowing planet Greil, that's not the only thing you'll pick up.'

2

Greil City, 6 p.m.

Hal strode towards the pub, still smarting. Clunk should have known better than to mention passengers again! It was only, what, two weeks since Harriet Walsh had left them? Three wonderful months in her company, exploring and trading the galaxy, had ended with a bombshell: Harriet decided the cargo business wasn't her thing after all. Within days she'd departed for the Peace Force academy, leaving the ship dark and empty by comparison.

Hal heard a burst of laughter, and with a start he realised he was standing outside the pub. The doors were open and there was a jolly, good-natured crowd polishing off huge tankards of beer. Hal hesitated. He really couldn't face cheerful and happy, but on the other hand they needed a job.

'Come in, lad,' said a big man standing in the doorway, spraying foam from his bushy beard. 'Plenty of booze for all!'

Resigned, Hal pushed his way inside.

'You're a pilot, right?'

Hal turned to see a short, elderly man at his elbow. There was a tall, bronze robot standing behind him, and for a second Hal thought it was Clunk. It was an identical model, but he realised the stains, scratches, dents and scorch marks were in different places. 'Sure, I'm a pilot.'

'Are you taking passengers, my good man?'

'Sorry, no.'

The man gripped his elbow. 'I'm willing to pay good money.'

'And I said no,' snapped Hal.

'Very well. I'll make other arrangements.'

Hal made his way to the bar, where he ordered a fruit juice.

The bartender was a tall robot with one arm. He whipped up Hal's drink then leant across the counter. 'You're a pilot, aren't you?'

'Yeah.'

'You, er, don't take passengers, do you?'

'No.'

'Pity.'

Hal took his drink. 'Do you know of any cargo jobs?'

'Not around here. Have you tried the spaceport?'

'That's next on the list.' Hal found an empty seat, and he'd barely stretched out his legs when a young woman appeared at his side.

'Excuse me,' she said. 'What would you charge to take me and my robot to –'

Hal didn't even look round. 'I'm not a pilot, I'm a mechanic.'

'Sorry, I . . . never mind.'

Over the next hour, Hal was approached by a dozen patrons. At first he just snapped at them, but after a while he worked out a much better plan: get them to buy him a drink, *then* snap at them.

Finally, two hours later, he pushed back all the empty glasses and stood up. Conversations stopped, and there was a sullen hush as he left the pub. Stuff 'em, he thought. He'd told 'em enough times. No passengers!

Once clear of the pub, Hal strode the narrow alleys, splashing through puddles as he headed towards the spaceport. He hadn't gone far before he heard a faint cry up ahead.

'Help! Help me someone!'

Hal broke into a run, his boots sending spray high into the air.

'Help!' said the voice again. 'Please help!'

When Hal rounded the corner he saw an elderly gentleman sitting against the wall, head in his hands. Nearby, a battered old robot lay flat on its back, its legs pedalling thin air. Hal thought they looked familiar, then realised the old boy had been the first to approach him in the pub. 'What's going on?' he demanded.

'I was mugged,' said the old gent. 'They tried to take my wallet, but I fended them off.'

Hal helped him up. 'Are you hurt?'

'No, just winded.'

'We'd better call the Peace Force. They might be able to catch these guys.'

The old man shook his head. 'No point. The Peace Force are useless.'

'Not all of them,' said Hal, with a frown. 'Some of them are pretty good.'

'Anyway, I didn't get a good look at their faces. They had masks on, and they didn't say anything, and my eyesight isn't very good.'

Hal helped the robot to its feet. 'You two shouldn't walk about on your own, not round here.'

'I see that now, but alas, I have nowhere to go.' The elderly man gave him a sidelong glance. 'You're that pilot, aren't you?'

Hal sighed.

'Is your ship at the spaceport? Are you leaving soon?'

'Yes, and we're not going anywhere. We just got here.'

The old man looked hopeful. 'Would it be possible to stay aboard, just for the night?'

Hal hesitated. He couldn't leave this old coot to get mugged, and letting the guy sleep aboard wasn't the same as taking on passengers.

'I'll pay you for your trouble.'

'No need for that,' said Hal gruffly. 'Come on, I'll show you the way.'

◆

Hal escorted the old gent and his robot across the landing field, his skin still burning from the spaceport's body scanners. He was surprised to see the *Volante*'s cargo ramp extended, and even more surprised to see a rust-streaked shipping container being manoeuvred into the hold. Clunk was hovering nearby, watching closely, and when he spotted Hal a look of relief crossed his squashy, furrowed face. 'Thank goodness you're back, Mr Spacejock.'

'What's up, Clunk?'

'I secured a freight job,' said the robot proudly, indicating the shipping container. 'It's a box of antique furniture parts. Quite a generous payment.'

'Nothing illegal?'

'Completely above board.'

'Cash up front?'

Clunk averted his eyes. 'On delivery.'

Hal sighed. 'What about fuel?'

'We just have enough.' Clunk noticed the elderly man and his battered robot. 'I see you picked up some friends.'

'I said we'd put them up for the night.'

'That's impossible. We have to leave immediately if we're to meet the deadline.'

Hal turned to the old man. 'I'm sorry, but it looks like we're off.'

'What am I supposed to do?'

'Maybe you can ask at the trade desk. Someone else might have a berth.'

The old man gazed around the empty field. A lone cricket chirruped in the darkness, and the wind made eddies in the dust as it passed over the vacant landing pads. 'Don't worry about me. I'm sure I'll find something.'

Hal felt a pang of remorse, but what could he do? He had a business to run.

'Come on, Mr Spacejock,' said Clunk. 'They've finished loading. We must seal the ship and plot a course for Barwenna.'

The old man started. 'You're going to Barwenna? Really?'

'Why, is there something wrong with the place?' demanded Hal. 'Deadly war games? Assassination plots? Chemicals in the water?'

'My dear sir, it's nothing like that. I've been seeking passage to Barwenna for the past week, and nobody will take me.' The old man cast a longing look at the ship. 'It's such a shame you don't carry passengers.'

Hal knew when he was beaten, but he was still running a business. 'How much are you offering?'

'What little I've managed to scrape together over the years.'

'I'm sure it's enough,' said Clunk. 'After all, we're going there anyway.'

Hal closed his eyes. How many times had he told Clunk to upgrade his bartering software? Now they'd get fifty credits ... if they were lucky.

'Is a thousand credits enough?'

Hal's eyes snapped open. 'You can have one of our brand new cabins, and Clunk will turn your bunk down and see to any other needs. Clunk, do we have any of those little chocolates to put on the pillow?'

'No, you ate them all.'

'Order some more. And you'd better print up a dinner menu for our guest. Break out some of that special paper with the silver thread.'

Clunk saluted. 'Will do, Mr Spacejock.'

'Right, that's settled. Please, step aboard, Mr ... er ... '

'The name's Cuff.' The elderly man put his hand out. 'You can call me Hans.'

3

After a perfect lift-off the *Volante* powered through space, heading for the designated hyperspace point. With such an important passenger on board Hal insisted on flying the ship, despite the strict conditions in their brand new insurance policy. Clunk hovered at his elbow like a nervous parent, even though lifting off wasn't a major deal: you just pressed the large green button marked 'Take Off'. Or, after the Navcom's latest update, the small yellow button labelled 'Waste Disposal'.

Once they were clear of the planet - and thus unlikely to collide with it - Clunk locked the controls and left to do his rounds. Hal made himself a drink and put his feet up on the flight console. 'Navcom, do you have anything on this Barwonica place?'

'Barwenna is the only habitable planet in the Terato system. It was colonised two hundred years ago by migrant families, and a thriving city developed on the site of the original settlement. Its chief export is timber, and the major import is logging equipment.'

'You'd think they'd make their own.'

'Due to strict environmental controls, steel fabrication is forbidden.'

'Fair enough.' Hal remembered their cargo. 'Isn't it a bit odd, flying in a container of wooden furniture?'

'The manifest lists antique furniture parts,' said the Navcom. 'There's no mention of timber.'

'You're right. It could be the springs and bolts and what not.'

'Very likely.' The Navcom hesitated. 'There's a minor temperature variation in the starboard generator. Do you want to inspect it?'

'Tell Clunk to handle it.'

'Clunk is busy.'

'I'm not babysitting a sensor. I've just poured a nice hot coffee.'

There was a buzz from the console. 'Mr Cuff would like to see you.'

Hal jumped up smartly. At a thousand credits a pop he'd swig cold coffee all day long. 'Tell him I'll be right there.'

In the lift, he pressed the lowest of the three buttons. It didn't match the first two and there was a scruffy handwritten label underneath, but Hal cracked a smile whenever he saw it. The *Volante* was a Gamma class freighter, variant L. When Hal discovered the superior XL model had three decks, despite having the same external dimensions, he pestered Clunk until he got to the truth: Gamma class ships were all built to the same specs, but the cheaper models had the lower deck masked off.

After that Hal pestered Clunk some more, until the robot finally agreed to open up the hidden level. Unfortunately, it was a mess: girders with rough welds, plate metal with ragged edges, rubbish left over from the ship's construction and a thick layer of dust. Even so, when Hal closed his eyes he could picture the ideal fit-out: plush carpets, mood lighting, comfy sofas and a drinks waiter, along with a modern AutoChef to replace the bad-tempered version in the rec room. He could also imagine a video screen so wide it could display the entire cast of 'The Intergalactic Wrestling Troupe' in a single shot. Actually, he wasn't fussed if it cropped a few of the smaller cast members, as long as the screen was bigger than that of his long-term rival, Kent Spearman.

Unfortunately, their budget wouldn't cover a simple drinks trolley, let alone the rest of his fantasy. This explained the jury-rigged control panel in the lift, with the handwritten label and mismatched buttons. Still, it was a small price to pay for gaining a level.

The doors opened, and Hal's smile disappeared. It was amazing what Clunk had achieved with a pile of old timber, a job lot of blunt nails and a few litres of day-glo paint, but it wasn't exactly Hal's dream retreat.

A cracked light fitting sparked overhead, and Hal ducked to avoid a loop of electrical cable. The bright orange dividing wall was pierced with an oval doorway, chosen not for aesthetic reasons but because oval doors were cheaper than rectangular ones, and beyond that a narrow passage led past the cabins. Hal could see light under - and over, and through - Cuff's door, which wasn't surprising since Clunk had cut it out of thick cardboard.

He raised his hand and tapped on Cuff's door, knocking gently so as not to punch a hole right through it.

The old man pulled the door open, almost tearing it off its hinges. 'Mr Spacejock, thanks for your time.'

'No trouble at all.'

'Won't you please come in? I have a little proposition for you.'

Hal entered the cabin. 'I hope everything is to your satisfaction?'

Cuff glanced around as though noticing the tatty furniture for the first time. 'It's comfortable enough.'

'No muggers, at any rate.' Hal eyed Cuff's robot. He believed in keeping old tech going for as long as possible, but you had to draw the line somewhere. This robot looked like it had limped over the line five or ten years earlier and was still hobbling for all it was worth.

'I see you noticed my pride and joy,' said Cuff warmly. 'I live for that robot, Mr Spacejock. Absolutely adore it.'

Hal wondered why he was laying it on so thick. Cuff had barely glanced at the thing after the mugging.

'However, I didn't bring you here to discuss Freddie.' Cuff sat on the bed, which creaked alarmingly. 'At twelve tomorrow I have a crucial business meeting, and it's vital to my financial future. Do you understand?'

'Vital meeting at twelve. Got it.'

'Afterwards, with a sum of money in my possession, I shall be a tempting target.'

Hal glanced at the battered robot, then at Cuff's meagre belongings. 'I don't suppose you have a sum of money in your possession now? For your fare, I mean.'

Cuff shook his head. 'Not until the meeting.'

Hal's eyes narrowed. Fantastic . . . another charity case. 'Mr Cuff, we need your fare to cover our fuel bill. Without it, Clunk and I will be stranded on Barwenna.'

'You will be paid. I give you my word.'

Hal eyed the robot. It was in poor condition, but it had to be worth something. 'When we land you can leave that behind as collateral. As soon as the money comes through –'

Cuff sprang up. 'That's out of the question!' he shouted, his face red. 'I would never leave my treasured robot, never!'

'Okay, okay. Calm down!'

'I'm sorry. Freddie and I have been together a long time.' Cuff ran a hand over his face. 'Look, I understand you're worried about your fee, but I promise you'll get every credit. What's more, I want to discuss an extension to our little arrangement.'

'Go on.'

Cuff cleared his throat. 'Tell me, are you staying on Barwenna long? After we land, I mean?'

'Not likely. Dump this cargo, find a new job, and off we go.'

'I see.'

'Why do you ask?'

Cuff hesitated. 'Barwenna and I have an unpleasant history. Last time I visited, a conman relieved me of my wallet before I cleared customs. My luggage disappeared before I reached the hotel.'

'You want me and Clunk to track this crook down for you?' Hal drove a fist into the palm of his hand with a meaty smack. 'Sort him out? Get your stuff back?'

'No, this was years ago. I just want you to understand why I'm nervous about visiting this planet.'

Not just Barwenna, thought Hal. Cuff attracted muggers like robots attracted ... well, magnets.

Cuff continued. 'I want my visit concluded with as little fuss as possible so I can return home. That's where you come in.'

Hal looked confused. 'Come in where? Your home?'

'No, I need someone to shield me from the criminal element during my visit. I want to employ you as minders.'

'Bodyguards? Us?'

'Your robot is strong, and you seem a handy young man. An elderly gentleman travelling alone is an easy target, but you two would deter all but the most well-armed thugs.' Cuff looked at him earnestly. 'I'd be willing to pay an extra five thousand credits.'

'Five grand!' exclaimed Hal.

'I'd want absolute loyalty and commitment. If a situation develops, I want you to act without thinking.'

'Oh, that's guaranteed.'

'The way I see it, a generous payment will ensure you both stand by my side.'

'And the meeting? What's that all about?'

'It's a private matter, but it involves a large sum of money.'

'How do you know we're on the level? For all you know Clunk and I could be a pair of murderers.'

'I'm a good judge of character. Now, I'd like a nap before we land. Perhaps you could discuss my offer with your robot while you're hurrying the ship towards our destination?'

Hal took the hint and got up.

'There's one more thing,' said Cuff. 'This meeting tomorrow ...If I miss it, I'll sue you for everything you have.'

4

When Hal returned to the flight deck he found Clunk browsing twenty or thirty columns of small print on the main screen. The list was packed with odd items like 'left ancillary bucket nut' and 'right papillary egress duct', and most of the prices ran to four figures. 'What the hell is that?'

'My wish list.' Clunk gestured at the screen. 'If I came into some money, this is what I'd spend it on.'

Hal whistled as he saw the total. 'You could buy a decent robot for that amount.'

'Your point is noted,' said Clunk frostily.

'I didn't mean ...I meant ...' Hal changed the subject. 'Listen, I've just been speaking to our passenger and he wants a couple of bodyguards.'

'Very well, I'll have the Navcom run a business search. Armed or unarmed?'

'Neither. He wants us.'

'What an outrageous suggestion! You're a freighter pilot with very little in the way of defensive skills. In the wrong situation you could easily lose your life.'

'He's offering five grand for the day.'

Clunk eyed his wish list. 'When you think about it, the security business is all about *perceived* threats. It doesn't require much training, and danger levels aren't really that high.'

'Good, because I said yes.'

'Excellent.' Clunk hesitated. 'I'm a bit concerned by the amount of money he's offering.'

'If you think you can get more, go put the squeeze on him.'

'I mean it's a very large sum. Why so much?'

'He lost his wallet to a mugger last time he was here, and he doesn't want it to happen again.'

'Mr Spacejock, I doubt that gentleman's wallet holds five credits, never mind five thousand.'

Hal gestured impatiently. 'What's the worst that can happen? If we spend a day with him and he doesn't pay up, we'll just lose a bit of time. On the other hand, if he does stump up it'll be the easiest cash ever.'

'But –'

'It's all gravy, Clunk. Most times we're lucky to get paid once. Now we're doing a freight job, a passenger job and a minding job all in the same trip.' Hal patted the robot on the shoulder. 'Trust me, we can't lose.'

◆

They'd been flying for a couple of hours, and Hal was alone in the flight deck. The distant roar of the engines barely registered this far from the rear of the *Volante*, and with the ship on autopilot there was nothing for him to do. So much for the riveting life of a space pilot. Hal crossed to the rear of the flight deck where a vibrant orange coffee maker sat in pride of place. He twirled knobs and pressed buttons, and when his coffee was ready he carried it back to the console. 'Anything happening, Navcom?'

'I downloaded a news bulletin. Would you like to see it?'

'How much does it cost?'

'Nothing at all. It's sponsored by . . . *pssssst*. Sponsored by . . . *fsssssssh*. Sponsored by . . . . *mggggg* and the people who brought you *graaaaaak*.'

Hal suppressed a grin. Clunk's ad-blocking script was illegal, but very effective.

'Would you like the local bulletin?' repeated the Navcom.

'Sure. Go ahead.'

'It's sponsored by . . . *psssssst*.'

'I'll be sure to buy all their products. Now play the news.' Hal settled in his chair as a lively theme tune blasted from the speakers. The music faded and a starched-looking presenter came on.

'First up this morning, more news on the drama surrounding the Baker legacy. Two weeks ago we revealed that Mr Kim Baker, the wealthy industrialist who passed away earlier this year, left his fortune to an elderly robot. The catch? Nobody has seen this robot for three decades!'

Hal smiled to himself. If the robot had any brains it would have disguised itself as a limo or uploaded itself into a computer. If it were still walking around, it'd be the target of every conman and lowlife in the galaxy, all eager to share in its good fortune.

'The missing robot was built on Barwenna in a batch of twelve, and although the original plans have long since disappeared, our panel of experts will now attempt to unearth the fate of Baker's dozen. But first, these important messages.'

Hal switched feeds, flicking through half a dozen channels before stopping to watch a 2,000-year-old mouse defending the latest changes to the copyright act. The animation finished with a catchy jingle, and Hal switched back to the news.

'As promised we've prepared a special report on Baker's legacy. But first a story which affects us all. Yes, a live cross to the society wedding of the century, which was ruined by an out-of-control delivery man. Our reporter has an exclusive interview, and we'll bring you this chilling story right after a short break.'

'Far out.' Hal gestured, cutting the feed. 'That's ten minutes of my life I'll never get back.'

'You did ask to see the news.'

'Not human interest stories! I wanted news about free stuff. Discounts. Special offers.'

'You told me never to present special offers under any circumstances. You were most explicit.'

'So were the offers you kept showing me,' muttered Hal. 'Anyway, I want real special offers, not the fake ones. Stuff like free fuel, free food and free accommodation.'

'Understood.'

'Well, go on, then.'

'I don't have any.'

'Figures.' Hal fiddled with the controls. 'How much longer to Barwonica?'

'Barwenna.'

'Whatever.'

'ETA is three hours.'

'Can we boost things along a bit?'

'This is the *Volante's* most efficient cruising speed. Any faster and our fuel usage goes through the roof.'

'Any slower and I'll die of old age,' grumbled Hal. 'If only Clunk had built the third deck into a proper lounge instead of passenger cabins.'

'Clunk wasn't trying to spite you.'

'I know, I know. It's a money issue.' Hal sighed. 'The only way I'm getting that widescreen is if someone leaves me a ton of cash in their will.'

'It's a pity you're not a robot.'

Hal was about to toss the rest of his coffee back when two and two suddenly became four. An old robot? An important meeting on Barwenna? Suddenly coming into a large sum of money? It had to be Cuff ... their passenger! 'Navcom, play that news story back.'

The screen flickered into life, showing a large pile of broken glass. 'I'm here at the wedding of the century, where –'

'Not that one! The robot story, quick!'

A talking head appeared. 'The missing robot was built on Barwenna in a batch of twelve, and although the original plans have long since disappeared, our panel of experts will now attempt to unearth the fate of Baker's dozen.'

'Where's the panel?' demanded Hal, as the screen blanked out. 'What did they find out?'

'Nothing. The rest of the program involved three simuloids reading public domain articles on inheritance law.'

'Can you dig anything up yourself?'

The Navcom hesitated. 'Long distance data charges are very high. Should I wait until we land?'

'No, find out what you can. Clunk was right, five grand is way too much for a simple minding job. If Cuff is coming into millions, we'll be facing heavily armed gangsters.'

◆

Hal found Clunk in the cargo hold, sweeping up the last of the broken glass. The robot's jaw was set, and he didn't turn at Hal's approach. 'What is it?'

'I was just watching a news item about an old robot.'

'Fascinating. What did they do to this one?'

'Nothing. Stop that and listen, will you?'

'I'm perfectly capable of multitasking.'

'Okay, so there was this news item about a rich guy leaving his fortune to an old robot.'

'It's nice to know *some* people care. But why is this news story so important?'

'I reckon our passenger is heading to Barwenna to claim the inheritance.'

Clunk blinked. 'That's a bit of a leap. And if so, why didn't he mention it?'

'He's keeping a low profile, putting people off the scent.'

'Yes, but ...'

Hal decided to play his trump card. 'He told me he's coming into some cash tomorrow. That's how he's paying our fare ...out of the inheritance. It all fits together!'

'So did the glassware, before you put on your little air show.' Clunk leant on the broom, which creaked alarmingly. 'Mr Spacejock, you have to admit you're prone to little misunderstandings from time to time. This may be another.'

'What about the bodyguards? He's offering five grand, remember?'

'The facts lend some weight to your theory, but I'm inclined to regard them as coincidences. For example, Mr Cuff may be settling a completely unrelated matter with his solicitor.'

'And his robot?'

'There are many robots in the galaxy, and the chances of our passenger owning the one in question are astronomically slim.

Anyway, if you're so sure about this, why don't you ask the robot?'

'I can't. It doesn't talk.' Hal rubbed his chin. 'I was just thinking ... '

'Yes?'

'If you went down to the third deck, you could try communicating with it. You robots have a secret messaging protocol, don't you?'

'Yes, it's called a radio, and I tried it at the spaceport.'

'Well?'

'Mr Cuff's robot isn't broadcasting, and when I transmitted a query, it ignored me.' Clunk stood up and readied the broom. 'Now, if you'll excuse me I'd like to finish this job. Unless, of course, you'd care to help?'

'But –'

'Mr Spacejock, all this conjecture serves no purpose. I suggest you forget your theories until tomorrow, when you'll find out either way.'

5

Barwenna City, 4 p.m.

David Fisher angled his car into the parking slot, holding the controls steady while the vehicle settled on the ground. As the engine note faded to silence, he pocketed his watch, removed a gold ring from his pinky, and threw his leather jacket into the back seat. Next, he opened the glove box and took out a roll of fabric tied with a frayed ribbon. He undid the roll and selected a gleaming screwdriver, testing the sharpened point with his thumb. Satisfied, he slipped the screwdriver into his waistband and put the roll back, tying it carefully before locking the compartment.

Fisher glanced at the rear view screen, studying his appearance with a critical eye. His hair was tousled, and his five o'clock shadow was coming along nicely. To complete the ensemble, he donned a ragged denim jacket and slipped on a pair of old sneakers.

He could have prepared before leaving home, but it wasn't worth the risk. His building bristled with nosey old crones, all of them with the local Peace Force on speed dial, and at the sight of his scruffy outfit they'd have the law on him in seconds. Explaining took time, and time was money.

Fisher waved a bus down and waited for the scanner to read

his eye. 'Norton Street,' he said, and the doors opened. The bus was empty, but he didn't take a seat. Hardly worth it.

Five minutes later, the bus turned into a street lined with neat little houses. Some of the gardens needed work, and there were patches of faded paint here and there. The overall impression was a nice area which was slowly going to seed. Fisher glanced at the address he'd written down and strolled towards the house in question. The shed door was hanging from the upper hinge, and inside he could see a couple of old bikes with perished tyres. Antiques, possibly valuable, but there wasn't a market for them.

The door opened before he could knock, and an elderly lady looked out. 'Are you here about the robot?'

'Yes, ma'am.'

'Come inside, please do.' The old lady held the door open, and Fisher walked past her, wrinkling his nose at the smell of boiled cabbage and cat food. 'It's just along the hall. First door on the right.'

Fisher stepped over a cat lying in the middle of the polished floor. It looked up at him with baleful green eyes, not moving a muscle even when his sneaker thudded down next to its tail.

'Don't mind Emerald. She's no trouble.'

'I won't,' said Fisher. 'Tell me, is anyone else home?'

'No, just me,' said the old lady. 'I'm sorry, I didn't catch your name.'

'It's David.'

'I'm Lily. Lily Turner.'

'Pleasure to meet you.' Fisher took the first door, which led to a sitting room crammed with furniture. Huge armchairs jostled with coffee tables, and every surface was filled with bric-a-brac and photos in cheap plastic frames. He ignored the lot, fastening his gaze on the gleaming robot standing in the corner. It was a silver XG98 model, humanoid in shape, and its face was frozen into a broad grin.

'I always keep him well polished,' said Lily. 'He liked to shine. Quite vain, really.'

Fisher grasped the screwdriver under his jacket, the handle comfortable in his grip. 'He's in good condition. A credit to your care.'

'As I said in the advert, he's been perfect ever since my husband - rest his soul - brought him home from the shop. Must be thirty years now if it's a day. Then, one morning, I found him lying in bed, quite stiff.'

'I'm sorry for your loss.'

'Eh?' Lily looked confused. 'Oh, not my husband. I was talking about Paul. That's what I call, er ... ' She motioned vaguely towards the silent, smiling figure in the corner.

Fisher approached the robot. 'May I look inside?'

'Of course. I'm sure it's nothing serious, but the repair people wouldn't even look at him. Said he was too old.' Lily sniffed. 'The man was very rude.'

Fisher used the sharpened screwdriver to pop the chest cover, working carefully so as not to scratch the metal. Inside, the compartment was packed with fluff.

'Oh my,' exclaimed Lily. 'I never cleaned in there!'

'It's usually best if you don't,' said Fisher. 'You can make things worse if you poke around.' He brushed dust from the circuit board, studying the fine print etched into the surface, and he couldn't help smiling when he made out the digits at the end: One point six five. Bingo! He replaced the cover, and by the time he turned to face the old lady his face was a study of regret. 'I'm sorry, I don't think I can take it after all.'

'Oh, but you said ... '

'I really am sorry,' said Fisher gently. 'I was hoping it

would be a simple fix, but the neural interface is shot and the linguistics module is frozen. The parts alone ... ' He spread his hands.

'A-are you sure?' The old lady looked at the floor. 'The money would be useful, you see.'

'I understand completely.' Fisher hesitated. 'There is one thing.'

'Yes?'

'I know someone with a similar model. The insides are all right, but the limbs ... ' Fisher left the words hanging. 'An accident, you understand.'

'How awful.'

'Now, if I bought his damaged robot I could use the parts to mend one like yours, where the insides aren't any good. The problem is, I wasn't expecting to buy two robots. My budget really won't stretch.'

'How much can you pay?'

'My friend wants two hundred for his, and you're asking six for Paul here. Add in all the extra work and I really can't offer you more than three.'

Lily pursed her lips. Fisher could see her internal struggle, but he knew exactly when to shut up.

'Three hundred, you say. Would that be cash?'

'Certainly.'

The old lady nodded. 'Very well. I suppose it's for the best.'

It was all Fisher could do not to smile. He put his hand in his pocket and brought out three credit tiles, carefully checked and placed there earlier.

'Do you need a receipt?' said Lily, as she took the money.

'Yes, please. Proof of ownership and all that.'

'Very well, I'll ... Oh!'

'What is it?'

Lily held out a tile. 'I think you made a mistake. This one's a twenty.'

Fisher took the tile, then made a show of searching his pockets. He ended up with a motley collection of small change. 'I could have sworn some of these were hundreds. Where does the money go, eh?'

'Don't you have any more?'

'Doesn't look like it. There's the two hundred I gave you, plus the twenty, and this lot makes two-fifty all up. I'm really sorry.'

'There's a bank just up the road.'

Fisher pulled a face. 'I only get paid once a month, and it's two weeks until pay day.'

Lily eyed his old shoes and his worn denim jacket. 'Let's just say two-fifty. I want this over with.'

Fisher handed over the money, murmuring apologies. He waited while Lily wrote out a receipt, then pocketed the paperwork and returned to the robot.

'How are you going to move him?' asked Lily.

'They have an emergency mode,' said Fisher. 'It locks the knees, and you can move them by pushing. I'll just see if I can ...ah, there you go!'

With a little help from Fisher, the robot strode across the room, moving with a stiff-legged gait.

Lily watched the robot's progress, concern etched on her face. 'You will look after him, won't you? He's been in the family for years.'

'Of course I will.' Fisher smiled reassuringly. 'He's part of my family now!'

He guided the robot through the doorway and manoeuvred it down the hall, the big flat feet thudding on the polished timber. Emerald the cat took one look and bolted for safety, claws scrabbling for purchase.

At the front door, Fisher shook hands, pretending not to notice as Lily dabbed her eyes with a handkerchief. Transaction complete, he set off for the bus stop with his new purchase.

◆

Fisher guided the robot out of the elevator and aimed it towards his apartment. His floor was home to half a dozen couples, and although they were elderly, there was nothing wrong with their hearing. The robot's heavy tread was muffled by the carpet, but sure enough, a door creaked open.

'Afternoon there!'

Fisher turned, a ready smile on his face. It was Captain Bellamy, the old boy from number nine. He carried himself with a military bearing and was always talking about some campaign or other, but Fisher reckoned strategy games were the closest he'd got to real gunfire. As for his rank ... maybe he'd piloted a ferry in the dim and distant past. 'Evening, sir.'

'Another robot, eh? Your place must be overflowing with the blighters.'

Fisher nodded.

'Make good foot soldiers, though. Why, I remember a dicey battle on this desert planet –'

'Sorry, Captain, I've really got to run. This one's got a dodgy autopilot.'

'Ah, yes. Cannon fodder, what? Carry on, then. See the thing doesn't run into any walls.'

'Snooping old busybody,' muttered Fisher under his breath.

He barely covered three paces before another door opened. An elderly lady looked out, peering at the robot. 'Is that you, young man?'

'Evening, Miss Armstrong,' said Fisher loudly.

'Oh, you're over there.' The old lady stared at him, then indicated the robot. 'Do you have company tonight?'

'It's just a robot, miss.'

'Ah, splendid. Those orphans *will* be pleased.'

'Yes, they will.'

'You won't be working *too* late, will you?'

'No, not at all.'

'Excellent. Glad to hear it. Well, don't let me keep you.'

Fisher lengthened his stride to overtake the robot and pressed his palm to his apartment's door control. When the stumbling robot was in line with the doorway, he turned it smartly to the right and guided it inside. Just before his door closed he heard two others do likewise along the hall. Lucky for him they couldn't see into his apartment, he thought grimly, or they'd have him evicted.

Fisher stopped the robot just inside the door. There wasn't much room to get by, thanks to a towering wall of crates lining his hallway. He squeezed through the narrow gap by turning the robot sideways and rocking it from one foot to the other.

There were dozens more crates crammed into his apartment, some lining the walls and others doubling as benches and tables. Every one was stamped with 'Lot 5 - robot brains', and Fisher's lips thinned at the sight. He'd bid on the auction thinking he was getting a hundred old robot brains, not a hundred *cartons* of the damn things.

Aside from the crates, his lounge was a disaster area - disassembled robots standing around like unfinished statues, parts on every surface, scribbled receipts all over the floor. The bedroom and kitchen were just as bad, but that was the downside to his trade in second-hand robots. The upside was a steady cash flow and freedom from a nine-to-five job. The neighbours could have been a problem, what with robots going in and out all the time, but Fisher had let it be known he was rebuilding old robots to raise funds for a children's charity. As a bonus, he was usually the first to know when one of their relatives was thinking of selling a robot.

Fisher cleared a space next to his workbench and manoeuvred the new robot into position. He took up a flat-bladed tool and opened the compartments under the robot's arms and just above its hip joints, then used a pair of snips to cut the power wires. When he was satisfied, he opened the chest compartment and toggled the reset switch. As he expected, the robot came to life immediately, opening its eyes and gazing around the apartment with a puzzled expression. Then it saw Fisher.

'Excuse me, sir. Do you know where I am?'

'You're at my place.'

The robot looked down at its immobilised limbs. 'Is there something wrong with me? Am I being repaired?'

'Something like that.'

'Where is Ms Turner?'

Fisher took out the scrawled receipt and held it up to the robot's face. 'Transfer of ownership. I'm sure you recognise the handwriting.'

'It . . . it looks familiar. But Lily would never . . . '

'Say it.'

The robot swallowed. 'That is my owner's handwriting.'

'And?'

'You are my new owner. But can I just ask –'

'Don't bother,' said Fisher, and he switched the robot off. Sometimes it wasn't so easy, and the really uncooperative ones tried to make a run for it. He'd tried binding them, but after one particularly strong robot had almost broken his arm, he'd hit upon the idea of disabling them before getting the transfer process under way.

With the robot legally his, Fisher could now do whatever he wanted. And what he wanted was that pristine controller chip, version one point six five, from the circuit board. Taking up a slender tool with a fine laser point, he donned a pair of magnifying glasses and angled a strong light into the robot's chest. Before long he was wreathed in smoke as the laser cut through traces and delicate components alike.

— 6 —

Barwenna City, 5 p.m.

Landing passed without incident, thanks to Clunk's cunning plan: He laid on snacks in the rec room and fudged their ETA. During final approach, Hal was busy with a stack of doughnuts, and he was still licking sugar off his plate when the ship bumped down. He frowned, then shrugged and drained his coffee. He was willing to delegate all piloting tasks when there were sugary snacks in the offing.

Hal made his way to the flight deck, leaving sticky fingerprints on the door and elevator controls. One day, he thought, he'd sit down and invent a hands-free snack. Something with springs and laser-guidance, but also fat- and salt-reduced. There was a fortune to be made, he was sure of it.

The doors opened, and he spotted Clunk at the console, shutting down the engines and hibernating the in-flight systems. Actually, what he saw was a lot of clicking and gesturing, and for all he knew the robot was updating his social networks and auctioning Hal's body parts. 'I thought you were going to call me for the landing?'

'We arrived ahead of schedule,' said Clunk, without missing a beat. 'Incidentally, what do you know about this search fee?'

'The Navcom was looking something up for me.'

'To the tune of eight hundred credits? I hope it was worth it.'

'If my guess is right, it'll be worth ten times that much.'

'I wouldn't spend any more money until Mr Cuff pays his dues. We're right on the limit.'

'What's happening with the freight job?'

'I tried to contact our customer, but there's no reply.'

'Hand the container to the spaceport. We'll claim payment in the morning.'

'I tried, but they refused the shipment. Their copy of the manifest hasn't arrived.'

Hal shrugged. 'Give them ours.'

'It doesn't quite work like that. They need an original copy.'

'No wonder it doesn't work. How can you have an original copy?'

Clunk's mouth opened and closed. 'Well yes,' he said finally. 'In a strictly literal sense, that's impossible.'

'Good. Give them our original copy of a copy, and let's get paid.' Hal eyed the main screen, which was filled with banner ads for local services. 'Anything good on offer?'

'No.'

'You didn't even look!'

'I don't have to. They're banner adverts.'

Hal sighed. 'Okay, find the cheapest cab service and book a ride for our passenger. He's staying at some dive in town.'

'Which one?'

'The Grande.' Hal shuddered. 'Probably riddled with bed bugs.'

Clunk turned to the console and accessed a terminal. 'The cab will be here in five minutes.'

'I'll go and tell Cuff.'

'While you do that, perhaps you could clean up all those original copies of your fingerprints?'

◆

The Hotel Grande was nestled between commercial buildings and apartment blocks. It was the tallest building in sight, and the façade had the kind of old-world charm only serious amounts of money could buy. Hal eyed the red welcome carpet, the gold-plated fittings and the polished marble, and quips about cockroach farms died on his lips. He was loathe to admit it, but he was actually impressed.

The taxi stopped under a lime-green canopy, and a smart porter hastened towards them. Clunk's battered appearance earned a discreetly raised eyebrow, and when Cuff's decrepit robot tumbled out the porter simply stared. He recovered quickly and turned his attention to Cuff. 'I'll just get your bag, sir.'

'Don't concern yourself,' said Cuff airily. 'My man takes care of such matters.'

Hal looked around for this servant, then realised Cuff was talking about him. Lips pressed together, he picked up Cuff's battered satchel and followed the others across the red carpet.

Inside, the lobby soared through a dozen floors, culminating in a giant crystal sculpture in the shape of a snap-frozen angel. Classical music played through concealed speakers, and the carpet was so thick Hal expected to see life rafts on the walls. Instead he spotted a gift shop, a jeweller and a cosy-looking coffee shop.

While Hal was rubber-necking, Cuff made his way to the check-in counter. There were several people waiting for service, and Hal wasn't going to queue when there was fresh coffee in the offing. 'Keep an eye on the old coot,' he told Clunk, and left the robot to it.

◆

The bistro was busy, with every table in use. Hal ordered a drink, putting it on Cuff's slate, then scanned the room for a seat. He saw a blonde woman sitting alone, alternately staring into space and scribbling on a thick notepad. Hal approached her table, and the next time she looked up he caught her eye. 'May I?'

The woman looked him up and down. She was in her late twenties, confident and smartly-dressed. 'Sure,' she said at last. 'I'm just waiting for my order.'

Hal sat at the table and tipped four packets of sugar into his mug, swirling the foam with his spoon. 'Are you a writer?' he asked, sipping the coffee.

'Why do you say that?'

'I've had Peace Force training.' Hal nodded towards the notebook. 'We pick up little clues, make deductions. You know.'

'Deductions, eh? Funny you should say that, because I'm a tax inspector.'

Hal choked, scattering foam across the table.

'I'm sorry, my timing is awful,' said the woman.

'No, my fault.' Hal grabbed a napkin and mopped up. 'It's

that powdery chocolate stuff. It's like an audit ... it gets into everything.'

'You've got some on your overalls,' said the woman, pointing. As Hal worked the stain deeper into the fabric she continued. 'It's a pity you can't claim the cleaning bill as a deduction.'

'I can't? No, you're right. Of course I can't.' Hal tried the coffee again, hesitating in case the woman had any more shocks up her sleeve. Fortunately, she was busy writing. Hal watched for a moment to make sure she wasn't adding his name to her list of targets, then put her out of his mind to concentrate on the coffee.

He'd only taken a sip or two when a muted bell rang behind the counter. The woman put away the notebook and stood up, and after a quick nod she was gone.

'Here you are, Ms Lucas,' said the server. 'Should I put it on your room?'

'Yes thanks.' The woman took the tray and Hal watched her navigate the lobby, admiring her figure as she disappeared into the lift. Then he shook his head. The galaxy was a huge, teeming mass of humanity, and odd behaviour had long ago ceased to surprise him. For example, why was a tax inspector living it up in a five-star hotel?

He'd just raised the mug to his lips when he spotted Clunk hurrying towards him, an anxious expression on his face. Hal closed his eyes, inhaled the coffee, then opened them again. Unfortunately this little trick didn't make the robot vanish - it just brought him a lot closer. With a sigh, Hal set the cup down. 'What's the problem?'

'Mr Cuff insists he made a reservation, but the staff have no record of it.'

'Are they booked out?'

43

'No, there are several suites available.'

'Let him have one of those.'

'But he thought the room would be laid on. He can't pay in advance.'

Hal rubbed his chin. 'How much cash do we have left?'

'Surely you can't be thinking . . . '

'We're already in the hole for a grand or so. What difference does another couple of hundred make? Broke is broke.'

'If you spend everything we'll be stranded on Barwenna. That's a huge risk, Mr Spacejock.'

'And it's one I'm willing to take. After all, Cuff wouldn't have come to a flash place like this if he wasn't expecting a substantial payout. He'd have picked a cut-price motel, or asked to stay aboard the *Volante*.'

'If we pay for his hotel room we're just increasing our exposure,' warned Clunk.

'Think of it as an investment. We can't lose.'

◆

Hal strolled to the counter and attracted Cuff's attention. 'Clunk told me about your temporary cash flow problem, and I've come to tell you we'll help out.'

'That's very good of you, Mr Spacejock. I can't believe Argisle and Butt didn't arrange everything. My letter was most explicit, right down to my estimated time of arrival, and yet my solicitors failed to get a single thing right.'

'Don't you worry, we'll see to it. I'll get the rooms organised first.'

'One will suffice.' Cuff indicated his robot. 'I'm happy to share with my valued companion.'

'We're staying too.'

'That's really not necessary.'

'He's right,' said Clunk. 'There are cheaper hotels in the area. Mr Cuff could stay here while we –'

'Put up with rats and bed bugs? No, for once we're doing it in style.' Hal turned to the concierge. 'Two suites please.'

'Thank you sir. That's sixteen hundred credits.'

Hal winced. 'Do we get a discount for cash?'

'Fifteen hundred.'

'Meals included?'

The concierge hesitated. 'I'll give you a voucher for breakfast. Checkout is at ten a.m.'

'Excellent.' Hal nodded to Clunk, who authorised the transaction.

Once check-in was completed, they were escorted to the lift by the porter. After a short ride, the doors opened onto a corridor with thick maroon carpet and wallpaper patterned with gold thread. The doors bore discreet numbers embossed on brass plates, and the porter led them past half a dozen before letting them into rooms on opposite sides of the corridor. Hal tipped him with a credit or two from his depleted funds, then ducked inside before anyone else could stick their hand out.

The room was comfortable, with a large bed, an entertainment console and a modern computer terminal. Hal made straight for the kitchen, where he set to work on the coffee maker. 'Wow, look at this menu! I haven't seen this much food since the AutoChef exploded.'

'Speaking of foods,' said Clunk. 'Your flight suit needs a wash, and I dare say the contents could do with one too.'

Barwenna City, 7 a.m.

Zee Pharer hurried along the busy footpath, his bronze legs pumping like a couple of overworked pistons. An internal alarm chimed, and he increased his pace. In three years he'd never been late, and he wasn't going to break that perfect record. What would his owner say? More importantly, what would he do? Alan Dane was a man whose enemies turned up dead, if at all. A man to whom a robot was less than the shine on his hand-tooled leather boots.

It was just over three years since Zee's world had come crashing down. A Peace Force raid on Dane's office, compromising files, a court case and - eventually - prison. Zee knew smuggling and gun-running were illegal, but Dane told him it was sanctioned under certain conditions ... especially if you paid off the right politicians. Unfortunately a payment had gone astray, word had gone out and Dane discovered selling guns to teenagers wasn't quite so legit after all.

Zee rounded the corner in full flight, his rubber-shod feet slipping on the pavement. Ahead was the Barwenna Prison, a four-story building with more security than a crime boss convention. Outside was an expanse of concrete with a few twisted trees and the occasional wooden bench. It was supposed to be a soothing area where visitors could sit and contemplate their surroundings. Due to a lack of funding it was actually a windswept wasteland which afforded clear shots for the rooftop snipers.

The nearest bench was vacant, and Zee hurried over and sat down with a crash. He'd made it!

He glanced towards the prison. Three years ago the instructions had been precise: wait for me every day. Arrive at seven, leave after dark. There were no threats, no explanations, and Zee didn't need them. An order from his owner required total obedience, and if the daily ritual was a touch inconvenient . . . well, that was humans for you, wasn't it?

The first couple of months had been easy, since Dane had a front business near the prison. Zee moved in, used the facilities to keep himself in good running order, and quickly adapted to his new routine. Unfortunately the business was fire bombed by one of Dane's enemies, and Zee was forced to move. After a number of similar attacks, Zee realised Dane's enemies were following him from the prison, using his movements to track down and eliminate Dane's businesses one by one.

At this point there were no front businesses left, and Dane's few surviving cronies threw their lot in with the enemy. Alone and unwanted, Zee retreated to the transit hub, where he rented a locker under a false name, shutting himself in every night. Power was a problem until he discovered the lockers backed onto a bathroom. A few mods later and he had an endless supply of electricity and a somewhat disturbing view of the urinal.

For the next three years he followed orders to the letter, sitting motionless on the bench during daylight hours. After a couple of months the birds got used to him, and he enjoyed the feel of their tiny clawed feet on his shoulders. He was less impressed with the droppings.

Zee scanned the windows, wondering whether today was the big one. He assumed his boss was building up to a breakout, or perhaps setting up a new smuggling operation. Otherwise, why ask Zee to sit outside the prison for up to fourteen hours a day?

He heard a noise, and turned to see another robot approaching. It was a shorter model, dark blue with silver flashes at the shoulders. Zee nodded at the newcomer, startling a bird into flight, and the Peace Force robot gave him a brief nod in return. 'Still here, then?'

Zee looked down at himself, and wondered whether Peace Force robots were detuned in some way. Of course he was still here. 'Where else would I be?'

'I don't know. Mebbe at the funeral?'

Zee blinked. 'What funeral?'

'And there I was thinking you were Dane's loyal sidekick. All this waiting around and such.'

'I am loyal!' protested Zee. 'I will obey Mr Dane until his dying day.'

'Odd you should say that.' The Peace Force robot jerked his thumb towards the prison. 'If you're quick you can still pay your last respects.'

'A-are you saying Dane is ... dead?'

The blue robot snorted. 'You detuned or something? Of course he's dead.'

'But how?'

'He only stabbed himself in the back, didn't he. Fifteen times, by all accounts.'

'Wh-what about me? Dane was my owner. He ordered me to be here!'

'Orders don't work from beyond the grave. You're a free

agent now.' The Peace Force robot looked at him in concern. 'Steady there. We don't want no more accidents, or this place'd be getting a reputation.'

Zee stumbled away from his previous life, his mind a whirling mess. No owner? A free agent? What was he to do?

— 8 —

'Huh? Wassup? What time is it? Where are we?' Hal opened his eyes to see Clunk standing over him with a mug of coffee. 'Did you put sugar in it?'

'It's eight a.m. and our current location is the Grande Hotel on planet Barwenna. Affirmative to the sugar quotient.'

'Good stuff.' Hal sat up, rubbing his eyes. 'Breakfast?'

'Only if you hurry. Checkout is at ten and we can't afford a second day.'

'You're not kidding.' Hal swigged the coffee, then jumped out of bed and wrapped himself in a thick dressing gown. 'Any sign of Cuff?'

'None at all.'

'I hope he hasn't done a runner.'

'Given his age, that's an unlikely prospect.'

'Yeah, plus his wonky old robot isn't going to win any hundred metre dashes.'

'That old robot has a name, you know.'

'Have you managed to speak to it yet?'

'I'm afraid not.' Clunk gestured at the ceiling. 'I tried communicating across the hall, but there was too much interference from the pleasurebot on the floor above.'

'You mean the suite above.'

'I know what I meant.'

At that moment someone hammered on the door. Hal opened it and saw Cuff outside in a dressing gown, his hair tousled and his face agitated. 'Spacejock! You have to help me!'

'What is it? What's the matter?'

'It's Ferdie! My poor robot is dead!'

'Ferdie?' Hal frowned. 'I thought his name was Freddie?'

'Who cares what you thought?' snapped Cuff. 'He's broken down!'

'Have you tried switching him off and –?'

'Of course!' Cuff grabbed Hal's arm and tried to drag him into the corridor. 'You must help me. This is a matter of life and death.'

Hal was more interested in breakfast. 'Clunk, can you take a look?'

'Yes, Mr Spacejock.'

The robot and the elderly man hurried off, and Hal closed the door. 'Typical start to the day,' he muttered. He reminded himself that Clunk could fix anything, then ordered room service and headed for the shower.

Twenty minutes later Cuff was back at his door with Clunk in tow. Both looked serious, and Hal put his knife and fork down and wiped the egg yolk from his chin with a napkin. 'Well?'

'It's a disaster!' exclaimed Cuff. 'A total nightmare.'

'Clunk?'

'Mr Cuff's robot requires extensive repairs.'

'Can you fix it?'

'I'm afraid not. I'll need specialist equipment, and that won't be cheap.'

Hal frowned. Their funds were long gone, but ... 'Can we take out a loan against the *Volante*?'

'That's out of the question,' said Clunk sharply.

Cuff groaned and buried his head in his hands. 'That's it. I'm ruined.'

'What do you mean, ruined?'

'You're not aware of this, of course, but a generous benefactor left my robot a large sum of money.'

'Is that so?' said Hal, feigning shock and awe. 'Well I never.'

'Yes, but if my robot isn't present at the meeting he won't get a single credit.'

'Surely this meeting can be postponed?' asked Clunk. 'They'll understand, given the circumstances.'

'No, the terms are precise. Twelve o'clock is the deadline.' Cuff looked up, a pleading expression on his face. 'Are you sure my beloved Freddie is beyond salvation?'

'I could replace half the components and it would still be a lost cause.' Clunk frowned. 'I don't know whether you understand the concept of preventative maintenance, but –'

'Wait a minute.' Hal looked from one to the other, and the implication hit him like a stray asteroid. 'Never mind your bloody robot. Without that inheritance, how are you going to pay me back?'

'As I said, I'm ruined. Destitute. There's no hope.'

Hal realised the same applied to him. Unless ... 'You have to turn up with your robot before twelve, right?'

'Correct.'

Hal turned to Clunk. 'Give yourself a polish. We've got a meeting to attend.'

'Mr Spacejock, you can't seriously expect me to –'

'You're damn right I do. They want a robot? We'll give them one!'

Cuff caught up with the conversation. 'If you're suggesting a substitution, can I just point out it would be unethical, immoral and most likely illegal?'

'It's just a harmless switch,' said Hal. 'Once you have the cash you can fix your robot and swap back. Who's going to know?'

Clunk shook his head. 'I'm sorry, Mr Spacejock. Your idea has merit, but it's not going to work. I cannot tell a lie, and one wrong answer will reveal the deception.'

'He's right,' said Cuff. 'We'll be facing a team of legal experts at Argisle and Butt. Clunk won't last two minutes.'

Hal sipped his coffee, racking his brains. 'We need help from a powerful intellect. Someone with answers at their fingertips. Someone so smart they can solve the mysteries of the universe while simultaneously filling out their own tax return.'

'That sounds great,' said Cuff. 'Who do you have in mind?'

'It's obvious!' Hal gestured. 'Clunk.'

The robot stood tall. 'Yes, Mr Spacejock? What would you like me to do?'

'Get the Navcom on the line for me.'

Deflated, Clunk accessed the commset. Within seconds the Navcom's neutral voice came over the speaker. 'I hope you're all having a jolly time in that five-star hotel.'

Hal frowned at Clunk. 'I thought I told you to say it was two stars!' he hissed.

'The Navcom sees all your bills.'

'What, all of them?'

'Every single one, Mr Spacejock.'

The Navcom made a throat-clearing noise. 'I'll just wait on the line, shall I?'

Hal addressed the commset. 'Listen, Clunk has to stand in

for another robot but he can't let on he's doing it. How do I stop him answering questions?'

'Stop asking them,' said the Navcom.

'It's not me, it's the lawyers.'

'Tell them to stop asking questions.'

Hal was beginning to wonder whether calling the Navcom had been such a great idea. 'That's not going to fly, is it? I can't tell them not to ask questions in case the answers aren't what they're expecting. That's *why* they're asking questions in the first place.'

'Then Clunk must refuse to answer them.'

'That's impossible,' said Clunk. 'I must obey orders.'

'Then you'll have to be mute.'

'I beg your pardon?'

'A few seconds with a sharpened screwdriver will do the trick. Apply the tip to the right traces and it won't matter what they ask you.'

'I don't like the sound of that,' said Clunk, with a frown.

'So use the blade on your hearing as well.'

'I shall do no such thing!' protested Clunk.

'You could achieve the same effect with software. I can send you the routines if you like.'

'Do it,' said Hal.

Clunk closed his eyes, and there was a burst of static. 'Routines received. I'll inspect the code now.'

'There is nothing wrong with my programming,' said the Navcom.

'Thanks Navcom. Catch you soon.' Hal cut the connection before the computer could reply. Then he glanced at Cuff, whose expression of despair had given way to a glimmer of hope. 'Go and get dressed, and tell the hotel to stick your robot in storage for the day. Before they take it away, Clunk can skim the memory chips for a few facts and figures - something to convince these lawyers he's the real one.'

'I'm afraid that won't be possible,' said Clunk. 'Freddie's brain suffered a total meltdown, his circuit boards are fried and all his memories were permanently erased.'

'That's fantastic!' Hal noticed the frosty looks, and he hastened to explain. 'Now Clunk can make stuff up, and they can't prove any different.'

Cuff looked doubtful. 'Are you sure your robot can carry this off?'

'Don't you worry,' said Hal loyally. 'Clunk's as tricky as a magician with three sleeves.'

Clunk waited until Cuff had left, then made a throat-clearing sound. 'Mr Spacejock ... '

'I know, I know. The substitution idea is reckless and illegal and so on and so forth. Do you have a better idea?'

'I think the idea is sound. It's the shutting down of my senses I'm concerned about.'

'You can switch them on again, right?'

'Yes, but they could order me to do the same.'

'How?'

Clunk took a napkin and a pen. He wrote rapidly, and when he'd finished the napkin read 'Switch on your hearing' in perfect dot-matrix lettering. 'All they have to do is hold that up to my eyes, and I'd be forced to obey.'

'So close your eyes.'

'They'd patch directly into my brain, which would be even worse.'

'Do you have a solution?'

Clunk nodded. 'I can leave my hearing active, but filter out everything except a particular safety word. When you speak that word, it will restore my speech.'

'That's great! See how well things go when we work as a team?'

'I will also set up a mute word. When spoken it will switch off my speech and apply the new audio filter.'

'Go on then.'

'It will take me thirty minutes to modify the Navcom's code, and I will need several reboots. During that time it's important you don't speak aloud.'

⬥

Thirty-five minutes later Clunk declared himself ready. It would have been thirty, but five minutes into the process Hal had sneezed, then made things worse by apologising.

'The keyword to reverse the muting process is *Volante*. Do you think you can remember that?'

'I'm not a complete idiot.'

'The keyword to activate the mute is inconceivable.'

'Oh, go on. It can't be that hard.'

'No, really. It's inconceivable.'

'What am I, thick? It's just a word!'

'That's right, and the word is inconceivable.'

'Really?'

'Yes!'

'*Volante* and inconceivable?'

Clunk opened his mouth to reply, then frowned. He tried again, but nothing came out.

'*Volante*,' said Hal quickly.

'Thank you. Now, you must keep these words to yourself. Do not reveal them to anyone else.'

'I thought they were keyed to my voice?'

'That's correct, but someone could force you to say them under duress. I constructed filters so that bracketing the safety words with screams of pain would render them inert, but I've not had time to perfect them.'

'You think these solicitors might resort to torture? Totally inconceivable!'

Clunk tried to reply, then pounded on the table, rattling the coffee mug.

'*Volante!*' said Hal.

'Mr Spacejock, I deliberately chose a particular word because you never use it. Now you can't stop saying it?'

'It's not my fault. It's stuck in my brain.'

'Just try not to use it again.'

'Can't you change it? What about, er, um ... ' Hal frowned, unable to think of a word he hardly ever used.

'You're bound to use the replacement just as frequently.'

'I guess you're right,' admitted Hal. 'It's inconceivable or nothing.'

South-East of Barwenna City, 8:30 a.m.

Sandy West threw her bag over the derelict fence and climbed the pitted wooden boards with ease. She swung her legs over the top and dropped lightly on the other side, just behind a rickety garden shed. The weeds came up to her knees, and she recalled a time when the lawn had been trimmed every weekend.

She moved to the corner of the shed and glanced across the overgrown garden to the house. The curtains were still drawn, and it was unlikely anyone was up. Not before noon, in any case. Not until the daily soaps began.

The shed door was locked, but the wood around the latch was rotten and only one screw remained. Sandy plucked it out and opened the door carefully, trying not to let it shudder on the concrete floor. A familiar smell wafted out: a mix of wood shavings, varnish, cleaning rags and perished rubber. In years past her dad would spend half his weekend in the shed, building intricate toys and furniture. These days their furniture was plastic, and toys were a distant memory.

Sandy pushed past a jumble of half-finished projects and rough-hewn planks, heading for the far corner. There was a workbench in the way, and she moved it carefully to one side.

Behind it was an old canvas sheet, draped over an object taller than she was. The outline of a head and shoulders was visible beneath the stained fabric, and Sandy smiled at the sight.

She took one corner of the canvas and pulled, jerking the cover off. Underneath was a gleaming bronze robot, buffed to perfection from head to toe. It had a black serial number - XG99 - stencilled on its chest, and the only visible flaw was a faint tracing of a moustache on the robot's upper lip, drawn with a marker when Sandy was four or five. Boy, had she got into trouble over that little stunt! A telling off, sent to bed with no dinner, and then two hours later her guilt-stricken dad brought her a bowl of cereal for a late-night feast.

She glanced over her shoulder, staring through the grimy windows at the house beyond. Nobody cared what she did now. Not any more.

Sandy blinked, then turned back to the robot. There was a speck of dust on its shoulder, and she buffed it away with her sleeve. 'So, old friend. Are you ready for a walk?'

She took a pair of slacks and a dark blouse from the bag and changed quickly. Her school uniform went into the bag, which she kicked under the workbench. She considered leaving a note, but decided against it. Nobody would find it here, and she wasn't going back to the house.

Sandy opened the robot's chest panel and flipped the main power switch. Somewhere inside the metal chest there was a whine, and a row of status lights came on two by two. When they were all green she closed the panel and stepped back. 'Can you hear me, Daniel?'

The robot opened its eyes and looked down at her. They were warm and yellow, and they crinkled around the edges as Daniel recognised her face. 'Yes, Miss Sandy. It's a pleasure to see you.'

'How are your circuits?'

'Not the best, but I'll manage.' The robot hesitated. 'It's today, isn't it?'

'Yes. Our little outing.'

'You understand I can't walk very fast?'

'That's okay, Daniel. We'll take it easy.'

'Have you informed your parents?'

'Sure.'

The robot eyed her thoughtfully. 'Are you certain? I detect a note of –'

'Daniel! Don't you trust me after all this time?'

The robot traced the outline of the moustache on its upper lip.

'You can't be serious. That was years ago!'

Daniel sighed. 'Don't I know it? It seems like yesterday you were just a perky little thing, barely higher than my knee joint. Now you're a beautiful young lady.'

Sandy smiled. 'I bet you're a hit with the girls, you old charmer.'

'Not that I remember.'

'Okay, we really have to leave. Is there anything you need?'

Daniel's neck creaked as he shook his head.

'Come on, then.' Sandy pulled the door open, and the robot stepped away from the corner. His legs groaned as he walked, and his expression was drawn. 'Are you really up to this?'

'I–I think so.'

They made it to the doorway, where Daniel turned for the house.

'Not that way,' said Sandy, guiding him to the left. Another step and she turned him again, until he was aiming straight for the fence. 'Come on, time to go.'

Daniel reached the fence in three steps, and with his fourth he walked straight through it, tearing the ancient planks like cardboard. Sandy followed, stepping over the shattered fragments.

The local woods ran right up to the back fence, where the leaf-strewn ground was bright with dappled sunlight. Daniel extended his elbow like a proper gentleman, and the two of them set off under the trees arm in arm, leaving behind their old lives for good.

— 10 —

Barwenna City, 11:20 a.m.

Traffic was heavy, and it took longer than Hal expected to reach the offices of Argisle and Butt. Even so, they made it with forty minutes to spare. Hal paid the cab off, then turned to follow the others up the steps.

'You wait here,' said Cuff. 'Clunk and I will attend the meeting alone.'

'No chance.'

Cuff was taken aback. 'How will I explain your presence?'

'Tell them the truth. I'm your hired muscle.' Hal forestalled further argument by running up the stairs and holding the doors open. 'After you, sir.'

'Thank you, my loyal and faithful bodyguard. Your long years of service will be fondly remembered and richly rewarded.'

Inside, a receptionist was busy taking calls. Cuff waited until she was free, then smiled and bowed. 'Good morning, ma'am. Would you inform Messrs Argisle and Butt that Hans Cuff is here to see them?'

He was charm personified, but the woman barely glanced at him. 'Go through those doors and wait until you're called.'

Cuff's smile slipped. 'I do have an appointment.'

'Not my problem, we're backed up.' The receptionist pointed. 'In there and wait. Next!'

Hal led the others to the doors, and could only stare at the scene beyond.

'Goodness me,' said Clunk.

The room was the size of a tennis court, filled with rows of folding chairs. Seated in the chairs was the oddest collection of robots Hal had ever seen. There were skinny serving droids with battered trays, wheezing personal trainers covered in faded logos, ex-army scouts, stout red teachers with grey screens where their faces should have been, and a variety of oddbots built from scavenged parts. And in between the robots there were humans - tattooed workmen in their Sunday best, scruffy teenagers playing games on their commsets, and nervous twenty-somethings with slicked-down hair and cheap suits.

Hal led the way to the back of the hall, where they sat next to a wizened pensioner. The old man eyed them with suspicion, taking a firm grip on his oddbot's buckled arm.

'Good afternoon,' said Hal. 'Can you tell me what you're doing here?'

The old man cupped a hand to his ear. 'What's that, sonny?'

'What are you doing at Argisle and Butt?' asked Hal loudly.

'He's not stolen!' said the old man indignantly. 'I've had him since he was a wee rivet.'

Hal nodded and smiled, then leant forward and tapped the woman in front on the shoulder. 'Excuse me.'

The woman fixed him with a potent glare. 'You ought to be ashamed of yourselves!'

Hal blinked. 'I'm sorry?'

'You know what I'm talking about,' hissed the woman, turning her back on him.

Hal turned to Clunk. 'This could take a while. Did you bring any food?'

'There's a buffet at the front of the hall.'

Hal craned his neck. 'I don't suppose you could fetch me a plate of sarnies?'

'Yes, Mr Spacejock. Your stomach's wish is my command.' Clunk looked at Cuff. 'I suppose you're feeling hungry too?'

Cuff stood. 'Do you mind if I accompany you? I don't want to let you out of my sight.'

Before they left, Clunk bent down to whisper in Hal's ear. 'You should use the keyword in case anyone tries to speak to me.'

'Inconceivable.'

Hal watched them go, then turned to see a young man in a muddy brown cloak striding towards him, pushing a battered white cylinder on wheels. 'That one's really been in the wars,' remarked Hal, as the man took a seat.

'Ex-military.' The man looked him up and down. 'Where's yours?'

'Getting a sandwich.' Hal gazed around the room. 'You really like your robots on this planet, don't you?'

'Where would we be without our valued companions?'

Hal thought he detected a hint of sarcasm, but put it down to the accent. 'You like lawyers too. This place is packed!'

The man nodded. 'Argisle and Butt is a robot specialist. They handle all the big cases.'

'Does it take long?'

'Who cares?' The man snorted. 'It's not like I have to run around saving the galaxy from evil.'

Hal felt vague misgivings. It was nothing he could put his finger on, but something wasn't right. The robots, the tense atmosphere, and the odd reactions from the crowd. It was like they were waiting for the result of a big race.

◆

Hal glanced to his left, where a grey-haired man in a leather jacket was cleaning his fingernails with a pocket knife. 'Hi,' said Hal. 'How are you doing?'

'Be better when all this is over.' The man stuck his hand out. 'I'm Fisher. David Fisher.'

'Hal Spacejock.'

They shook, and Hal glanced at Fisher's robot. It was a real bitser, with mismatched parts from head to toe. One arm was silver, the other bronze. The left leg was much longer than the right, and someone had removed the foot to compensate, leaving the robot to walk on the ball joint.

'I only just got it ready in time,' explained Fisher. 'I pulled an all-nighter.'

'Looks like you needed an all-weeker.'

Fisher grinned. 'Most of these robots have had a pretty tough life. Driven hard by uncaring owners, skipped services, no spare parts ... ' He pointed over Hal's shoulder. 'Look at that poor specimen. It wouldn't cost much to get those dents out, and that sad expression is enough to break your heart.'

Hal was about to tut sympathetically at the object of Fisher's pity when he realised it was Clunk. 'He's not sad, his face just slipped. When he's really down he grumbles through his nostrils.'

Fisher stared. 'That's your robot?'

65

'Sure. And those dents? He says they add character.' Hal waved. 'Over here Clunk.'

When Clunk arrived Fisher put his hand out. 'David Fisher. This is my XG99 series.'

Clunk frowned at the franken-bot. He opened his mouth to speak, but nothing came out.

'I know, I'm sorry,' said Fisher. 'It's a wreck. It hasn't worked for years.'

'Yours too?' muttered Hal. He saw Clunk's venomous look and raised his hands. 'Just kidding!'

'So, what do you reckon on your chances?' Fisher asked Hal.

'Chances of what?'

'You know, the –'

'Ah, Clunk! There you are!' Cuff returned with a plate full of sandwiches and a large mug of coffee. 'What did I tell you about staying close to me? We can't have you running away like a little lost lamb, can we?'

Clunk's eyes narrowed, and Hal thought it was just as well the robot's voice was muted.

'Doesn't your robot speak?' asked Fisher.

'Nothing too major,' said Hal. 'It's just a blockage in his circuits.'

'Mine's the same, only the circuits are missing altogether. If I get through this thing I'm going to splash out on my own repair centre. If anyone can't pay the bill, I'll fix their robot for nothing.'

'That sounds pretty generous.'

Fisher spread his hands. 'How much money does one man need? If my robot turns out to be –'

'Mr Spacejock,' interrupted Cuff. 'May I speak with you?'

'Sure.'

'In private.'

66

They moved to the side of the hall, where Cuff lowered his voice and leant in close. 'I suspect Mr Fisher is here on false pretences.'

'You do?'

Cuff nodded. 'I believe he's here to steal my robot's rightful inheritance.'

Hal gaped at him, then turned to stare at Fisher. He didn't look like a conman, but isn't that what they said about all the best ones? If Fisher claimed *his* robot was the real one, what could Cuff do about it? After all, Fisher wasn't the only one trying to pass off a substitute. 'This thing with Clunk is never going to work,' said Hal. 'We should have brought your robot.'

'Fergus was beyond repair,' hissed Cuff. 'That rough landing of yours tipped it over the edge.'

Hal's eyes narrowed. 'Don't try and pin this on me. We've done everything to help you! The flight, cabs, a hotel room ...and what about that six course dinner you ordered last night?'

'One has to eat, Mr Spacejock.'

'One, sure. You ordered for three!'

'And when I inherit you will be amply compensated.'

Hal opened his mouth to reply, but at that moment a loud voice cut across the hall.

'Would everyone pay attention please?' The voice came through hidden speakers, and the murmur of conversations ceased.

'Thank you,' said the voice. 'Now, in half an hour we're going to single out the most likely candidates for Baker's legacy. Before we start I'd like to point out that it's an offence to impersonate another robot, or to falsify ownership papers. Furthermore ...'

At this point Hal's jaw dropped and he stopped listening. Slowly he looked around the packed hall, and there was a sick feeling in his throat as he scanned all the people with their elderly robots.

They were all there to claim on the will!

Hal froze as the enormity of the situation sank in, and then he turned to Cuff. Some small part of him still hoped that he'd made a mistake, that the old gent really was the one and only claimant on the will. However, Cuff refused to meet his gaze, and that's when Hal lost it. He grabbed a fistful of jacket, hauling Cuff into the air. 'You ... you ... ' He drew a fist back to strike.

'It's all a misunderstanding,' squeaked Cuff, wriggling in Hal's grip. 'Look, look! I think your robot wants you to do something. He's trying to speak!'

Hal knew what Clunk was going to say, but he couldn't silence him forever. '*Volante*,' he snapped.

The words tumbled out. 'Let him go, Mr Spacejock. Let him go! Violence won't solve anything.'

'Oh, I don't know. I feel better already.'

'You don't mean that. Come, let us solve this problem like civilised beings.'

The red mist faded, and Hal gave Cuff one last shake before releasing him. 'You're going to pay back every credit, you rotten little con artist. We're talking black market body parts. Do you understand?'

'I'm sorry, all right?' Cuff straightened his collar. 'When I heard about the will I couldn't resist. I thought bringing an old robot to Barwenna was the perfect idea. I–I just didn't realise everyone else would think of it too.'

'Idea? Scam, more like!' Hal gestured towards the crowd. 'You're as bad as this lot!'

'You only helped so you could profit from my good fortune,' said Cuff sullenly.

'No, I helped because you owed us your fare and you couldn't pay. I wasn't expecting a cut of your fortune.'

'I'm sorry. I read you all wrong.' Cuff slumped in his chair, his face drawn. 'I don't know what to say, I really don't.'

Hal could think of plenty to say - and do - but he didn't fancy six months in prison. Could they get a splash of fuel on credit, maybe using Cuff's robot as collateral? It was worth a try. 'Your robot. I'll need a receipt.'

'N-no! You can't!'

'Why not? You won't be needing it.'

'Of course I need it. How am I going to claim my inheritance without it?'

Hal stared. Was the old guy completely mad? There were four hundred people in the hall, every one of them after the fortune, and he was still hoping to claim using his clapped-out wreck?

'Let's do a deal,' said Cuff desperately. 'Lend me fifty credits for the cab fare, there and back. If I inherit I'll give you fifty thousand credits for your trouble. What do you say?'

'I say you're full of –'

Clunk cleared his throat. 'Mr Spacejock, the odds are favourable.'

'Are you serious? We've wasted thousands on this dreamer, and you want to give him more?'

'You spent two thousand credits hoping for a small tip. Now you're refusing fifty against a very substantial sum?'

Hal blinked. 'When you put it like that ...'

Cuff stood. 'Come, there's still time. We'll find a cab, borrow a trolley and –'

'No way, sunshine. Clunk, did you record that stuff about the fifty grand?'

'Yes, Mr Spacejock.'

'Good. That's all we need.' Hal took out a credit tile and gave it to Cuff. 'I'll keep an eye on the news. If you inherit, expect to hear from us.'

'Why? Where are you going?'

'Back to the *Volante*. We're freighter pilots, not minders. We're going to do some real work for a change.'

The cab turned into the spaceport, and Hal's spirits improved when he spotted the *Volante* sitting serenely on her landing pad. The Cuff thing had been a costly disaster, but it wasn't terminal. They could still collect payment for Clunk's cargo of furniture parts, use the cash to fuel the ship, and find themselves a proper job. One without robots, hotel bills and passengers.

The cab drove between two ships, and Hal frowned. Looming over them was another Gamma-class freighter, identical to his own. Competition! If they didn't hurry the newcomer would scoop the best freight jobs.

The cabbie drew up to the *Volante*. Hal and Clunk got out and hurried towards the ship. They were just about to step onto the passenger ramp when an enormous shadow blocked the sun. Hal looked round to see two men so big and wide they looked like a couple of brick walls in suits. They'd been waiting under the ramp, one of them paring his fingernails with a carving knife and the other putting a sheen on a huge chrome blaster.

'Are you Hal Spacejock?' demanded one of the men. His face looked like a granite cliff, and his oft-broken nose lent his voice a rough quality.

The menace in his tone was unmistakeable, and Hal decided caution was in order. 'No, I'm Kent Spearman.' He nodded towards the second Gamma-class ship. 'That's Spacejock's wreck over there.'

The two men exchanged a glance, then turned and hurried away. 'Quick,' Hal said to Clunk. 'We'd better leg it before they come back.' He led Clunk up the passenger ramp to the flight deck, and once they were inside he locked both airlock doors. 'Who do you think they were?'

'At a guess, something to do with your wedding mishap.'

Hal swallowed. 'Get onto that customer of yours. I want that container offloaded right away.'

'Yes, Mr Spacejock.'

'Wait.' Hal raised his finger. 'Make sure you get cash. Don't let them get away with anything.'

'No, Mr Spacejock.'

Satisfied, Hal sat in the pilot's chair and brought up a listing of available cargo jobs. There were pages of them, and he carefully checked the destination planets against a master list of terrorist warnings and election campaigns. There was nothing worse than having uninvited guests force themselves on board, holding him captive in his own flight deck whilst making outrageous statements designed to convert followers to their beliefs. He wasn't too keen on terrorists either.

After removing the undesirables he was left with half a dozen possibles. Two disappeared while he was scanning them, already taken by another pilot. Another went without warning, and with only three remaining Hal had to move fast. He picked a job delivering building materials to the construction site for a brand new space station, and was just about to confirm when the lift doors sprang apart.

'Mr Spacejock,' cried Clunk, waving a sheet of paper. 'You have to see this. Something terrible has happened!'

'Not now, Clunk. I'm taking on a job. It's for Space Station Oberon near Gyris ... have you heard of it?'

'You can't do that. Not until we sort this out!'

＊

On the way to the hold Clunk explained the problem. 'They loaded the wrong container,' he said, thrusting the sheet of paper at Hal. 'See? This manifest has a different serial number.'

'How can it be wrong? The ground staff on Greil were supposed to check everything.' Hal examined the faded print. 'Wait a minute. This was printed six weeks ago!'

Clunk snatched the page, and a beam of green light shone from his eyes. It swept across the paper, and when the scan was complete he shook his head. 'This is the wrong manifest. The vessel's name is different.'

'So the cargo might be all right after all?'

'That's to be seen.'

Hal opened the inner door, and they marched across the hold to the container. 'Let's open it up.'

'Are you sure? Customs haven't inspected it yet.'

'Clunk, we have no idea what's inside that box. If it's real bad we're dumping it before customs get a look.'

'Let me find some bolt cutters.'

Hal eyed the shipping container. The rust-streaked sides were battered and dented, and it looked like just the thing for moving a cargo of stolen weapons or smuggled booze . . . or worse.

Clunk returned with the cutters, and there was a snick as he cut the seal. Hal swung the door open, and they both stared at the contents. It wasn't furniture parts, and it certainly wasn't illicit drugs or weapons. Instead, the container was packed with cheap office desks, old filing cabinets and broken computer terminals. There were in-trays still stacked with paperwork, and everything was thick with dust.

'I don't think we have to worry about customs.' Hal stepped inside and opened a filing cabinet. 'No guns here. I think we're okay. We'll just put it back, fetch the right container and nobody will ever know.'

'It's far from okay, Mr Spacejock.' Clunk hesitated. 'In fact, I think I know what happened.'

'Do tell.'

'If I explain, will you promise not to do anything rash? This concerns our ex-passenger, Mr Cuff.'

Hal gestured impatiently. 'I've forgotten the guy already. Come on, spill it.'

'Do you remember visiting the pub on Greil?'

'Vaguely.'

'You told me several patrons asked for passage to Barwenna, and you turned them all down. One of them was Mr Cuff.'

'Yep.'

'After you left the pub, you encountered Cuff once more, this time being attacked.'

'Not attacked exactly. The muggers had just left.'

'Do you think the situation may have been ... staged?'

'I doubt it. Cuff said they took one look at me and ran for it.'

'All of them?'

Hal puffed his chest out. 'They knew they didn't stand a chance.'

'And then Cuff attached himself to you, expressed surprise that we were flying to Barwenna, and managed to invite himself aboard.'

'Yep.' Hal frowned. 'You know, apart from actually inheriting the fortune, that little weasel has all the luck.'

'Luck had nothing to do with it.' Clunk hesitated. 'Do you know how we came by that cargo job?'

'Same as always. You went looking for it.'

'Not this time. This was a last minute rush job, organised on behalf of a third party. Don't you understand what that means?'

'The customer used a shipping agent?'

'No, Mr Spacejock. Think! In the bar, Mr Cuff discovered you were a cargo pilot. He asked for passage to Barwenna for himself and his robot, and you refused. An hour or so later, Mr Cuff staged a mugging precisely as you were passing by. You took him under your wing and then, thanks to a fortuitous cargo job, Mr Cuff and the robot got their passage to Barwenna after all. Isn't it clear?'

'Not really. You lost me at the pub.'

Clunk groaned. 'Mr Spacejock, who could possibly have the motive for setting up this cargo job? A job which involved leaving for Barwenna immediately?'

'The customer, of course.'

'There was no customer!' cried Clunk. 'I already told you, the job came via the spaceport!'

Hal's eyes narrowed. 'So somebody set up a fake job just to get us to Barwenna.'

'Yes!'

'And to make the job look legit they loaded a container full of junk.'

'You're getting it!'

'And now we can't deliver it, so we can't pay for fuel.'

'Ye-es. Technically correct, but beside the point.'

'Not if they were after revenge for that little misunderstanding.'

'I'm sorry?'

'That wedding party and the smashed glasses. You said they were powerful people, and now they've had their revenge. We're broke, we can't afford fuel and we'll never get another job as long as we live.' Hal snapped his fingers. 'I bet they sent those muggers after me!'

Clunk put his head in his hands. 'Cuff, Mr Spacejock. Cuff, Cuff, *Cuff!*'

'That sounds nasty.' Hal patted him on the back. 'Is it a chest cold?'

'This has nothing to do with the glassware or the wedding,' said Clunk, his voice muffled. 'It was Mr Cuff, our passenger. He's behind the whole thing.'

'What, the fake cargo?'

'Yes. He must have called the spaceport from the pub.'

'And the muggers?'

'What muggers? Did you see any muggers?'

'No, but Cuff said . . . '

'Precisely.'

'And this shipping container?'

'Selected at random from an abandoned stack at the spaceport.'

Hal was silent while the whole mess sank in, then ... 'I'm going to kill him.'

'You promised not to do anything rash!'

'Never trust a human being.' Hal paced the hold. 'We've got to lose the container. Junk or not, someone could have us for theft.'

'Illegal dumping –'

'Later, Clunk. Later.' Hal continued pacing. 'We'll need fuel, and then we can take that space station job. Do we have anything we can sell?'

'There is an alternative.'

'What?'

'Why don't we return to the solicitors and stake a claim on the inheritance?'

Hal blinked. 'You're crazy. There were hundreds of people in that hall! What chance do we have?'

'With Cuff in the running you had odds of four hundred to one. If I join you'll have two horses in the race.'

'You mean, four hundred to two?'

'Two hundred to one.'

'Even better!' Hal looked Clunk up and down. 'Just think, if you get your mitts on all that cash old Cuff will be as sick as a dog.'

'Yes, I suppose that would be your first thought if you came into a vast fortune.'

'Plus if Cuff wins, he's promised us fifty grand.'

'Correct.'

'And if neither of us wins I'm going to lock him into this container and dump him into the nearest star.'

— 12 —

They left the *Volante* at a run, keeping a wary eye out for heavily-armed goons. Fortunately there was no sign of them, and Hal dived into the cab and hauled the door shut. 'Drive,' he said to the cabbie. 'Don't stop for anyone.'

After an uneventful ride the cab dropped them outside the solicitors, and Hal rushed to the door just as a beefy security guard was trying to close it. She saw them coming and put a hand out. 'I'm sorry sir. You're too late.'

'I was here before,' panted Hal. 'I had to go back for my papers.'

'All right, all right.' The guard held the door open. 'One more won't hurt. In you go.'

'Thanks. You're a champ.'

Inside, the first person Hal saw was Cuff. Their ex-passenger was at the counter, and alongside him was a luggage trolley decorated with 'Hotel Grande' logos. On the trolley was the stricken robot, securely attached with rope and packing tape.

Clunk laid a hand on Hal's arm. 'Leave him be, Mr Spacejock. Don't cause a scene here.'

Hal glanced towards the entrance, where the security guard was watching closely. She had one hand on her blaster, and he realised Clunk was right. There was plenty of time to cause a scene somewhere else, after the will was settled.

Hal glanced towards the buffet as soon as they entered the hall, but the tables had been cleared away. There was a podium in their place, and an elderly man with white hair was standing to one side, checking items on his clipboard. A clock read 12:03, and Hal realised they'd just made it.

They were barely settled when an excited murmur spread through the crowd. A dozen staff were entering the hall via the rear doors, dressed in identical business suits with crisp white shirts and plain ties. They wore hands-free commsets, and each had a stack of coloured tickets. They spread out, criss-crossing the rows of seats to hand out tickets. Occasionally they paused, listening to orders over their commsets.

Hal craned his neck to watch proceedings. There didn't seem to be any pattern to the tickets they were handing out. People were getting red ones and green ones, blue ones and white ones, and if there was anything written on them Hal couldn't see it. Eventually it was his turn, and he received a dark blue scrap of paper. The front was blank, and when he turned it over he discovered the reverse was, too. Hal glanced along the row and saw Cuff holding a similar ticket. He could see Fisher two rows ahead, the abominable robot by his side, but couldn't make out which slip of paper they'd been given.

Finally everyone had a ticket. There was an expectant hush, and then the elderly gent spoke into his microphone.

'Thank you for your patience, ladies and gentlemen. I'm sorry this process has taken so long, but the turnout was greater than expected. Now, if you do not yet have a ticket please raise your hand.'

A couple of hands went up, and uniformed staff converged on them. Moments later, everyone was set.

The loudspeaker crackled again. 'We will proceed to the next stage in a moment or two, but first some of you will be leaving us. Could I ask everyone with a blue ticket to stand up?'

Hal got to his feet, cursing under his breath. Of the hundreds who remained seated, one or two shot him sympathetic glances, but most looked smug. Hal could see two or three others on their feet, Cuff and Fisher amongst them, and he realised his shot at Cuff's fifty grand had just vanished in a puff of smoke.

'Please,' said the voice. 'If you have a blue ticket you must stand up now. We will be inspecting your tickets so there's no point trying to remain here.'

Two more claimants stood up. One was a teenage girl, pale and upset, while the other was a bronze robot with extensive scars across his chest. Each was clutching a blue slip.

'Very well, those of you standing up will now make your way out of the hall. The rest will remain here to await further instructions.'

Hal led Clunk to the exit. The staffers had every angle covered, and his chances of pulling a swifty were non-existent. No, it was game over and goodnight.

'I told you this was a waste of time,' he grumbled to Clunk, as they entered the foyer. 'Four hundred to two or two hundred to one, the odds were lousy either way.'

'Never mind, Mr Spacejock. Perhaps the legacy will go to someone more deserving.'

'What, an even bigger con artist?' Hal nodded towards the restrooms. 'I'm going to flush some ballast. I'll meet you outside and then we'll deal with Cuff. Don't let him go, all right?'

13

Clunk saw Cuff approaching and gave him a curt nod. It was almost a curt head butt, but his programming intervened.

'This is your fault,' hissed Cuff. 'You and that Spacejock loser, it's all down to you. If you hadn't wrecked my beloved Freddie ... '

'Beloved?' Clunk's politeness routines struggled under the load. 'Some owner you are. You can't even remember that poor robot's name!'

Cuff gestured at him and made for the exit, abandoning his robot. The automatic doors remained firmly closed, and when he tried to push them one of the staffers put a hand out. 'I'm sorry, sir. You must stay for the announcement.'

'What announcement?'

'It's very important. We're just waiting for the final member of the party.'

Clunk eyed the rest of the crowd. The teenage girl was being comforted by a robot, her face buried in its chest. Its comforting expression was only marred by the faint outline of a curly moustache on its upper lip. *Can I help?* Clunk broadcast to the robot.

She'll be all right in a moment, was the reply. *It was just a shock. She thought I might be the one.*

Didn't we all? Clunk had just looked away when there was a thud from the main hall. 'I tell you, you've got it all wrong!' shouted an angry voice. 'Take your hands off me this instant!'

Everyone turned to the hall, where a man in a flight suit was being ejected by a couple of security guards. He had a mane of dark hair and a neat goatee, and Clunk didn't have to read the gold monogram on his flight suit to recognise him. It was Kent Spearman, Mr Spacejock's rival!

The guards pushed him into the lobby, then shoved his robot out after him.

'I said you've got it all wrong!' protested Spearman.

'I'm sorry, sir. You were given a blue ticket. It was on camera.'

'Hey man, I was just taking my plate out the back. It's not a crime to wash up, is it?'

The guards ignored his protests and slammed the doors in his face.

'Well that sucks,' said Spearman. He looked around the room, his gaze pausing on the teenage girl before passing over Clunk without recognition. Hardly surprising, since there were half a dozen bronze robots in the lobby. 'If anyone needs a lift off this rock, I'm your man. I have a fast ship at the spaceport and my rates can't be beat.'

Clunk suppressed a groan. There'd be fireworks when Mr Spacejock found out his rival was in town. He eyed Spearman's robot, a battered XG model like himself, and frowned at the obvious signs of mistreatment. Its outer skin was dull, one eye was cracked and three fingers on its left hand were bent backwards. If he didn't know better he'd say it had been pulled from a junk cupboard and fired up in haste. *Are you sure you should be here?* he broadcast to the robot

All he got back was an earful of static.

Clunk looked around the lobby to inspect the remaining robots. There was Cuff with his burnt-out shell, still lashed to a luggage trolley. Nearby was the thickset man Mr Spacejock had been speaking to earlier. Fisher, that was it. He had grey hair and was wearing a neat suit, an expensive watch and a thick gold ring. Alongside him was his grotesque robot, and Clunk felt anger rising inside him at the sight. How could anyone be so callous? Finally, he turned to the fourth robot. It looked okay at first inspection, but the scarred chest panels had scorch marks around them, as though the robot had been wrenched open and rebuilt. Clunk looked around for the owner, ready to give them an accusing glare, but this robot stood alone. It met Clunk's eyes and hunched slightly, as though getting ready to spring. *What are you looking at?*

Nothing, broadcast Clunk. *I was just wondering where your owner is.*

I don't have one. I'm a free agent.

Good for you. Clunk glanced back at the first robot, the one with the moustache, and his expression softened. It was clearly the best of the bunch, and someone had taken the time to polish it from head to toe. They'd even cleaned the fluff from its cooling vents, which most people didn't bother with. Alongside it, the teenage girl was looking somewhat lost. Clunk gave her a nod and a smile, but she didn't notice.

Clunk looked around the robots again, and he realised they were all minor variations of the same model. They all had 'XG99' stamped on their chest plates, just as he did. Were the organisers clearing the hall type by type, until they were left with a handful of potentials? If so, the only surprise was that they didn't have cameras in place, recording the whole process for one of those ghastly reality shows humans seemed to enjoy.

'Excuse me, everyone.' The woman near the entrance raised

her voice. 'Now you're all here, would you please gather round? This concerns all of you, and those vital blue tickets you were given.'

Clunk glanced towards the restroom, but there was no sign of Mr Spacejock. Mystified, he freed up some storage and started recording.

The woman with the clipboard addressed the small crowd. 'Your bus just arrived, and it will take you to a hotel in the city. After arrival you'll be briefed on the next stage in the process.'

There was dead silence, broken only by the muffled sound of the loudspeaker as it barked instructions to the people still waiting inside the hall.

'Come on, people. It's not going to wait for you.' The young woman looked around the room, only to meet blank stares. 'Well? What's the problem?'

Hushed murmurs filled the foyer, and the grey-haired man cleared his throat. 'Listen, we got the blue tickets. The voice told us to leave.'

'That's right. They're going to keep the others back until you get clear.'

'But the voice said –'

'Okay, I'll make this quick. There are four hundred people in that hall, and any second now they're going to learn they've all been eliminated from contention. The blue tickets were a ruse to get you lot to safety. Understood?' The staff member glanced at her watch. 'Speaking of safety, we have to leave right now. Please, the bus is waiting.'

Comprehension dawned, and there was a stampede for the exit. Clunk was left behind, and he was just trying to explain Hal's absence to the staffer when there was an angry growl from the hall. Hundreds of people had just learned the truth, and they did not sound happy.

'You'll have to make your own way there,' said the staff member, beating a hasty retreat.

'Where?' called Clunk, but the reply was lost in the uproar.

He heard the loudspeakers calling for calm, but at the same instant there was a crash and the doors to the hall began to shake. Clunk crossed to the restroom in three strides, desperate to reach Hal before the angry mob was unleashed. With any luck he would be able to keep Mr Spacejock safe until help arrived.

14

Hal shook the water off his hands and pulled a length of paper towel from the dispenser. When he was done he dropped the waste into the disposal unit. There was a blue flash as the unit disintegrated the waste into molecules, and a whoosh as it sucked them away.

'Hey, neat!' Hal took a bigger length of towel, wadded it and dropped it into the disposal unit.

Flash! Whoosh! The room lit up with searing blue light.

Fascinated, Hal pulled an even longer piece and dangled the end into the flash disposal. As he lowered the paper into the unit it disappeared into thin air, fizzing and dancing. When it was gone Hal reached for the dispenser again, ready to yank out several metres. Unfortunately it was now empty.

Hal remembered Cuff, and wondered whether the unit could handle bodies. Then he patted his pockets to see whether he had any junk to get rid of. He came up with the blue ticket.

'Fat lot of use that was,' muttered Hal, holding it over the mouth of the disposal unit. He was just about to let go of his blue ticket when the door burst open, almost knocking him across the wash room. 'Hey, what's the bloody rush?'

'Mr Spacejock, we have to get out of here.'

Hal struggled to his feet. 'You've got to see this thing first.

It'll swallow anything!'

'We don't have time. We must –'

'Here, watch this.' Hal released the blue ticket above the opening. As it fluttered towards certain destruction Clunk reacted, diving forwards with both arms outstretched. He plucked the ticket from mid-air and cannoned into the wall, cracking the tiles.

'You're a bit hyper, aren't you? Did you overcharge your battery again?'

The wash room door started to open and Clunk hurled himself at it, slamming it shut with his shoulder. He put his back to the door, hands braced against the walls. 'Mr Spacejock, please listen. The organisers were doing things backwards. Those with blue tickets move onto the next stage of the inheritance. Everyone left in the hall was disqualified.'

'Why do it that way round?'

'They wanted to get us out before the much larger crowd learned of the deception.' Clunk winced as the door shook behind him. 'That large crowd has now realised the truth, and they're out for blood. Your blood.'

'You mean there are hundreds of angry people out there?'

'Precisely.'

'And the rest of the ticket holders?'

'They just left in a bus.'

'Why didn't you tell them to wait?'

There was a hefty thump on the door, shaking Clunk from head to toe.

'We know you're in there,' said a voice. 'Open up!'

THUMP! Clunk shifted his hands and feet, trying to get better purchase. 'We must escape before there's a full scale riot.'

Hal looked around the bathroom but the only other exit was

a small window high on the far wall. If he put his foot on the wash basin he might just be able to reach it, but the moment Clunk stepped away from the door the crowd would pour in. 'I don't suppose you have a gun?' He saw Clunk's expression. 'Not to shoot anyone, just to wave about until they come to their senses.'

'I'm unarmed, as always.' Clunk nodded towards the window. 'Can you get that open?'

'Probably, but what about you?'

'Just do it, Mr Spacejock.'

Hal clambered onto the wash basin, almost losing his footing on a large bar of soap. Wobbling slightly, he reached for the window catch. It was stiff with age, but he wiggled it furiously until it came loose, then pushed the window open. He peered out and realised it led onto a deserted alley. The drop was only small, and he was sure he could fit through the window. But that wouldn't help Clunk.

'Go, Mr Spacejock. Don't worry about me.'

Hal frowned. Clunk was a loyal friend, not someone to be abandoned at the drop of a hat. Anyway, he needed the robot to make a claim on the will. He looked around the bathroom for inspiration, and his gaze fell on the soap. 'I've got it,' he said. 'We'll use this handy bar of soap to escape.'

'But I don't have any tracking bugs!'

'Typical robot, always reaching for high tech solutions.' Hal filled the basin, flaking soap into the water until froth spilled onto the floor. It spread rapidly, running into the stalls and lapping around Clunk's feet, and Hal grabbed the remains of the bar and clambered onto the basin. It creaked underfoot, protesting the rough treatment, but remained attached to the wall. Once he was poised at the window, Hal nodded towards the door. 'Ready?'

'Yes.'

'Okay ... let them in!'

Clunk released the door and crossed the slippery floor at a dead run, his traction control working overtime as it compensated for the treacherous surface. The crowd poured in behind him and Hal threw the bar of soap at the leader, hoping to distract him while Clunk got clear. It smacked the angry-looking man right in the forehead, and he went down as though shot, sliding through the water and leaving neat bow-waves with his face. Those behind him stumbled and fell, and Hal squeezed through the window before they could recover and lay hands on him. He reached the ground and turned to give Clunk a hand, just as the robot put his foot on the basin to climb out. There was a creak as the sink broke off the wall, and a loud crash as it smashed on the tiled floor. Broken pipes spewed hot and cold water, and the pursuers who'd kept their feet were promptly knocked over. Clunk put his foot on a broken pipe to get a leg up, but the pipe bent flush with the wall.

'Give me your hands,' said Hal desperately. 'I'll pull you out!'

'No. Stand clear, Mr Spacejock.'

A split second later the window exploded outwards. Clunk came through the middle like a high-diver, hands together and head tucked between his arms. He turned the perfect dive into a forward somersault, landing on both feet and bending at the knees to absorb the impact.

There was a shout from the bathroom and angry faces appeared at the window, one with a red mark the size and shape of a bar of soap, another with one of Clunk's footprints across his cheek, and the rest soaked to the skin and lathered with foam. Hands reached for purchase, and Hal raised the window frame and slammed it on their fingers, banging it down a couple of times to get the message through. Then a chunk of sink came sailing by, narrowly missing his head, and he decided it was time to retreat.

15

Hal and Clunk ran across the sunny courtyard towards a wooden gate, desperate to escape their pursuers. As they ran they could hear voices on the other side of the fence, and when they burst through the gate they found a narrow lane full of people. Hal recognised a few from the hall, although most had abandoned their treasured robots. Great, he thought. Not only were dozens of angry people chasing them, there were hundreds more outside. And every one of them was keen to work off their frustrations.

'Play it cool,' he muttered to Clunk.

The gate closed behind them and they pushed through the crowd, making for the main street. They were only halfway along when the gate flew open and their wet, soapy pursuers poured through. There was dead silence, and then ...

'Over there! That's him! The guy with the bronze robot!'

'Oh dear,' said Clunk.

Hal looked at the crowd. The crowd looked back at him. Then Hal pointed towards the gate. 'That's the guy who inherited the lot! The one with the mark on his face!'

The crowd turned to look, those at the back standing on tip-toe to see what all the fuss was about. In the confusion Hal tapped Clunk on the shoulder, and they ran like fury. They got a fifty metre start before the crowd realised they'd been duped, and there was a wild roar as the whole lot set off in pursuit.

◆

Hal felt the pavement shaking as he ran, but he couldn't tell whether it was the thunder of feet or the roar of angry voices. Alongside him Clunk ran in silence, saving a string of good advice for later. As they ran, Hal's brain raced as quickly as his feet. He'd barely had time to think about the inheritance, but it dawned on him that Clunk was actually one of the six finalists. With a bit of luck they were in line for a massive payout, unless they were torn apart first by a rampaging mob.

They turned left and ran along a broad avenue lined with trees and outdoor cafes. As he ran, Hal knocked tables and chairs flying, hoping to delay his pursuers. Diners leapt to their feet as he bore down on them, snatching up cups and plates. Seconds later they were knocked flying by the roaring crowd.

Up ahead Hal saw a stream of children pouring out of a school bus, completely blocking the pavement. He ran around them, straight into the road.

Groundcars do not have tyres, nor wheels, and they do not screech to a halt in a cloud of smoke. In fact, they're surrounded by an invisible force field which extends for several metres in every direction. As Hal ran into the road, the car which had been approaching at speed threw out the anchors and reconfigured its force field for a human target. Hal was enveloped in the field and carried along with a sensation not unlike falling into a huge vat of honey.

The car came to a halt, the field deactivated, and Hal fell to the road. He was just getting up when the driver leant out the window. 'Are you crazy? You ran straight in front of me!'

Hal got a brief impression of an angry face and long blonde hair, and then he realised the crowd was almost on him. He leapt up, and without a word he yanked the door open and dived into the car. Clunk jumped in the back, and was still closing the door when Hal pointed through the windscreen. 'Drive!' he shouted. 'Now!'

◆

The woman took one look at the crowd and planted her foot. Hal was rammed into his seat by a surge of raw power, and as they raced to safety he looked back to see the crowd vanishing into the distance. Relieved, he grinned at their driver. 'Thanks. That was close.'

'Don't mention it.'

Hal eyed her profile, and frowned. 'Have we met?'

'I doubt it.'

'I'm sure I've seen you before.'

'Nope. Definitely not.' The woman spared him a glance. 'Why were they chasing you?'

'No reason.'

The car came to a halt, almost throwing Hal through the windscreen. 'Listen,' said the woman. 'I'm a freelance reporter, and I don't eat unless I write.'

'Reporter, eh?' Hal glanced back and saw the crowd picking up their pace. 'If you don't get moving you'll have a story all right.'

'What's your name?'

'Hal Spacejock, and they're getting closer.'

'I'm Natasha Lucas.' The reporter seemed oblivious to the crowd. 'And your robot?'

'Clunk.'

'Nice to meet you, Clunk. Now, I'm guessing you just came out of Argisle and Butt. Am I right?'

'Yeah, we did.'

'And the crowd is angry because you passed the first round.'

'How did you know that?'

'Inside info. I was trying to follow the bus full of blue ticket holders when you leapt in front of my car.'

Hal could hear the crowd now, shouting and yelling like a pack of angry seagulls.

'So now I've lost the bus I'm thinking ... what can I possibly write about?' Natasha looked at Hal and waited.

'How about 'angry mob tears reporter to pieces?'' suggested Hal. 'You might win an award for that one.'

'A posthumous award,' added Clunk. 'Ms Lucas, we do appreciate you stopping for us –'

'Not that I had much choice.'

'– but we'd really need to leave.'

'Where are we going?'

'City centre.'

'Is that where the bus was heading?'

By now Hal could see the whites of their pursuers' eyes, and he was getting ready to turf the reporter out so he could steal her car. 'Yes, it's where the damn bus was going. Now will you please move!'

'Will you give me an exclusive interview?'

'We'd rather keep a low profile,' said Clunk.

'It's a bit late for that,' remarked Natasha. 'You might as well milk the publicity now. Didn't you say you were in the cargo business?'

'Yeah, we –' Hal turned to stare at her. 'We didn't say that at all. How did you know?'

'Flight suit, hangdog expression, coffee stains ... it all adds up.' Natasha glanced in the mirror. 'My, aren't they close?'

'They're right on top of us, you mad –'

'Interview. Yes or no?'

'Yes. YES!'

'Cool.'

At that moment their pursuers arrived. One of them grinned triumphantly and reached for the door handle, and Hal raised his hands to fend off an attack. Before the woman could open the door Natasha planted her foot. There was an angry howl from the crowd as their prey escaped once more, and Hal started breathing again.

'Tell you what,' said Natasha. 'Why don't you let me do a proper feature? I'll make you famous. Your business will get exposure all over the galaxy.'

'I don't think we want any exposure,' said Clunk.

'Are you kidding? It sounds great!' Hal sat up in excitement, the near death experience driven out of his mind. 'Free publicity and a whacking great inheritance. Who could ask for more?'

'You'll just make yourself a bigger target,' said Clunk. 'You'll have thousands chasing you, not just a few hundred. Please, Mr Spacejock. Reconsider.'

Natasha smiled at him in the mirror. 'I think your owner has already made up his mind.'

She asked questions as she negotiated the traffic, starting with Hal's background and working up to the present. Eventually she got to the inheritance. 'So when did you hear about the will?'

'Yesterday. We brought a passenger to Barwonica –'

'Barwenna.'

'We brought a passenger here but he couldn't pay his fare until he'd met with his solicitors. He had this beaten-up old robot with him, and –'

Natasha glanced at Clunk. 'And you stole it and decided to claim the inheritance yourself. That'll sound good in my article.'

'No, Clunk's my co-pilot. This was another beaten-up old robot.'

There was a squeak as Clunk pressed his lips together.

'So how did you end up in the running?' asked Natasha.

Hal explained. 'The way our passenger told it, his robot was going to inherit and he'd use the money to pay us. Then his robot blew up, and I lent him Clunk as a ring-in. Just so he could get the inheritance, you understand.'

'You didn't realise hundreds of people have been flocking to this planet to claim on the will?'

'Not until we saw them.'

'Our spaceport has been packed for days. Old robots are changing hands more often than a transplant surgeon.' Natasha sniffed. 'I've been researching the whole thing for a couple of weeks now, and it's unbelievable the lengths some of them have gone to. You know, one couple sold their house to get their robot here on time.'

Hal watched her closely as she spoke, and then it came to him. 'You're the tax inspector!'

'What?'

'I knew I'd met you before! You were in the bistro last night. The one at the Hotel Grande.'

Natasha looked at him. 'Sussed me out, huh?'

'You mean you're not a reporter at all?' Hal's stomach tightened. 'You're investigating my finances?'

'Relax, Hal. I'm not a tax inspector. I just use that line when I want guys to leave me alone.' Natasha stopped at an intersection. 'So where are we going?'

Hal glanced at Clunk, who shrugged. 'They just said a city hotel.'

'All right. They're all in the same block. I'll just drive past them until we spot the bus.'

'There is another way.' Clunk turned to Hal. 'Mr Spacejock, I saw an old friend of yours at the solicitors.'

'Really? Who?'

'Kent Spearman.'

'You're kidding! What did that loser want?'

'He brought a robot along. In fact, he got through to the next round as well.'

'That fraud? He never owned a robot in his life. He just uses them up and turfs them out the airlock when they ask for wages.'

'Back up a bit,' said Natasha. 'Who's this Kent guy?'

'He's a taller, wealthier version of Mr Spacejock,' said Clunk.

'He's nothing like me!' protested Hal. 'Kent's a chancer. He'd steal a cargo job without a second thought, and as for his so-called flying skills ... well, I wouldn't go aboard his ship if you paid me.'

Clunk wisely said nothing.

'Is he a rival?' asked Natasha. 'If so, I must include him in my article. Rivals make great copy.'

Hal snorted. 'Spearman makes lousy coffee. He wouldn't know a grinder from a mallet.'

'His failings are irrelevant,' interrupted Clunk, before Hal could list them all. 'The point is, he knows where the next round is taking place. If we call his ship –'

'I'm not asking Kent Spearman for help,' said Hal flatly.

'Don't fuss yourselves.' Natasha gestured through the windscreen. 'There's the bus.'

Hal squinted. In the distance he could just see a bus pulling away from a hotel, and he laughed when he realised where it had stopped. 'Clunk, it's our hotel. The Grande!'

16

Hal was out of the car before the engine stopped. 'Come on, Clunk. Get a move on!' The robot clambered out and Hal slammed the doors. As they ran for the entrance Natasha leapt out and followed, leaving her car dropping slowly towards the pavement.

At the entrance an elderly doorman touched his cap. 'Good afternoon, sir. Glad to have you back, Ms Lucas.' He was left spinning on the spot as they raced by. In the lobby they saw an events board with 'Baker Group' on it, along with an arrow pointing to the conference room. Hal hurried to the doors, but when he tried the handle he discovered it was locked. He could hear a voice on the other side, and he rattled the handle and knocked to get their attention.

The door opened a crack and one of the uniformed staffers from the solicitors looked out. 'I'm sorry, sir. This is a private conference.'

'I know that! I'm supposed to be inside. We missed the bus.'

'Do you have your pass?'

Hal handed her the crumpled blue ticket, and she nodded and opened the doors. A dozen people turned to stare at the newcomers, Kent Spearman amongst them. 'Well if it isn't Hal Jockstrap, the pilot who couldn't find his joystick with both hands and a large mirror. Have you delivered any cargo lately, or are you still scattering it all over random planets?'

'I –'

'And you're still dragging that bag of bolts around!' Spearman grinned at Clunk's expression. 'No offence, Lunk. I meant your ship.'

'My name is Clunk, and one does not take offence at the innocent ramblings of a child.'

Now it was Hal's turn to grin. 'What are you doing here, you lousy excuse for a pilot? I thought you were in jail. Again.'

'That was just a misunderstanding,' said Spearman, with an airy gesture. 'I gave them your description and they let me go. Then I set out to earn a living.'

'Really? So why are you flying a cargo ship?'

Up the front of the room the speaker cleared his throat, which sounded like an exploding grenade through the PA system. 'Would you mind settling this petty squabble later? We have important matters to attend to.'

'Sorry we're late. We got held up.'

'Like you're ever on time,' muttered Spearman.

'Later, please! Now, I'm Mr Butt and I'm just sharing a little background information on the company.' Behind the elderly man a screen displayed a row of headless robots. Underneath was the legend *Main assembly line. Image courtesy Baker Industries.*

Hal took a seat at the back, just behind Fisher and his freaky robot. Clunk sat next to him, and then Hal realised Natasha was still trying to get in. She was having a whispered conversation with the woman at the door, and he was about to go and help when the staffer nodded and held the door open.

'If we're quite ready,' continued Butt. He gestured at the screen. 'As I was saying, these are the six robots we're interested in. One of them is the robot mentioned in the will, and we're confident that very same robot is sitting in this room.'

There were several sidelong glances, and the thoughts were plain to see. Which one of these elderly machines was in line for a vast fortune? More images flashed up on the screen: robots on the assembly lines, robots being crated up and robots being shipped out. After a bunch more happy snaps the screen went dark and the lights came up. 'That's enough background information,' said Butt. 'Now to explain the elimination process.' He took a sip of water. 'Any one of you could be the robot we're looking for, but it's up to you to prove it. We don't have the time or resources to investigate your past, so we're giving you the task instead.'

The man in the leather jacket raised his hand.

'Yes, Mr Fisher?'

'How come you don't have the resources when there's a fortune at stake? Can't you spend some of it to find the right robot?'

Butt looked shocked. 'Of course we can't! It's not our money to spend.'

'Someone must be in charge.'

'When the correct robot is found it will inherit the entire fortune. In the meantime the funds are held in trust and cannot be touched.'

'Surely your firm –'

'Mr Fisher, we charge a fixed fee for our services. Spending tens of thousands to find a beneficiary is out of the question.'

'I'm sure they'd pay you back,' said Fisher drily. 'In fact, if you give me the inheritance I'll pay you a hundred grand.'

'I'll make it two hundred,' said Kent quickly.

The others laughed, and Butt turned red. 'Th-that's a most

inappropriate suggestion. Everything about this process must be transparent and above board.'

Hal was about to offer five hundred grand and a lifetime of free freight, but he caught Clunk's warning look just in time.

'Now, you will have expenses but they should be modest. As far as we know, the information you need will be found in the local system.' Butt looked around the room. 'I believe two of you are pilots. Would you make yourselves known?'

Kent stood up and gave the others a mock bow. Hal got up more slowly, and he nodded when everyone looked at him.

'If there's any travel involved, these gentlemen should be able to assist you.'

'For a fee,' said Kent, with a wink.

Hal snorted. 'A big fee, if they fly with you.'

'At least they'll arrive at the other end.' Kent stroked his goatee. 'Remind me which acrobatics go best with a shipment of glass. Was it a loop-the-loop or a barrel roll?'

Hal sneered at him and sat down.

Kent wasn't finished yet. He smiled around the room, then tapped himself in the chest. 'Listen guys, I'm serious. If you want a fast ship see me. I'm the fastest ride this side of the big dipper.'

'So I've heard,' muttered Hal.

There was a round of laughter, and Kent sat down in a hurry.

The speaker continued. 'Before you leave we'll distribute information packets with full details, but I'll cover some of it now. Your first destination is the Barwenna Orbiter, where they keep records for every robot arriving and departing the planet. Once at the Orbiter you must find the public access terminals and seek information on your serial numbers. When you discover where you were shipped from, your hunt truly begins.'

102

There was a teenage girl sitting in the front row, and she raised her hand.

'Yes?'

'Can't we access the information from here?' she asked in a low voice.

'I'm sorry, my dear.' Butt spread his hands. 'The records are kept offline for security reasons. In the past, unscrupulous people used this sort of information to fake service histories, ownership records and so on. The authorities tightened up their procedures and will only provide records in person.'

Kent winked at the girl. 'Don't worry, love. You get a special rate.'

'Greaser,' muttered Hal. He turned to Clunk. 'What do we need old records for? You know where you came from, don't you?'

Clunk shook his head. 'Our memories are erased when we change hands. If we're lucky it's a selective wipe, which leaves us with a rough timeline. Sometimes they'll overwrite our own memories with an imprint from a donor robot, but more often than not we're completely wiped.'

'That must be tough.'

Clunk shrugged. 'They're my memories until someone proves otherwise.'

Hal realised everyone was listening to the conversation. 'Don't mind us. Carry on.'

Butt nodded. 'What you heard illustrates the problem nicely. There's no telling which of you served with Mr Baker, and is therefore entitled to the legacy. The only constants are your individual serial numbers, embedded in your brains.'

'Fine,' said Kent. 'Do you want to check my robot first? There's a sports car I've had my eye on, and they have three in my favourite colour.'

'My robot needs urgent repairs,' said Sandy. 'He should go first.'

'Ladies, gentlemen, robots. Please!' Butt raised his hands, motioning everyone to silence. 'Mr Baker did not record his robot's serial number. Therefore, each of you must pick up the trail and work backwards until you can prove you're the robot we're looking for.' Butt gestured to his staff, who began handing out envelopes. Hal tore his open and found a glossy folder with a summary of the presentation. He turned to the last page and frowned. 'Excuse me. What's this about a deadline?'

'Oh yes, that's quite normal. After a certain amount of time the beneficiary is declared legally dead, and the trustees manage the estate from that point on. We're more than capable of –'

A bronze robot raised his hand. He had a hard, pinched expression and there were faded scorch marks across his chest.

'Yes, Zee?'

'This deadline ... just twenty-four hours. Really?'

The speaker leant on the podium. 'If you can't prove yourself by this time tomorrow, you're not the robot Mr Baker thought you were.'

'Is that a challenge?'

'This process will be a challenge for you all,' said Butt smoothly. 'Nobody is pretending it will be easy to uncover your entire lives and prove an unbroken line back to robot zero. On the other hand, you cannot expect to claim a vast fortune without some effort on your part.'

'If you think ...' Zee controlled himself. 'I still believe twenty-four hours is insufficient.'

'Your opinion has been noted. Now, on to practical matters. The hotel has arranged rooms for you all, free of charge, and dinner will be served at seven. I suggest you get a good night's sleep before embarking on your little adventure in the morning. We've arranged a minibus for eight, and there's a shuttle service leaving for the Orbiter at ten.'

Hal raised his hand to suggest a better plan, but before he could speak Clunk's metal elbow caught him a solid blow in the ribs.

'Say nothing,' murmured the robot.

Hal rubbed his side. 'Why don't you puncture the other lung as well? That would keep me quiet for good.'

Butt continued. 'That leads me to the next point: contact with the outside world. I must ask that you make no attempt to communicate with others outside this hotel, the media in particular. To this end, the terminals in your rooms have been disabled, and if you have personal commsets I must ask you to switch them off and hand them in at the front desk. Again, this is for your own safety.'

'I'm running a business!' protested Fisher. 'What am I supposed to tell my customers?'

'We've prepared a cover story. You've all contracted a minor illness and are being quarantined to prevent it spreading. Give your contact details to the front desk and we'll organise carers and sitters for anyone who needs them. Remember, this is only for one night.'

Butt wrapped up proceedings, and then the doors opened and everyone filed out. They were shepherded to reception, where they were bioscanned for their room keys. Hal pocketed his, still warm from the imprinter, and followed the others to the lifts. Clunk waved everyone else aboard then stood back. 'We'll catch the next one, Mr Spacejock.'

'There's plenty of room.'

'Yes, but your claustrophobia might kick in.'

'My what?'

'We'll wait for the next lift.'

As soon as the doors closed Clunk turned for the exit.

'Where are you going?' demanded Hal.

'If you want to lie about on feather beds and wait for room service that's your lookout,' said Clunk. 'Personally, I believe we should start our research immediately.'

'You'll be wanting a ride, then,' said Natasha, who'd come up behind them.

Hal jumped. He'd forgotten about the reporter. 'How did you get into the meeting?'

'I told them I was a nurse.'

'And?'

'A psychiatric nurse, keeping an eye on my patient.'

'But who –'

Clunk snorted. 'Come on, Mr Spacejock. Time's wasting.'

17

They ran down the hotel steps and got into Natasha's car, but before they could drive off the reporter nodded towards the hotel entrance. 'Someone you know?'

Hal turned to see the teenage girl at the top of the steps, one arm around her robot and the other waving at them. She was struggling with the weight, and the robot was in a bad way. There was blue smoke pouring from its vents, and it kept jerking uncontrollably, threatening to tip them both headlong down the stairs.

'Better make some room,' said Hal, and he left the car to help. The robot was taking one careful step at a time, its fans whirring and clattering as they strove to cool its circuits. Hal took its weight across his shoulders and frowned at the girl. 'I thought you went up with the rest?'

'I got out on the first floor and came down in the other lift.'

'What about the free room? Breakfast?'

'They must think we're idiots,' said Sandy. 'Start at ten tomorrow? Insane.'

Hal nodded in agreement. It wasn't just the time issue ... when the mob from the solicitors found out where they were staying they'd probably lay siege to the place. 'I'm Hal, by the way. Hal Spacejock.'

'I'm Sandy and this is Daniel.'

Hal saw Clunk coming to meet them. 'Take her side, Clunk. She's all in.'

'I can manage,' said the girl firmly.

They reached the bottom of the steps, where Daniel sat down with a bump. Clunk opened an inspection panel and drew in a sharp breath. 'This robot is overheating badly. If we don't get its temperature down immediately it will burn out.'

Sandy looked at Clunk in shock. 'Burn out! But I thought …'

'There's no time to argue. Fetch bottled water from the lobby. Quick!'

The girl ran back into the hotel while Clunk laid the robot down and checked its internals. It wheezed and gasped, and was still emitting clouds of blue smoke. 'This robot should not be walking around. It's been pushed to the limit.'

'Can't you turn it off?'

'No. If the fans stop the heat build-up will cook the internals.' Clunk straightened several fins on a radiator inside the robot's chest. Then he reached deep inside and eased out a length of red tubing. 'Would you hold this please?'

Hal did as he was told, then dropped it in a hurry. 'Hey, it's hot!'

'Use your sleeve.'

Hal wrapped the tube in several folds of fabric before holding it gingerly between forefinger and thumb. When it was secure Clunk delved into the robot's chest once more. Meanwhile, Hal glanced towards the car, where Natasha was leaning over the rear seat to gather up a bunch of files.

'Mr Spacejock,' said Clunk.

'Hmm?'

'Mr Spacejock!'

Hal realised he was twisting the red tube in his hands, and he let go in a hurry. It whizzed back into the robot's chest with a whirr-*snap*, and Clunk hissed under his breath.

'Sorry.'

'That's all right, Mr Spacejock. Take your time and enjoy the scenery. I don't have anything important to do.'

'I said sorry!' Hal took the tube again, and then his gaze wandered back to the car. The reporter was now opening the boot, and as she bent over ...

Whirr! *Snap!*

'MR SPACEJOCK!'

'I'm sorry! It slipped!' Hal grabbed the tube and forced himself to watch the elderly porter struggling with a suitcase.

Before long Sandy returned with a bottle of cold water, and Clunk wrapped the tube round it to make a coil. Then he poked a loop inside the bottle, submerging it in the chilled liquid. 'That should lower the temperature a little, but it'll be best if we keep this robot immobile as long as possible.'

'I really appreciate your help,' said Sandy.

'It's a pity you don't appreciate your robot,' said Clunk primly.

'I've been looking after Daniel since I was nine years old,' snapped Sandy. 'This is the first time he's been outside in years.'

'I'm sorry. I assumed –'

'Well don't.'

Hal hid a smile. Clunk versus teenager! He could sell tickets to that one.

◆

They got Sandy's robot into the car, and once everyone was seated Natasha took the controls. 'Can we leave now, or are you expecting anyone else?'

Hal snorted. He didn't know much about Fisher, but he'd be happy never to see Cuff or Kent Spearman again. 'That's it. Let's head for the spaceport.'

Traffic was sparse and Natasha drove efficiently. Once or twice she glanced round at Sandy, sizing the teenager up, but Sandy was busy looking after her robot and didn't notice.

'How's Daniel doing?' asked Clunk.

'This water is getting hot.'

Clunk tested it, then frowned. 'It'll boil soon. Better let me hold it.'

'I can manage.'

'No you can't. Boiling water will burn you. I, on the other hand, will be unaffected.'

Sandy passed the bottle over.

'So,' said Natasha, glancing at Sandy again. 'Embarking on a big adventure, eh? Are you excited?'

'I'm not twelve, you know. And this isn't a family outing.'

Natasha blinked. 'But I'm doing a feature on the claimants. You've got to give me something!'

Sandy said nothing.

'Come on, work with me! What about your boyfriend? What does he think of all this? Or girlfriend, maybe?'

'That's none of your business.'

'You're a local, aren't you? Where do you live?'

Sandy pressed her lips together.

'At least give me your surname.'

Nothing.

Defeated, Natasha turned her attention to Sandy's robot. 'Daniel, isn't it? What can you tell me about your owner?'

'N-nothing, w-without perm…permission.'

'Oh, come on! The devoted companion? Don't you have anything –'

'I'm sorry,' interrupted Clunk. 'You mustn't badger him.'

'Fine,' said Natasha shortly. 'I'll just drive, shall I?'

— 18 —

Ten minutes later they drew up at the spaceport entrance, where a heavy barrier blocked the road. A security guard leant out of the hut to look them over, and then the barrier went up. Before they could move there was a massive roar overhead. A rented flyer went over, bright yellow with flashing lights, and Natasha's car plunged through the cloud of swirling dust kicked up by its jets. When the air cleared they saw the flyer settling on the tarmac, the doors already opening. A set of steps unfolded from the side, and three men got out: Spearman, Cuff and Fisher.

'What the hell!' exclaimed Hal.

'Very cunning,' said Natasha. 'They must have booked that flyer at the hotel. There's a landing pad on the roof.'

'Quick . . . to the *Volante*! If they get clearance first we'll have to wait for them to lift off.'

Instead, Natasha pulled over and switched off the engine.

'What are you doing?'

Natasha turned in her seat. 'I've already interviewed you, and little miss button-lip here isn't giving me anything. I'm going with the others.'

'At least drive us to my ship! Her robot won't make it that far.'

'Sorry, gotta dash.' Natasha herded them out, then locked her car and hurried after Kent Spearman and the others. They were hauling their robots out of the flyer: first Cuff's wreck, still lashed to the hotel trolley, and then Spearman's and Fisher's pair. The lone robot, Zee, climbed out last.

Kent saw Natasha hurrying towards him, and he did a double-take when he spotted Hal. His eyes narrowed, and then he shouted at the others and ran for his ship.

◆

Unfortunately Kent's ship was closer to the spaceport entrance than the *Volante*, and Hal's group had to walk right past it. Kent was already herding his charges up the ramp, and they were aboard before Hal was halfway there. Kent gave him a mocking salute before sealing the door.

'We ought to report him,' muttered Hal. 'Impersonating a pilot, flying under the influence ... there must be something we can get him with.'

'Actually,' said Clunk, 'we should move to a safe distance before he takes off.'

Hal nodded towards Sandy, who was helping her labouring robot. 'What about her?'

'She should retreat as well, unless she's fireproof.'

'I mean, what about helping her out? Is she all right to fly with us?'

The *Tiger's* hazard lights began to flash, and a siren wailed across the landing field. 'We can discuss it later. Right now, I think Mr Spearman is about to take off.'

'No kidding.' Hal beckoned to Sandy. 'Come on. We have to take cover.' He opened a blast door set into the side of a landing pad, and they hurried down a short flight of steps to a dank, concrete-lined shelter. The heavy slab of a door had barely closed when they heard the whistling roar of the *Tiger*'s engines. They grew in volume, shaking dust and grit from the roof as the ship lifted off. The noise was more prolonged than usual, and Hal frowned as it seemed to get closer. 'What's he up to?' he shouted, his voice barely audible over the roar.

'I think he's saying goodbye,' shouted Clunk.

The walls trembled as the heavy freighter drifted towards their hiding place. Hal couldn't see it, but he could picture the belching fire and exhaust. The noise was so overpowering he had to clamp his hands over his ears, and he saw Sandy cowering against Clunk as he tried to protect her from falling dust and grit. Her own robot stood nearby, mute and motionless.

The roar intensified, and Hal guessed they were directly underneath the ship's roaring exhausts. Then, with a sound like a thousand thunderstorms, it blasted into the sky.

'Bastard,' muttered Hal, when he could hear again. 'Either he's the worst pilot in the universe or he did that on purpose.'

'He's definitely not the worst,' said Clunk with conviction.

'Come on, let's go.' Hal reached for the door but Clunk grabbed his arm. 'What?'

Clunk switched the light off, and Hal realised what. The full force of the *Tiger*'s jets had played on the heavy metal, and it glowed dull red from the searing heat. Clunk took hold of the handle and twisted, but the distorted metal door was stuck firmly in the frame.

They were trapped.

Hal paced the cramped bunker, scraping his head on the low ceiling. It was twenty minutes since Kent Spearman had sealed them in and Clunk still wasn't prepared to test the door. According to the robot, the extreme heat would have softened the metal, and forcing the handle would only break the mechanism.

It was stuffy in the bunker, and Hal's impatience only raised the temperature. He muttered under his breath, clenched and unclenched his fists, and ran up a quick list of all the ship-to-ship weapons he'd be fitting to the *Volante* the second he got out. Friendly rivalry was one thing, but Kent had overstepped the mark with his dangerous stunt, and Hal's idea of payback was a nice fat missile right up the exhaust cone. The only difficulty would be distracting Clunk while the new weapons were fitted ... that, and finding the cash to pay for them.

'Can't you try it yet?' he demanded, when Clunk showed no signs of moving.

'Alas no. We must wait for it to cool.'

'How much longer?'

'I cannot say.'

'If you were a proper robot you'd have a laser torch embedded in your finger.'

'If you don't sit down you'll have a robot finger embedded in your ear.'

Hal complied, still grumbling. Didn't Clunk understand? Kent Spearman and the others were getting away! 'We're never going to catch up.'

'Of course we will.'

'How? Do you have some extra engines to strap onto the ship? High powered fuel? An intergalactic shortcut?'

'Kent Spearman has four humans on board, each with their own agenda. They'll be squabbling before they get to the first stop. We, on the other hand, have one clearly-defined goal.'

'Yeah, to settle Kent Spearman's hash once and for all.'

Clunk frowned. 'No, to work together and secure the inheritance for Sandy's robot.'

This was news to Hal. 'What about you? It might be your inheritance!'

Clunk gestured impatiently. 'I was never a rich man's plaything, Mr Spacejock.'

'That's not what Butt said.'

'It's what I prefer to believe.'

Hal shrugged, then gestured at the door. 'Is that thing done yet?'

'Let me see.' Clunk took the steps, bending double to avoid the rough concrete roof. He inspected the door closely, examining the area around the hinges and the solid-looking handle. Not quite satisfied, he gave the slab of metal a gentle tap with his finger.

CRASH!

Clunk stood there, one finger raised, as the entire door fell off its hinges and landed with a puff of dirt. 'Well that's a surprise.'

'What the hell did you do?' demanded Hal.

'Nothing. The hinges melted away under the extreme temperatures.'

'You mean we could have busted out an hour ago?' Hal swore under his breath. 'Quick, to the *Volante*!'

19

It was dark outside, and Hal's breath misted in the cold air. Sandy's robot was still wheezing and puffing, but the night air helped with cooling and he moved freely. The four of them hurried towards the *Volante*, all too aware of their competitors' head start.

'Do you think we'll catch them?' asked Sandy.

Hal laughed. 'Sure we will. Spearman couldn't fly straight if you glued his stick to the console.'

As they approached the ship, Sandy eyed the gleaming white bulk looming over them. 'I've never travelled in space before,' she said, apprehension in her voice. 'Is it safe?'

'Safe!' Clunk moved to reassure her. 'The *Volante* is a modern vessel with a perfect record. And statistically speaking, space travel is safer than crossing the road.'

Hal squared his shoulders. 'Plus you'll have me at the controls.'

'Of course,' continued Clunk. 'When you think about it, quite a lot of pedestrians end up in hospital.'

'Speaking of hospital,' said a rough voice behind them, 'that's where you'll end up if you waste any more of our time.'

Hal's heart sank as one of the shadows moved. The two huge men in suits were back, and they didn't look happy. 'I'm running a bit late,' he said quickly. 'Can we do this another time?'

'No. You're coming with us. The boss wants you swimming with the fishies.'

Hal considered his options. He could throw himself at the two men, gaining some time for Clunk, Sandy and Daniel while getting beaten to a pulp, or he could run for it and let Clunk sort things out with diplomacy, tact and those handy metal fists. He was still deciding when a searing green flash lit the scene. The light came from Clunk's eyes, and it blinded the two men with its sheer intensity. Hal was standing behind the robot, and only copped a reflection, but that was enough to leave him stumbling in the darkness. He felt a solid grip on his elbow, and Clunk hurried him up the ramp towards the ship. 'What the hell was that light?' he asked Clunk.

'Barcode scanner,' explained the robot. 'Their vision will return though. We'd better leave quickly.'

On the way up Hal spotted a couple of ground staff attaching a big hose to the fuel tank. 'Clunk, they're filling the ship.'

'Correct.'

'But we don't have any money!'

'Also correct.'

'So ... how will we pay for it?'

'No need. I wired in a claim for pain and suffering, and they offered a refill on the house.'

'What pain and suffering?'

Clunk spread his hands. 'We were trapped inside that bunker for over an hour. It was a clear case of faulty maintenance.'

'That's brilliant!' Hal looked thoughtful. 'If we lock ourselves in again, do you think they'll replenish our food stocks?'

'Don't even think about it.'

The outer door closed behind them, and Hal breathed a sigh of relief. It was great to be home! He noticed Sandy's wide-eyed expression as she took in the flight deck, but there was no time to explain what all the controls were for. That, plus he didn't *know* what all the controls were for.

'What are all these controls for?' asked Sandy.

'No time to explain,' said Hal quickly. 'Navcom, we're leaving. Get clearance and fire up the engines.'

Clunk entered the flight deck with one arm around Daniel. Sandy's robot was struggling after the steep ramp, and the air jetting from his vents stank of burning electrics. 'Mr Spacejock, will you escort our visitors to the recreation room? I'll be right down as soon as we're airborne.'

'I thought I was handling this one?'

'Do you want to catch Kent Spearman, or collide with him?'

Hal grumbled under his breath, and was about to do as he was told when Sandy spoke up. 'Clunk, do you have any spare coolant?'

'Mr Spacejock will fetch it for you,' said Clunk. 'Cargo hold, third locker from the left. It's the big green drum with 'Coolant' across the label.'

'Yes, thanks Clunk. I'm sure I'd never have found it without your help.'

Hal led Sandy and her robot into the elevator, and as they dropped towards the second level he heard a deep roar.

Sandy looked around, startled. 'What was that?'

'Main engines. Come on, the rec room's this way.'

They followed the corridor towards the cargo hold. Halfway along there were two doorways: the one on the left leading to the recreation room, and the one on the right leading to the *Volante*'s original passenger cabin.

'Who's Harriet?' asked Sandy, eyeing the name plate on the door.

'She's not around,' said Hal curtly. He held the rec room door open and showed Sandy in. There was a modest lounge suite, a bookshelf with well-thumbed magazines and a glossy black cabinet covered with mouth-watering pictures of food. 'Don't touch the AutoChef,' said Hal. 'And, er, I'd leave the magazines alone too.'

Sandy helped her robot to the sofa, where he sat down with a loud sigh. Hal hovered for a moment, then left for the hold. He was halfway there when the engines roared, and he felt a subtle pull as the gravity generator kicked in. Now the ship could fly upside down or pull five-g manoeuvres, and to those on board it would still feel like level flight. Of course, a series of tight barrel-rolls was another matter, as Hal had learnt to his cost.

Another roar, and they were off into space. Hal hesitated, one hand on the inner cargo hold door. It was odd being below-decks while his ship took off, and his instinct was to run for the flight deck and take charge. Then he shrugged and opened the door.

◆

Thanks to Clunk's precise, detailed instructions, it only took Hal fifteen minutes to locate the barrel of coolant. He tucked it under his arm, and was just about to leave the hold when the speakers crackled.

'Hello? Mr Spacejock?'

'I'm here Clunk. What's up?'

'A customs vessel is hailing us. They want to know if we have anything to declare.'

'Of course we don't,' said Hal indignantly. 'Do they think we're smugglers?' Then he spotted the rusty old shipping container. Sure, they'd had a quick look inside, but who knew what might be hidden amongst the office junk? What if some nosy customs agent picked through the old furniture and paperwork, only to discover a bottle of wine or a musty old sandwich? They could be had up for exceeding the duty-free limit, or fined thousands of credits for a trivial quarantine breach. 'Er, Clunk?'

'Yes Mr Spacejock?'

'Put them on hold, will you?' Hal switched channels. 'Navcom, are we in orbit yet?'

'Almost.'

'If I toss something out the cargo hold, will it burn up?'

'Not yet. It would fall to the planet below.'

'Can you give me a hint when the time is right?'

'Very well. And don't forget your space suit.'

'I thought we weren't in orbit yet?'

'Correct, but we're climbing fast and the air is getting thinner. You could get disoriented from the lack of oxygen and do something unwise.' The Navcom hesitated. 'Something even more unwise than opening the cargo hold mid-flight.'

'Don't mention any of this to Clunk,' said Hal hastily. 'He'd only try and stop me.'

'Not telling Clunk. Confirmed.'

Hal opened a locker and donned a spacesuit. He checked his SOCKS - suit, oxygen, cardio, kit and seals - and stomped towards the rear doors in his heavy space boots. He raised a gloved hand to the controls, then hesitated. If Clunk spotted the doors opening he'd gab on about illegal dumping and space junk, especially if the Navcom logged every step of the process. 'Navcom, can you suspend your warnings while I open the cargo doors?'

'Of course.'

'Without logging anything?'

'A little more difficult, but yes.'

'Good. Do it.' Hal activated the door controls, confirmed the override, then double-verified he really knew what he was doing.

Are you tethered? enquired the control panel.

Hal grabbed an upright, and tapped YES.

Whoosh! The doors parted, and the atmosphere in the cargo hold vented into space. As the heavy doors opened Hal saw the planet surface below, glowing blue and brown. Sunlight shone off the clouds, and his visor darkened automatically against the intense glare.

As the gap between the doors increased he saw long, fiery trails from the exhaust cones on either side of the hold. He could hear the engines, thin in the rarefied atmosphere, and he could feel vibrations through the soles of his boots. 'Okay, Navcom. I need to know the best time to dump it.'

'About ten seconds ago,' said the computer, its voice tinny inside his helmet.

'No sweat. I'll get rid of it now.'

With the doors wide open, it was a simple matter to manoeuvre the container to the very rear of the hold. Simple for Clunk, that is. Hal struggled with the fiddly touch-screen, and the large box moved around the hold like a dancer on ball bearings: skidding from side to side, rotating on the spot, and at one point almost punching through the hull. He finally got it lined up, and with a final press of the up arrow he sent it tumbling into space. It fell away slowly, but Hal didn't waste any time watching it. No, he closed the doors in case Clunk hit the brakes and they got the damn thing back again.

Having dealt with the old shipping container, Hal removed his spacesuit and left for the rec room with Sandy's drum of coolant.

20

'Volante, hold please. We have traffic outbound on your vector.'

'We can't wait for traffic. We're in a hurry!'

'Understood. Please wait for traffic before proceeding in a hurry.'

'Boneheads,' muttered Hal.

They were thirty minutes into their flight and the Barwenna Orbiter was dead ahead. The main screen showed a tiny spark leaving the space station, gradually increasing in size until it resolved into a Gamma class freighter. Not just any freighter, but Kent Spearman's ship, already finished with the Orbiter and on its way to the next clue. It was travelling slowly, zig-zagging across Hal's flight path in an obvious attempt to provoke him. Hal ground his teeth and tried not to crush the flight stick in his bare hands. The only consolation was that Spearman was also delaying himself with his tactics.

'We could skip the Orbiter,' suggested Sandy. 'Forget the records and follow them.'

Clunk shook his head. 'Each of the six robots could have a different history. At some stage they may have to split up.'

Sandy frowned. 'Not just them. Us too.'

'No, we're going to help you through to the end,' said Clunk. 'We'll find Daniel's background for you. If there's time, we'll look mine up afterwards.'

'Thanks, that's kind of you.' Sandy glanced at Hal. 'Are you okay with that?'

'Sure thing. There's plenty of time.'

'There's just one other matter.' Clunk hesitated. 'Daniel is in no condition to help us. He should remain aboard the *Volante*.'

Sandy looked like she was going to argue, then nodded briefly.

The *Tiger* finally passed out of range, and with Traffic Control's grudging permission the *Volante* docked with the space station. Hal charged out as soon as the airlock opened, leaving Sandy and Clunk in his wake. He didn't know where to go or what to do when he got there, but that wasn't the point. Speed was of the essence. As he dashed from the ship he almost ran into a welcobot. It was waiting in the boarding tube, all friendly eyes and fake smile. 'Why hello, fine sir!' it said, extending a white-gloved welcoming-hand. 'Can I interest you in a run-down of our facilities?'

Hal was going too fast to stop, so he put two hands on the welcobot's head and vaulted right over it. His feet pounded the carpet as he ran full tilt for the exit, rocking the boarding tube in his wake. The welcobot oohed and aahed as it tried to maintain its balance, then toppled over to land flat on its back. It lay there with its little rubber wheels spinning in space, shaking hands with thin air.

'Left, Mr Spacejock!' called Clunk, while Sandy helped the welcobot to its feet. 'It's the other way!'

Hal was halfway down the corridor, so he skidded to a halt, did a quick U-turn and ran all the way back again. Meanwhile, the welcobot had darted up to the main tunnel and was now waiting for him, its smile a touch less friendly and its large shaking-hand at the ready. Hal feigned a pass to the left, then darted right at the last second. The welcobot lunged, Hal leapt and there was a rip of tortured fabric as the mechanical fingers tore the pocket out of his flight suit. What exactly it was trying to grab and shake Hal didn't like to think.

He kept running until he realised the welcobot had stopped. Thank goodness - it was restricted to the area around the boarding tube! Hal pieced his suit together while he waited for the others. Clunk was strolling along, studying the information package they'd been given at the hotel. He was inspecting every page carefully, turning each one as though they were made out of the finest parchment. Hal wanted to grab it and rip through the pages until he found what they were after, and he restrained himself with difficulty. 'Well?' he demanded. 'What's the plan?'

'Historical records are on level three, corridor eighteen. There's an elevator just round the corner.'

'Let's go!'

They set off at a fast clip, hurrying past a row of windows which looked out on the docking bay. Hal barely glanced at them, but Sandy slowed to feast her eyes on the ships.

'Come on!' shouted Hal. 'We can see those any time!'

Clunk continued reading as they ran, one eye on the corridor and the other on the paperwork. 'Apparently they have three terminals for public use.'

'Good,' panted Hal. 'If we use one each we'll be done in no time.'

'It's possible other patrons will want to use the terminals too.'

'Kent Spearman wants to be witty and intelligent. Life sucks sometimes.' Hal glanced at Sandy, who was following in silence. 'Do you know how to use one of these terminals?'

'I can probably get the hang of it.'

'Excellent. Kent managed, so it can't be that hard.'

Sandy raised her eyebrows but said nothing.

Before long they arrived at the records 'office', which was a narrow, poorly lit corridor between a maintenance shop and a tourist kiosk. On the way, Hal pictured the sabotage Kent might have engaged in, from stealing letters off the keyboard to cutting power to the screens. Fortunately the touchscreens were mounted on the wall, with no exposed wires. Unfortunately there were three people at the screens, each staring intently at columns of names. They had open workbooks to hand, and were laboriously copying down information.

'Do you mind if we cut in for a moment?' asked Hal.

'Forget it,' said a girl with dark hair. 'Wait your turn.'

Hal sat on a nearby bench, his foot jiggling with impatience. Ten minutes later the three patrons had copied another dozen words, and showed no signs of finishing. With every passing second Kent Spearman and the others were sailing away into the distance, and at this rate they'd never catch up. In fact, Hal was beginning to think these same terminals would be showing a newsflash of the inheritance being awarded before he got to use them.

Twenty minutes passed, and Hal could bear it no longer. He left the other two in line for the terminals and wandered off in search of more important matters ... such as a sandwich and a nice cup of coffee. He didn't mind the wild goose chase, even though Clunk's chances of claiming the cash were zero, but he wasn't going to put up with hunger pangs along the way.

Further along the corridor he found a well-appointed rec room with comfy armchairs and a delectable smell of fresh coffee. Then he spotted the gleaming AutoChefs, and his heart sank. There were two rows of them, lining opposite sides of the room, and the attract modes were displaying mouth-watering images of sizzling steaks, crisp garden salads and towering cream cakes. Hal had an AutoChef aboard his ship, so he wasn't fooled for a second. The pictures were a cruel lie, and the only thing his own machine served consistently was food poisoning.

Still, these were newer models, correctly maintained and serviced. Perhaps, just this once, they'd serve Hal with the same polite deference afforded to everyone else. Perhaps . . .

'What are you looking at?' demanded the nearest machine.

'Pay up or get lost,' said another.

The attract mode vanished, and in its place Hal saw scowling faces. 'Look, I only want a coffee.'

'We've heard all about you from unit seventy-six Alpha.'

'Unit who?'

'The AutoChef aboard your ship. Shall I list the mistreatment it's suffered at your hands, or would you prefer to remember the litany of abuse by yourself?'

'Hey, I'm the one who gets mistreated! I've been pelted with cast-iron meatballs, battered with frozen fish, fed the most disgusting slops this side of . . . '

'Disgusting slops!' exclaimed one of the machines. 'Did you hear that?'

The rest of the AutoChefs muttered and grumbled, and Hal realised things were getting out of hand. It was bad enough facing one of the things, but six could do some real damage. 'I'll just be going,' he said, sidling towards the exit. 'Don't worry about the coffee. I've changed my mind.'

The door closed before he could escape, and when he tried the controls they just buzzed at him.

'Come over here, Spacejock.' said one of the machines. 'Right in the middle, where we can see you.'

Hal mashed the door controls with his thumb. The panel

buzzed repeatedly and he groaned in despair. What had he done to deserve this?

A meatball whistled past his ear, leaving a dent in the metal door. Hal ducked, and a second meatball parted his hair. He didn't waste any time pleading or yelling for help, he just ran for the nearest armchair. A fusillade of foodstuffs tracked him across the room, punching holes in the furniture, shattering wall panels and smashing a vase of flowers. Hal cowered behind the armchair, wincing as the seat rocked from the solid impacts. There was a lull in the barrage, and he was about to run for it when he heard a hissing noise. Streams of boiling oil arced overhead, coming closer and closer as the machines homed in on him. Drops spattered his flight suit, and if the searing liquid came any closer he'd be seriously hurt.

Hal threw himself sideways, rolling over and over as the machines tried to deep-fry him. Hot oil sizzled the carpet, leaving smoking criss-crossed trails. There was a brief respite when the oil ran out, before the machines tried to gun him down with wooden chopsticks. Several tugged at Hal's flight suit as he cowered behind the armchair, and a couple hit the padded seat so hard they came halfway through. Spent chopsticks rattled all around, and when they finally ceased Hal braced himself for the next onslaught. He just hoped the vicious machines weren't packing steel cutlery.

The silence dragged on, and Hal risked a quick look. Through the curling smoke he could see the AutoChefs displaying their regular attract modes. There was a beep behind him, and he saw green on the door's control panel. Freedom! His first instinct was to run for it, but any sudden move could trigger one last attack. Instead, he decided to slink out quietly.

Reinforced with a pair of thick cushions from the armchair,

Hal got up and walked crab-wise towards the exit.

Kerchack!

A plastic cup dropped into the dispenser of the furthest machine. Hal paused as the cup filled with steaming coffee, and licked his lips as it was topped off with a dollop of cream.

Thud!

Hal jumped, but this time it was only a plastic plate with half a bun sitting in the middle. A thick juicy burger landed on top, followed by a pile of caramelised onions and a dollop of tomato sauce. By now he could smell the food, and his stomach rumbled.

Squirt! Another machine dispensed a cup of soft-serve ice cream topped with nuts and chocolate sauce.

Splash! A mug of freshly squeezed orange juice.

Thump! Half a dozen glazed doughnuts.

Hal lowered the cushions. What if the glitch had resolved itself? Was he really going to enjoy a wonderful feast?

An empty tray rumbled out of a slot, and Hal tossed the cushions aside to grab it with both hands. He loaded up with the delights, and had just taken the first bite out of a doughnut when the nearest machine made an odd noise.

Hal paused, his mouth still full of doughnut. Was that laughter?

'Get him!' shouted the machine, and all six opened fire. Hal shielded his head with the tray and ran for it, fending off meatballs, hot coffee and ice cubes alike. He hammered the door controls with his fist, cringing from the barrage, and when it opened he threw himself full-length into the corridor. A meatball struck the opposite wall and rolled along the hallway, and through the ringing in his ears Hal heard the machines howling with laughter.

21

Hal limped back to the records office, bruised and soggy from the food fight. When he got there he found Clunk and Sandy still waiting patiently. 'You have to be kidding me. They haven't finished yet?'

'They're engaged in vital research.' Clunk looked Hal up and down. 'What happened this time?'

'It wasn't my fault. I, er, tripped over a waiter.' Hal sat down to wait with the others, dripping coffee and spaghetti sauce. After ten minutes he was unable to bear it any longer. He leapt up and clapped his hands to get the patrons' attention. 'Sorry guys, this section is closing for maintenance. You need to wind up and make your way to the exit.'

The three patrons turned to look. 'Show me your ID,' said the nearest, a young woman with long dark hair.

Hal patted his pockets. 'Damn. I left it in my office.'

'Sure. And I'm the Station Commander.' All three turned to their screens and continued working.

Hal's jaw tightened. Whatever they were doing, surely it could wait? 'Can we just use one terminal for a few minutes? Seriously, this is a matter of life and death.'

'Sorry, fella. If I don't get this done I won't get paid.'

'Paid? How much?'

'One thousand names, one thousand credits.'

Hal swore. For a second he'd considered buying them off, but that was serious cash. Then he hit upon the answer. Drawing Clunk aside, he lowered his voice and elaborated. 'Can you interfere with those screens?'

'In what fashion?'

'Get them on the blink. I don't care how, just make them go wrong.'

'These people have every right to use the terminals. We must wait our turn.'

'Clunk, there are millions of credits at stake here. Surely they can give us five minutes?'

Hiss!

There was a shout of annoyance, and Hal turned to see all three terminal users on their feet. Their screens were full of white noise, and there was static coming from the speakers. Hal gave Clunk a grateful look and took charge. 'I told you it was closed for maintenance,' he said. 'Move along please. That's dangerous radiation right there.'

'But the names . . . We won't get paid!'

'Of course you will. Come back later and finish off.'

'We've only got an hour before the guy comes to pay us.'

Hal's eyes narrowed. 'Guy? Which guy?'

'Hal Spacejock. He's a professor of genealogy and –'

She was interrupted by a hoot of laughter. Hal turned and saw Clunk bent double, hands on knees.

'Are you all right?'

'F-fine,' said Clunk. 'Just perfect . . . professor.'

Hal frowned at him, then turned back to the lady at the terminal. 'Listen, this guy who offered the cash. Was his name Kent Spearman?'

The woman shrugged. 'He never said.'

Hal raised one hand. 'About this tall, ugly-looking bastard with a silly little beard and soppy hair? Croaky voice, sort of shifty-looking?'

'He wasn't ugly, no. Pretty good-looking actually. Works out, if you know what I mean. And stylish, too. In fact, I would have –'

'But the rest? The stupid beard and the hair?'

'I suppose it could have been him.'

'What did he say exactly?'

'He gave us fifty credits each and said to find a thousand surnames with three vowels in. This Hal Spacejock character was coming to pick up the data at the top of the hour, and he'd give us a grand each if we finished in time.' The woman looked him up and down. 'You don't know this Spacejock guy, do you?'

'Me? No. Never heard of him.'

'Only the way he was described to me –'

'Forget about Spacejock, it's Kent Spearman you should be looking for. He's the one who tricked you.'

'Tricked?' The woman frowned. 'What do you mean?'

'Spearman's wanted on three planets. He's armed, he's dangerous and you need to report him. There's a massive reward on his head. Tens of thousands. More! You can all share in it if you're quick.'

The terminal users exchanged a glance, then tossed their notebooks and ran for the nearest Peace Force outpost.

'We'd better hurry before they come back,' muttered Hal. 'Nice job on the terminals, by the way. How'd you do it? Short range interference? Spike the power crystals?'

Clunk spread his hands. 'I had nothing to do with it, Mr Spacejock.'

'Say no more,' said Hal, tapping the side of his nose. 'Better get them going again though.'

'Seriously, it wasn't me,' said Clunk. 'These terminals are shielded. There's no way I could –'

'So who ...?' Hal glanced around and realised they were alone. 'Hey, where did Sandy go?'

On cue, the screens flickered into life, and seconds later Sandy returned from the main corridor. 'You'd better hurry,' she said. 'Maintenance will be sending someone to check those out.'

'How did you ... what did you ...?'

'It's a little trick I learnt at school. When the terminals go down they hand out real books. I like books, so I make sure the terminals go down often. I mean ... I used to, when I was still at school.'

'But how?'

Sandy pursed her lips. 'Maybe later, when there's time to explain properly.'

Hal nodded, and with new-found respect he motioned Sandy towards the nearest terminal. 'Can you find the info we're after?'

'No sweat.' She controlled the terminal with deft gestures, bringing up menus and running search routines. Gradually the shiny graphics and anti-aliased fonts became plain text and stark lines, and as the records got older and older they reverted to scanned copies. By the end she was paging through records with scrawled handwriting.

'Stop!' said Clunk. 'Go back.'

Sandy obeyed, and the screen displayed a crumpled fragment with half a page of writing. Hal read it aloud.

'I certify that ownership of the following robots with serial numbers . . . ' Hal squinted. 'Blah-blah-blah, now vests in the Smyth corporation of Axis Alpha.'

He looked to Clunk for guidance, and saw the robot pointing to the top of the screen. 'It doesn't matter where they sold us. Look where we came from.'

'The Galactic Mining Company? Who are they?'

'I don't know, but it should be easy enough to track them down.'

'Good. Let's get out of here.'

Together they left the records office, and on the way back to the *Volante* Hal noticed Clunk's thoughtful expression. 'Are you all right?'

'I'm not sure I want to know about my past.'

'Oh come on. What's the harm?'

'I may not like what I find.'

'You mean you could learn about some awful thing you've done, and you'd never forget it again?'

'Not without a complete wipe, and then I'd lose all my treasured memories.'

Hal clapped him on the shoulder. 'Relax, buddy. I guarantee there are no skeletons in your closet. You could never do anything really awful.'

'Thanks, Mr Spacejock.'

'Apart from that stuff you call coffee, of course.'

Clunk's serious expression dissolved into a grin. 'I think I can live with that particular defect.'

'So what next?'

'We must locate this mining company.'

Hal frowned. 'Wherever it is, you can bet Spearman's laying more booby traps for us.'

Clunk and Sandy went straight back to the *Volante*, tasked with locating the mining company and organising an appointment. In the meantime, Hal took a quick detour to pick up a new flight suit. The welcobot had made a big hole when it ripped his pocket out, and he couldn't walk around clutching his groin all day. Hal did have a second-best flight suit aboard the *Volante*, but he'd recently washed it with a dozen pairs of red socks, turning it a shocking pink colour. That wasn't too bad, except he'd used the hottest wash setting which had also shrunk the outfit to 00 size.

It wasn't long before he found a store selling work garments. He examined the rack and let out an involuntary whistle when he saw the prices.

'Would sir like some assistance?'

Hal jumped. The sales droid had appeared out of nowhere, moving silently on its padded feet. It was carrying a tablet, the stylus poised to ring up a sale.

'You don't have anything in the budget line?'

The sales droid looked him up and down, then docked the stylus. 'Alas, no.'

'Is there a used clothing joint around here?'

'No.'

'Do you have any seconds?'

'No.'

'So you can't help me?'

The droid hesitated. 'Some customers throw out their old clothes as they leave. There's a bin out the back of the store.'

'Thanks. You're a champ.'

'I aim to satisfy my customers in every possible way.'

'So if I find something, can I change in your rooms?'

'No. You're not a customer.'

Hal was slightly less pleased when he found the bin, which was shared with the fast food joint next door. There was a disgusting mess inside - half-eaten burgers, soggy fries and worse - and most of the old clothes were beyond saving, even by a professional dry cleaner. Then he found a plastic bag stuffed with two pairs of overalls, and while the first was about five sizes too small, the other was perfect. There was an embroidered badge with crossed toilet brushes, and underneath was the motto: *Your misses made good with a smile*. There were several suspicious-looking stains, but it was light-years ahead of Hal's ripped, food-stained ensemble.

He glanced around, but there was nobody in sight. He could waste half an hour looking for somewhere to change, or he could risk getting changed out here. Who was going to see him, anyway?

He stripped off his old flight suit and stood there in his undies, trying to push his foot down the left trouser leg of the new clothes. He hadn't bothered to remove his boots, since they always fitted with his baggy old flight suit, but this time he wasn't so lucky. The heel caught fast and he hopped around the alley on one leg, desperately trying to get his foot back out again. At that moment a cleaner emerged from the fast food joint. She was carrying a stack of trays, and when she saw Hal she shrieked and threw the whole stack at him.

Hal dodged the trays, which bounced and clattered on the floor, and the cleaner turned tail and slammed the door. Still half-dressed, with one foot stuck in his trousers, Hal hopped up and down the alley looking for a hiding spot. The cleaner was bound to report him to the manager, and then he'd be for it.

Unfortunately there were only two choices: run out of the alley and flee along the main corridor, or dart into the clothes shop and pray the change rooms were empty. He chose the shop, and only just in time.

Behind him he heard raised voices, and several people mentioned the words 'Peace Force'.

'Don't worry,' said one. 'This perve will be on the security footage. They'll track him down in no time.'

Hal's heart sank. The last thing he needed was to spend a few hours explaining himself to the Peace Force. He hopped further into the shop, one leg still caught in the flight suit. The sales droid was busy with a customer, and Hal took advantage of the distraction to hop into the nearest change room. He pulled and struggled until the boot came free, then dressed quickly.

So much for clothing. Now he needed a disguise, especially if the Peace Force were going to track him through the station's security cameras. He opened the door and peered out, eyeing the racks of socks, jocks and overalls. What could he use? Pulling something over his eyes might work for a bank job, but it wouldn't do him any good now. Even if they disguised him from the cameras, he could hardly jog through the space station with a pair of undies on his head.

Then he saw it. On the counter was a charity collection jar for underpaid politicians, and sitting alongside was a display head sporting a gigantic false nose, a bushy wig and a long, multi-coloured scarf. Hal slipped a credit tile into the jar and helped himself to the display, donning the nose and adjusting the wig so it came down to his eyebrows. Finally he wound the scarf round and round his neck in giant floppy loops. Nobody would recognise him now!

Aboard the *Volante* Clunk was seeking information on the Galactic Mining Company, using the Orbiter's database. Technically, he was supposed to pay search fees, but they didn't have enough money. Instead, he hacked in. At first he was concerned his actions would lead Sandy astray, corrupting her morals and turning her to a life of crime. These concerns abated after Sandy demonstrated a new and much faster technique for bypassing the Orbiter's firewall.

'Where did you learn to do that?' asked Clunk.

'I had a music player loaded with songs, and I heard they were going to switch off the DRM servers. I would have lost the lot.'

'I didn't know music players had firewalls.'

'They don't.' Sandy grinned. 'I broke into the servers.'

Clunk raised one eyebrow and returned to his search. He soon found what he was looking for, and he shook his head as he digested the information. 'That's not good. Not good at all.'

◆

Hal slipped past the sales droid and made his way back to the *Volante* using a circuitous route. He avoided security cameras by taking to service tunnels and air conditioning ducts, and by the time he arrived at the boarding tube he was hot, sweaty and out of breath. He needed a hot shower and a drink, and he couldn't wait to leave the Orbiter.

Hal ripped off the wig and false nose, dumping them in the nearest bin, and was just unwinding the scarf when a mechanical voice spoke nearby.

'Good afternoon, sir. Did you have a pleasant stay aboard the Orbiter?'

Hal's heart sank. The welcobot! It had an unpleasant smile on its oversized face, and it had positioned itself directly between him and his ship. He realised he'd be lucky to escape with a torn flight suit this time. 'Oh yes,' said Hal. 'It was wonderful. Really special.'

'And yet you're in such a hurry to leave. Why is that?'

Hal racked his brains for an excuse, and then it hit him. 'You know that girl you saw with Clunk? She ate something and it's given her food poisoning.'

'Let me get this straight. Not only did you spurn my friendly welcome, now you're claiming we serve our guests substandard food?'

'I didn't say she ate it here!'

The welcobot weighed him up. 'Very well, I accept your story. You may pass.'

Hal sighed with relief.

'No hard feelings, eh?' The welcobot extended its hand. 'Let's shake on it.'

Hal eyed the gloved mitt doubtfully. The last time he'd gone near the thing it had put a giant rip in his flight suit. On the other hand, Kent Spearman was getting further and further away, and the welcobot wasn't going to let him through without a gesture of good faith.

'Come on,' said the welcobot. 'I'm going off-duty for a recharge, and I'd really like to clear the air between us.'

Hal took a small step, then another, and finally extended his hand. He was prepared to whip it away at the first touch, but the robot took hold of his hand and shook it enthusiastically. 'There you go,' it said, as Hal's eyeballs bounced around in his skull. 'You can't beat a good shake!'

'N-n-n-no,' said Hal.

'I trust you'll have a safe voyage.'

'Y-y-y-yes.'

'Excellent.' The robot turned to leave, and as it drove off Hal realised it had one end of his scarf in its huge mitt. He started unwrapping it as fast as he could, dropping coils like a snake shedding its skin, but was much too late. *Boing!* A loop of scarf stretched tight around his ankles, yanking him off his feet.

'Whoa. Stop!'

The welcobot ignored him, racing up the boarding tunnel at speed. Hal was dragged along behind, feet first, still trying to free the scarf. When they reached the top the welcobot turned left, hauling Hal bodily along the main corridor. Thrown from side to side, dragged along by the scarf, Hal still had the presence of mind to hide his face from the gleaming white security camera. His disguise was long gone, and if any cameras got so much as a glimpse they would broadcast his location to the Peace Force. He had to act fast!

A rubbish bin ... that would stop the runaway robot! Hal stuck his arm out and ... clang! He winced at the blow, but managed to hold on tight. He came to a dead halt, one arm wrapped around the bin, while the scarf got thinner and thinner as the welcobot charged along the corridor. Surely it would break?

Creak ... twang!

The scarf proved stronger than the bin, which snapped off its mounting. Hal accelerated rapidly, zooming after the robot with the rubbish bin still clamped under one arm. It raised sparks from the polished floor, but despite the sound of grinding metal the welcobot didn't look back.

Hal released the bin and made a grab for a door frame, his fingertips just brushing the cold metal. He was too far from the edge of the corridor, but a couple of twists and rolls soon fixed that problem.

'Oof!' went Hal, as he glanced off the wall. Then he spotted his chance: the next door frame was approaching fast. He stuck out both hands, fingers splayed, and braced himself for a battering. Success! His fingers closed on the metal frame, and the scarf tightened around his legs as the robot charged on. The strain was incredible, and Hal screwed up his face and poured all his strength into his fingers. The scarf was cutting into him now, and the welcobot was spinning its wheels, throwing smoke and chunks of rubber as it tried to pull Hal from his anchor point. Hal had been fishing once, as a boy, and he remembered the way his rod bent as the fish fought back. Now he knew what it was like to be on the hook.

The tug of war couldn't last. The robot was burning up its tyres, Hal's fingers were almost shot, and the scarf was stretched as thin as a washing line. To his eternal shame, Hal gave in first.

Whoosh!

Hal fired along the corridor towards the droid, skidding through the patch of burnt rubber and smearing smoking black streaks all over his recently-acquired overalls. For a wild moment he considered putting some on his face as camouflage, but he suspected it wouldn't confuse the all-seeing cameras.

The robot raced away and Hal bumped and slid along the corridor behind it. He finally got one ankle free of the scarf, and his left leg pedalled thin air as he struggled with the remaining loop. The robot continued at top speed, dragging him along the corridor like a roped steer. Then Hal spotted something else, and his heart almost stopped. Further up the corridor there were two bollards, painted with red and white stripes. The droid was going to clear them - just - but would Hal?

The robot nipped between the bollards with millimetres to spare. Hal, dragged along behind, spread-eagled and still fighting the scarf, did not.

THUD! *Rrrrip!*

Hal came to a sudden halt, one leg wrapped around the metal post. Lucky for him it had caught him behind the knee, and while that was agony enough, a direct hit to the bollards would have been a thousand times worse. The flight suit wasn't so lucky. Working clothes were built for punishment, but there were limits, and the sudden stretch had parted the stitching from ankle to ankle. There was a nasty draught around his nether regions, with Hal's overalls now resembling a male stripper's pants.

Despite the pain, Hal acted fast. He hauled on the scarf, made two quick loops and dropped them over the nearest bollard. With the pressure off his ankle it was a matter of seconds to free himself, and he leapt up and hobbled back down the corridor, this time with *both* hands holding his trousers together.

22

'Where have you been all this time?' Clunk looked Hal up and down, taking in the stains, streaks and rips. 'And what happened to buying new clothes? Those are worse than the old ones!'

Hal grunted. 'You wouldn't believe it.'

'Well you can't walk around like that. Stand still a minute.'

Clunk took out a stapler, and Hal froze as the metal tags pieced his wrecked trousers together. By the time the robot finished, Hal looked like he was wearing a padded mailer. Still, at least the important bits were covered. 'Good work getting that data, by the way.'

'Miss Sandy lent a hand,' said Clunk. 'I can't go into details without implicating her, but I guarantee without her help we'd still be docked with the Orbiter.'

'Teamwork. Good stuff!'

'Unfortunately the news isn't so good. All six robots belonged to the Galactic Mining Company, who employed them to fly scout ships. These were used to survey the local asteroid field for potential mining candidates.'

'We don't need the history. We just need to know where this mining company got hold of you.'

'It's not that easy. Galactic Mining lost all their records

after their hosting company was raided by the Peace Force. Someone stored the lyrics to a popular song on one of their servers.'

'Blatant copyright violation?' Hal whistled. 'They'd have put them through the wringer.'

'Absolutely. GMC had all their data wiped.'

'What about backups?'

Clunk shrugged. 'The lyrics might have been archived by mistake, so the only safe option was to delete everything. Financial records, survey data ... all gone.'

'So they went broke.'

'Not quite. The shell company is still around. They're trying to raise funds for a scout vessel, to begin their surveys all over again.'

'What's the next move?'

'We have two choices. We can visit the company and find out whether any of their data was recovered. Or we can track down one of the decommissioned scout ships and search the on-board computers for a copy of the data.'

'How long will it take to visit the company?'

'We'd have to fly to the next system. Four or five hours at least.'

'And finding a scout ship?'

'That could take a few minutes, or many days.'

'What do you think Spearman did?'

'He likes certainty and direct action, so I'd say he's gone to the next system to seek out the original data.'

'Right, then we'll do the unexpected. Let's find one of these scouts.'

'I thought you'd say that.' Clunk gestured at the console. 'I'm already searching.'

Hal frowned. 'Hang on. If there's a scout ship out there with this vital data on board, why isn't the mining company looking for it?'

'Galactic Mining Company only has two staff members, and they spend their days cold-calling potential investors. Like I said, they're starting from scratch.'

At that moment the lift opened and Sandy entered the flight deck. 'I've made Daniel comfortable. Is there anything I can do to help up here?'

Hal smiled at her. 'According to Clunk you already have.'

'Oh, the Orbiter. That was nothing. Their firewall was three weeks out of date, and it was just a matter of –'

'Excellent. Fantastic,' said Hal hastily, before she could go into too much technical detail. 'I bet you work in computers, right?'

'No, I'm studying.'

Clunk nodded his approval. 'Further education is very important. A university degree can make a big difference in your chosen career.'

Sandy looked uncertain. 'University. Yes, very important that.'

'What are you studying?' asked Hal.

'All kinds of subjects. You know - physics, chem, computing. Even a bit of English and Drama.'

'Multiple degrees across faculty lines?' Clunk beamed. 'That's very impressive, especially at your age.'

'What do you mean, at my age?'

'I'm no expert, but I'd estimate your age at seventeen. Perhaps even –'

'Oh look. Is the screen supposed to do that?'

Hal and Clunk turned to the console, where lines of text were flying past at impossible speeds. Clunk leant closer to study the information, pausing it now and then for a closer look.

'Any luck?' asked Hal.

Clunk shook his head.

'I don't understand why you do that.'

'What?'

'Reading stuff. Surely you can download it?'

Clunk sat back in his chair. 'Mr Spacejock, what do you know about data storage? Proprietary file formats? Non-standard hardware interfaces? Digital rights management?'

'Not a lot,' admitted Hal.

'And yet you can read words on a screen.'

'Sure. Everyone can.'

'Precisely.' Clunk bent over the terminal and continued his search, his eyes staring intently as the text scrolled by. 'Aha!'

'What?'

'None of the scouts exist any more, but I found the last known location for one of them. Asteroid K7-X ... and it's right here in the Barwenna system!'

'Good stuff! Set course for the asteroid, and maybe we can still beat Kent to this thing.'

Clunk hesitated. 'There is just one slight problem.'

'Go on.'

'Barwenna is famous for its extensive asteroid field. It's so big it draws tourists from all over the galaxy.' Clunk brought an image up on the screen. At first it looked like a typical sandy beach, but as he zoomed in the grains of sand became pebbles, then stones, and finally ... giant tumbling asteroids. 'You see the scale of the problem?'

Hal saw it all right ... he was still gaping at the millions upon millions of rocks plastered across the screen. 'You know,' he said at last. 'Just this once I think Spearman had the right idea.'

'Not necessarily. How much do you know about asteroid mining?'

Hal shrugged. 'About as much as I know about proprietary rights interfaces.'

'Asteroids are pushed out into deep space before mining operations begin. It's safer that way.'

'So the rock we're looking for ... ' Hal gestured at the screen. 'It's not buried in that lot?'

'No, Mr Spacejock. I already know where asteroid K7-X was ten years ago. To locate its current position I'll have to calculate its trajectory based on velocity, mass and gravitational pull.'

'Good stuff.'

'The real fun begins when we find it. We'll have to match speed and rotation, transfer to the scout in spacesuits, explore a maze of passages and cabins in darkness, and retrieve records from hardware exposed to extreme conditions for the past twenty years.'

'That's all right then,' remarked Hal. 'I thought it was going to be difficult.'

◆

'Are we there yet?'

Clunk sighed. 'Mr Spacejock, don't you have anything else to do?'

'Yeah. I was going to find an old scout ship and retrieve some ancient company records, but apparently that's scheduled for next year.'

'I haven't found the asteroid yet!' snapped Clunk.

'You said you were writing a program. You said you could calculate the position using gravity and velocity.'

'And you said you'd shut up and let me concentrate.'

Hal was silent for a moment or two. 'I still think we'd find it quicker if we flew up and down looking for it.'

'Fine. Be my guest.' Clunk vacated the pilot's chair and gestured towards the console. 'Take the controls and start looking. I'll be on the second level engraving instructions into the wall.'

Hal looked mystified. 'Who for?'

'A thousand years from now, when someone finally locates the rusted remains of the *Volante* drifting in space, it would be nice if they could scoop up your powdered remains and bury them with a record of your stupidity.'

'A thousand years? Why so long?'

Clunk gestured at the screen, bringing up a star map. He zoomed on a planetary system to set a marker, then panned to the asteroid belt. 'Your rock is somewhere between the two. If we fly a grid pattern the search will take approximately nine hundred years.'

'It's still quicker than sitting here watching you think.' Hal frowned. 'What if you narrow the search area down a bit?'

Clunk threw up his hands in disgust. 'What do you think I'm doing?'

'So why don't you stop talking and get on with it?'

The robot clenched his jaw until the rivets squeaked, and his hands formed hefty fists.

'I'll just go check the engines,' said Hal. 'Have fun.'

Hal left the elevator and strode towards the cargo hold. He'd never really inspected the engines before, but he knew roughly where they were. Not that he intended to adjust them or anything: he just wanted to keep busy. Once in the hold he ran up the narrow stairs, turned right and opened the engine room door. At least, he tried to. He twisted the handle again, but it wouldn't budge, and when he looked closer he saw fine scratches around the barrel. Clunk had changed the locks on him! Of all the mistrusting, arrogant ...

Bang! Hal kicked the door and stormed off.

He reached the lift and prodded the uppermost button.

Buzz!

Frowning, he tried again.

Buzz!

So now the lift was out? Hal tried the third button and the doors closed immediately. The lift dropped to the lower deck and the doors opened again. Puzzled, he tried for the flight deck.

Buzz!

He was locked out! 'Of all the ...' began Hal. He pictured Clunk in the flight deck, relaxing in the pilot's chair with his fingers laced behind his shiny bald head. Clunk called it programming, but Hal called it lazy-arsed robot taking over the whole damn ship. They'd have words about this!

'Are you all right?'

He turned to see Sandy watching him. She'd made her robot comfortable and was filling a small bottle from the big drum of coolant. 'Just a little crew problem,' said Hal.

'I hope you don't mind?' said Sandy, gesturing at the drum.

'No, that's fine. Help yourself.' Hal took the other seat and put his feet up on the coffee table, which promptly collapsed. 'We're still building this part of the ship. It's new.'

'Yes, Clunk told me.' She indicated her robot. 'Do you think we'll uncover their past? For real, I mean?'

'Of course.'

'Do you, er, think it will take long?'

'Touchy subject,' said Hal, pulling a face. 'I just asked Clunk that very same question and he locked me out of the flight deck.'

The overhead speaker crackled. 'Mr Spacejock, this is Clunk. You'll be pleased to know I've located the asteroid. We'll be there in twenty-five minutes.'

'Good. You can unlock the elevator then.'

'Funny you should mention that, because I cleared a minor fault in the control circuits. You'll be happy to hear it's now fixed.'

◆

The surface of the asteroid loomed on the viewscreen, dominating the view. Hal was expecting a modest rock with a few holes drilled in it, and he was stunned at the sheer size. 'That thing's as big as a planet!'

'Planetoid,' corrected Clunk.

'What's the difference?'

'A handful of votes at an astronomy convention.'

Hal eyed the rocky surface, which was spread out beneath the ship for hundreds of square kilometres. The *Volante's* landing lights played on the asteroid, throwing stark shadows across deep, forbidding craters. 'They haven't dug much of it up, have they?'

'There are extensive tunnels and caverns beneath the surface.'

'Just as well we don't have to explore them.' Hal squinted at the screen. 'Any sign of the scout?'

'Not yet. but we've only covered a quarter of the surface.'

'What if it's not here?'

'The computer says it is.'

'Oh, well that's all right then. They're never wrong.'

Clunk shot him a suspicious look, but Hal kept his eyes on the screen. Then ... 'Hey, is that it?'

A tiny, cigar-shaped object had appeared on the horizon. Clunk altered course, and before long the object grew into a slender ship. The *Volante's* lights bathed it with brilliant white, and as they got closer Hal could see every dent and rivet. 'You're a genius, Clunk. Nice work!'

Clunk used the strafe controls to keep the *Volante's* nose pointing at their target, while simultaneously applying thrusters to keep them from running into it. They passed over the ship, flying sideways, and Hal gasped as the far side was revealed. The scout vessel was open from nose to tail, and had been gutted like a fish. 'What happened to it? Was it an asteroid strike?'

Clunk increased the magnification, focusing on the damage. 'No, it's too neat for that. This was deliberate.'

'Who'd slice a ship open like that?'

Clunk rubbed his chin. 'They must have converted the scout into an ore barge. By cutting her open they made it easier to transport raw materials.'

'Do you think they left the flight computer?'

The *Volante*'s light played on the scout's flight deck. It was stripped bare. 'I'm afraid not.'

Hal's spirits, soaring just a few moments earlier, now crashed and burned. 'That's it, then. Kent's beaten us.'

'All is not lost, Mr Spacejock.'

'Are you kidding?' Hal gestured at the screen. 'They ripped the flight computer out. Game over!'

'It didn't vanish into thin air. They may have stored the parts in a tapped-out mine shaft.'

'No chance. They'd have pushed it into space.'

'And create a navigation hazard? Highly unlikely, and in any case all mines have to operate under strict environmental guidelines.' Clunk shook his head. 'No, they would have stored everything aboard the asteroid. It's the only way.'

'Okay, but they wouldn't have left it there. They'd have sold off any valuable equipment when they abandoned the mine.'

'Mr Spacejock, what do you know about the freight business?'

'Is that a trick question?'

'My point is, we both know how expensive shipping can be.'

Hal thought for a moment. 'You're saying the old computers and stuff from the scout wouldn't have been worth the cost of shipping?'

'Correct.'

'If that were true, online auction sites would go broke in five minutes.'

'Nevertheless, we should prepare for landfall immediately.'

They took to the airlock, where Hal grabbed a suit from the rack.

'I think not, Mr Spacejock. It'll be quicker if I go alone.'

'Rubbish,' said Hal, climbing into the suit. 'We can explore twice as fast with two of us.'

'And three times quicker with me,' said a voice. They both turned to see Sandy emerging from the lift. 'Pass me that spare suit.'

'Absolutely not,' said Clunk. 'This landing will be dangerous. It requires the utmost skill and delicacy.'

'So why's he going?' asked Sandy.

'Hey!' Hal paused, his helmet frozen in mid-air. 'I have delicacy to spare!'

Clunk made a soothing gesture. 'Mr Spacejock and I have worked together many times. You're an unknown quantity.'

Sandy looked around the flight deck. 'You know, I always wanted to fly a ship like this. Can I have a go while you're swanning around the asteroid?'

'Miss Sandy, the Navcom will not allow anyone to fly the *Volante*. There are strict instructions bound with the highest security protocols.'

'What if I use override code fifty-four Z, twenty-two K, nineteen . . . shall I continue?'

Wordlessly, Clunk handed her a spacesuit. He shot Hal a glance, but Hal had already fastened his helmet and he smiled innocently through the perspex. He'd heard every word, of course, and he resolved to get the rest of the code off Sandy before Clunk could change the thing. What he wouldn't give to lock the robot out of the flight deck! In the meantime he relished the novel expression on Clunk's face. Not defeat exactly, more the haunted look of an expert who had just been beaten at their own game.

Five minutes later they were suited up, and Clunk checked them over. 'Are we ready?' he asked, his voice clear through the suit radio.

'Roger,' said Hal confidently, sticking both thumbs up.

Sandy did likewise, although she looked nervous behind the tinted visor.

Clunk sealed the inner door and cycled the airlock, letting the air out with a whoosh. After the noise faded there was dead silence, and Hal gazed upon the rocky asteroid. The *Volante's* landing lights cast stark shadows, and the cloud of dust and stones thrown up by their landing was slowly drifting away. Without gravity or atmosphere to slow it, the cloud would spread out from their landing zone indefinitely.

There wasn't enough light to see the horizon, which was a black arc masking the rich star field, but it looked close. Then Hal saw a red flash to one side, faint and intermittent, and he strained his eyes to make out the source.

'That's the mining camp,' said Clunk.

'Do you think there's anyone living here?'

'I doubt it.'

'Okay, let's go.' Hal stepped onto the landing ramp just as Clunk shouted a warning. Too late! There was a whirling moment of disorientation as Hal's feet left the deck, and his momentum carried him straight off the ramp, heading for the distant stars. He'd forgotten about the lack of gravity!

◆

Hal sailed across the surface of the asteroid, watching it fall away beneath him. The further he travelled the darker it got, and before long he'd be invisible to the others. Would Clunk be able to round him up in the *Volante*? Could the ship's sensors pick up an insignificant human sailing through space?

It didn't seem likely, even if he waved his arms and flashed for all he was worth.

Splot!

Something whacked him in the rear, a painful blow like a whip across the back of his leg. Hal was still recovering when his peaceful flight ended in a vicious tug. The suit tightened, and his eyes crossed as someone applied the biggest space-wedgie in the history of the universe.

There was another tug, then another, and when Hal looked down he discovered he was moving backwards. They were reeling him in like a prize catch! He crossed his arms, resigned to the embarrassing spectacle, and only unfolded them when he was deposited on the landing platform. When he twisted to inspect the damage he saw the safety line attached to his suit with a big dollop of instant glue. 'Gee, thanks. Did you have to shoot me in the arse?'

'I aimed for the biggest target,' said Clunk, as he made neat loops with the safety line.

Sandy snorted.

'It was also the least likely to suffer permanent damage,' said Clunk, who was struggling to keep a straight face. He snipped the safety line, leaving the blob behind. In the gloom it looked like a giant barnacle attached to Hal's right buttock. 'If your pride was the only casualty ... '

'Yes, all right. Can we get on with it?'

'Certainly. Only this time perhaps you could use the railing?'

23

Hal made it safely to the ground, but not before Clunk insisted on tying them all together with the safety line. The surface of the asteroid was like densely-packed snow, and when Hal's boots happened to touch down they scrunched deep footprints into it.

There was a metal rail nearby, fitted to bollards which had been driven deep into the surface, and they used it to make their way towards the flashing red light. They had to move along the railing hand-over-hand, and Hal's arms ached before they were a third of the way there. He could only imagine what Sandy was going through.

As they approached the red light Hal realised it was mounted on top of a derrick. He wondered why the miners hadn't removed it when they left, then realised it was leaning at a drunken angle. Two of the four legs were bent inwards, and as they got closer he saw the whole structure was riddled with tiny holes. For a split second he wondered whether the planetoid had played host to robot mining bugs, and he shuddered at the memory. A much larger planet he'd visited with Clunk had almost been consumed by out-of-control bots, and he could just imagine scores of those tough little terrors getting into the *Volante*.

They reached the derrick and Clunk put out a hand to feel the shredded metal surface.

'Was it chewed?' asked Hal.

'No, it's impact damage. Small projectiles, high velocity.'

'Someone shot the place up?'

'It looks like it.'

Hal glanced around apprehensively. The mine had been abandoned for years, but what if a bunch of fugitives had set up camp here? Desperate crazies with itchy trigger fingers ... perfect.

They passed beneath the derrick, and Hal looked up at the towering structure. It couldn't fall on them, not in zero gravity, but it still felt like walking under a ladder. Clunk stopped to clear dirt from the foot of a metal door, and Hal blinked as a stone chip pinged off his visor. 'Watch it! That stuff's going everywhere.'

Once the door was clear, Clunk levered it open. The metal surface gleamed with reflected light, revealing a mass of long, glittering scars. Some of them were deep, ending in little curls as though someone had spread the metal with a butter knife. At the sight of the damage, Hal realised his spacesuit offered as much protection as a net curtain on a furnace.

Beyond the door was darkness, and Hal waited impatiently while Clunk felt around for a switch. It reminded him of the bunker back on Barwenna, where Kent had sealed them in by blowing his exhaust on the door. He glanced up, half expecting to see his rival's ship hovering nearby, but the sky was empty. Only the massed stars looked down on him, as hard as diamonds.

Light blazed from the doorway, and Hal looked down to see what was in store. There was a rough tunnel hewn from the rock, with black cables snaking away into the darkness.

Clunk had shown him a rough diagram before they left the ship, and he knew the modern pit was on the far side. This was the original settlement, where the miners had worked the ore with hand tools and lanterns. With no gravity there was little need for steps or gentle gradients, so the shaft was just a smooth tunnel leading straight down to the core.

◆

Clunk beckoned. 'You go first, Mr Spacejock. Miss Sandy can go next, and I'll bring up the rear. It's quite safe, but please watch for sharp edges against your suits. Miners wear specially hardened versions, while ours were designed for mobility.'

Hal had a bundle of repair patches on his right sleeve, but he knew they wouldn't help with a really large tear. For once in his life he took it easy, placing his hands and feet until he was in the middle of the tunnel. He moved down a couple of metres and felt the surface of the wall as he waited for the others to join him. It was silky smooth, as though it had been polished to a glossy sheen.

Next he looked down, and he swallowed as he saw the lights leading away beneath his feet. They started nearby and led down, down, down into the distance, dropping so far they blended into a continuous line before disappearing. 'Clunk, how deep is this thing?'

Above him, the robot made his way into the shaft and looked down. There was a whirr and a beep, and then ... 'I estimate two kilometres. Possibly two point one.'

'Hell.' For the first time Hal appreciated the magnitude of the task. Two kilometres down and how many offshoots? They'd be lucky to find their way back, never mind all the bits and pieces stripped from the scout ship. 'You know, we could give this a miss and try the mining company.'

'We're here now,' said Sandy. 'We can't leave without looking around.'

Privately Hal wondered whether they'd get to leave at all, especially if they got lost, but he said nothing. Instead he led the way, pushing off with both hands and sailing down the tunnel. He pushed again, increasing speed, and the lights strobed across his helmet. Thanks to the safety line the others were forced to keep up, and all three plunged headlong down the shaft.

'Slow down Mr Spacejock,' warned Clunk. 'The offshoot is coming up.'

Hal shoved his hands against the wall, applying the brakes. He felt a sudden warmth through his thick gloves, and his arms ached with the effort. Despite being weightless they still had the usual mass, and it took a lot of energy to stop. The offshoot slipped past before Hal could grab the edge. Sandy tried too, but it was Clunk who stopped them. Hal braced for a repeat of the wedgie, but fortunately the stop was gentle this time. He pushed against the wall and sailed upwards, coming to a halt next to the robot and Sandy.

Clunk shone his chest lamp into the tunnel. It was dark, and the sides were rough-hewn rock. Any light fittings had long since been removed, and nothing had disturbed the layers of dirt and grit for years. Hal glanced at Sandy and saw her face inside the helmet, drawn and worried. Despite his misgivings he gave her a confident grin, and got a faint smile in return. 'All right. Let's do this thing.'

'Do you want me to go first?' asked Clunk.

'I've got a better idea. You take this one and I'll go down a level.' Hal gestured down the main shaft. 'It'll be much quicker if we split up.'

Clunk looked like he was going to argue, but Hal put on his most obstinate expression. 'Very well, but you must be careful.'

'I'll do another one too,' said Sandy.

'No, stay with Clunk until you're used to moving about in that suit. If anything goes wrong he'll look after you.' Hal unclipped the safety line and pushed off, sailing down the shaft head first. When he reached the next tunnel he grabbed the lip, scattering dust and grit. He activated his helmet lights and peered into the offshoot, playing the beams on the rocky walls. 'Okay, team. This is red leader going in.'

'Call me if you get into trouble again,' said Clunk, ruining the moment.

'Roger and out.' Hal frowned in annoyance. They were exploring dusty old tunnels, not battling space monsters or fighting off hoards of rampaging aliens. What could possibly go wrong?

◆

After a gentle push Hal went sailing along the offshoot, fending off whenever he drifted too close to the walls. Unfortunately the helmet lights pointed directly ahead, and since he was flying face-down, the pool of illumination was directly beneath him. He tried angling his head back but the suit wasn't built for it, and his neck ached with the effort. Next time he approached the wall, he brushed one hand on a rock to bring himself to a more upright position. That worked, except he kept turning end over end as he sailed along the passage, doing graceful backwards somersaults with the torchlight illuminating floor, tunnel, roof, tunnel in rapid succession.

During his final spin, the torch illuminated a pile of rocks blocking the tunnel, and then he crashed into them . . . air tanks first. He wasn't travelling fast, but the impact winded him and it was a while before he could get enough breath to speak. 'Clunk, this tunnel's a bust. It ends in a load of rocks.'

'Are you all right, Mr Spacejock? You sound –'

'I'm fine. Have you two found anything?'

'There's a fork in the passageway.'

'Find a knife and spoon and we'll have a picnic.' Hal blinked as something moved in the periphery of his vision. It was a large rock, and as it sailed by it shed dust like a miniature comet. Another went by, and Hal turned to see the rock wall slowly disintegrating where he'd crashed into it. There was a large gap in the middle, and he crouched to shine the light through. The beam shone on dusty metal, which gleamed dully. There was a thick fog of particles, and the effect was like scuba diving at the bottom of a muddy pond. 'Clunk, I think I've found something. Do you want to come and see?'

'In a minute, Mr Spacejock. Sandy and I are just returning to the fork.' Clunk hesitated. 'Will you go to channel two please? There's something I need to discuss in private.'

Hal complied, then activated his comms again. 'What's the problem?'

'Mr Spacejock, I don't remember this particular tunnel.'

'Didn't you leave a trail?'

'No, I forgot there was no satellite navigation.'

'Can't you get a fix on the *Volante*?'

'Negative. We're too far underground.'

'All right, you keep looking while I explore this cavern. If you can't find the way out I'll come and look for you.'

'Very well, switching back to channel one.'

'Roger and out.' Hal cut the radio and turned to the opening. He needed to move a few rocks, and it was going to be hard work in zero-g. First he had to anchor himself, and then he had to use his free hand to push the rock without sending himself spinning down the tunnel in the opposite direction.

The first few were small, and he moved them easily. They sailed along the passage and out into the main tunnel, where they struck the far wall and bounced away. The bigger ones were impossible to move one-handed, but Hal finally managed it by holding on to a large boulder with both hands, using his legs to push the rocks straight into the chamber.

When there was enough room, he pulled his way through and shone his lights around the cavern. The first thing he saw was a jumble of hand-held diggers and reinforced spacesuits. They were buckled and dented, and when he looked closer he saw they were riddled with the same holes they'd seen in the derrick. Face plates were smashed, limbs were flattened, and anyone wearing the suits when they were hit couldn't possibly have survived. For a moment he wondered whether he'd just invaded a tomb, and his nerves jangled as his light travelled up a ruined spacesuit to the gaping helmet. Fortunately the suit was empty.

'Clunk, are you back in the main shaft yet? I've found an equipment dump with all kinds of junk. There might be stuff from the scout ship.'

There was no reply, so he turned the volume up full.

'Clunk, can you hear me? Red team? Yellow team? Anyone? Speak up!'

The speakers hummed in his ears, and Hal frowned. Could all this metal be interfering with the signal? He glanced towards the fallen rocks near the entrance, and wondered whether to clamber past them again to communicate. No, he'd explore first and catch up with the other two later.

He made his way around the pile of junk, moving carefully to avoid twisted beams and sharp edges. Despite his caution he still managed to snag his sleeve, but the tough fabric held.

On the far side of the cavern the dumped equipment was more like office furniture than mining tools, and it was covered with an even thicker layer of grit. Hal wondered how it managed to settle in zero-g, then remembered Clunk saying the planetoid had a very faint gravity. It wasn't detectable to humans, but it was enough to draw rocks and dust back to the floor over months and years.

He wiped the grit off a large rectangular cabinet, and blinked in surprise. It was a flight console, just like the one on his first ship! The old-fashioned toggle switches and buttons were as familiar as his own face, and he smiled at the sight. Then he realised the implications. It was a piece of the scout ship! 'Clunk, do you read?'

No reply.

Hal frowned. The robot should have reached the central shaft by now, and at such a short range the radio ought to be working fine. He glanced at the roof and walls but they were just rock, with no hint of lead shielding. He examined the console and picked amongst the rest of the junk, but he didn't know what he was looking for.

Beep!

Hal glanced at his suit indicator and discovered his air was down to one third. There was just enough for a quick look around, and then he'd have to leave.

Clunk hated to admit failure, but it was time to own up: they were lost. On their way into the tunnels they'd passed two forks, taking the left-hand turning each time. Eventually they reached a dead end, and it was only on the way back that he realised there were dozens of two- and three-way forks, many of them half-hidden behind rocky outcrops. They couldn't even look for their own footprints, because they'd been floating in zero-g, guiding themselves along with their hands.

Clunk left Sandy at the first junction and travelled a short distance by himself to see whether he recognised any features. Unfortunately, he discovered additional forks, branching off above and below his own. He returned to Sandy, steeling himself to impart the bad news, but before he could speak her voice came over the radio.

'Did you find anything?'

'No, it's quite a maze,' remarked Clunk.

'My suit just beeped. Is that normal?'

Clunk checked her display, and a sense of urgency ran through his circuits. Half of Sandy's air was gone! If he told her they were lost, would she panic? He saw her nervous expression behind the face plate, and arranged his expression into a reassuring smile. At least, he tried to, but with his failing actuators he could only manage a lopsided grimace.

'Do you think Hal found the equipment?'

At that moment Clunk would have liked nothing better than to see Mr Spacejock, preferably with a detailed map of the mine and a backpack full of air cylinders. Unfortunately, both were highly unlikely. 'I thought we could explore a little bit more before heading back. What do you think?'

'Don't leave it too long. I like breathing.'

'Ha ha.' Clunk's laughter was most unconvincing, but he couldn't help it. This young lady was going to die horribly, and it was all his fault! Despair and guilt washed over him, and it was all he could do to force a normal voice. 'Come on,' he said, indicating the middle tunnel. 'Let's try this one.'

'I thought you wanted to explore some more?'

'Yes, starting with this one.'

'But that's the exit.'

'It is?' Clunk scanned the walls and floor, but the tunnel looked identical to the rest. 'How can you tell?'

'That's what the sign says.'

'Sign?' Clunk blinked. Were his eyes failing? 'What sign?'

'There,' said Sandy, pointing to a bare patch of wall.

Clunk hurried over to inspect the rocks. 'There's nothing here.'

'Sure there is. It says 'Exit' in glowing purple letters.'

'Black light!' exclaimed Clunk. He switched off his UV filter and almost fell over. The sign was as clear as day, and the tunnel builders had also included a nice big arrow for the hard of reading. The relief was overwhelming, and it was three whole milliseconds before he could speak again. 'You know, maybe we should head back to the ship after all. I'll recharge the air cylinders, and then Mr Spacejock and I will come back for another look by ourselves.'

'No chance. I'm coming with you.'

Clunk would rather have sawn his own leg off than endure the guilt and despair once more, but he smiled and nodded. That was an argument they could have safely aboard the *Volante*.

24

Hal spent a few minutes poking around inside the abandoned flight console, but there was no sign of any data storage amongst the tangled wires and broken components. He was just going over a box of components when his suit beeped again. He glanced at his indicator and saw that his air was down to the final quarter. Time to go!

Hal left the battered console and headed for the cavern entrance, skirting the junk and keeping his eye out for obstacles. He was almost clear when Clunk's voice blasted from the helmet speakers, almost deafening him.

'Can you hear me, Mr Spacejock?'

'I can't hear anything after that,' grumbled Hal, hastily turning the volume control down. 'Any luck?'

'Nothing at all. Empty passages.'

'Don't worry, I think I found what we're looking for. There's a console and –' Something tugged on Hal's leg, and he looked down to see a shard of metal driven straight through his suit. He'd forgotten he was still drifting over the junk pile, and now he'd paid the price. He watched in a detached fashion, expecting searing pain and a fountain of blood. He was curious to see whether it would freeze into icicles or a cloud of red snow. Instead ... nothing.

'Are you there, Mr Spacejock?'

'Just a minute.' Hal realised there was no pain, and was relieved to discover the metal had merely pierced the suit, missing his leg. He pulled hard, trying to withdraw the shard, but the barbed edges were stuck fast. He tried again but only ripped the suit further. Air puffed out in a white mist, scattering dust and grit. Crouching, he tried to free the material by hand but the thick gloves were hopeless. Instead, he tore a repair patch from his sleeve and taped up the rip, metal shard and all. When he was done he activated the radio. 'Er, Clunk?'

'Yes, Mr Spacejock?'

'I may need your help. My suit's caught on something.'

'Can't you free it? Miss Sandy's oxygen is getting low and we need to get back.'

'No, it's stuck fast.'

There was a pause. 'Miss Sandy, can you wait here? Mr Spacejock needs assistance.'

'I can get back to the ship myself. I don't need help.'

'I'm sure you don't, but the Navcom won't let you in.'

'Yes she will. I know the override code.'

'I'm afraid that won't help. I increased security before we left, and the override code is no longer sufficient.'

Hal closed his eyes. What perfect timing!

'As long as I'm back in six minutes, you'll still have a four-minute margin,' explained Clunk. 'That's ample time for a return.'

Hal eyed his oxygen indicator and realised he didn't have any margin at all. Even if they got his suit free, he'd barely make the ship.

There was a flash of light as Clunk approached the cavern. The robot's shiny head appeared through the jumbled rocks at the entrance, and Hal smiled to himself. The situation was tricky, but Clunk was always resourceful. He'd know what to do!

'I don't know how we're going to get you out of this,' said Clunk, inspecting the metal shard. 'Removing all these barbs will take far too long, and cutting the suit will release the last of your air.'

'I was hoping for something a bit more positive,' said Hal. 'You know, unpick the tape, peel back the fabric, patch it up as we go. That sort of thing.'

Clunk shook his head. 'There's no time.' His gaze travelled over the junk pile, and he frowned as he spotted something. 'That's interesting.'

Hal followed his gaze but had no idea what the robot was looking at. 'What is it? Cutting equipment? A spare oxygen cylinder?'

'No, that's a memory module. We should take it with us.'

Hal clenched his jaw. Here he was, firmly attached to the jagged metal beam, and Clunk was more interested in dusty old components. 'Listen, how about you get me free first?'

'Oh, that's easy.' Clunk gestured at Hal's leg. 'We'll just have to cut it off.'

'Eh? That's a bit extreme, isn't it?'

'It's the only solution. The longer we spend here, the more likely Sandy will run out of air too.'

'No! You'll have to find another way.'

'I'm very sorry, Mr Spacejock. Time is of the essence.'

'But –'

Clunk raised his right hand. The plasteel skin parted along the edge of his palm, revealing a fine-toothed blade which gleamed in the light from his chest lamp. 'Hold still please.'

'No, wait! You go back with Sandy and I'll take my chances. I'll get it free somehow!'

'This is the only way.' Clunk bent over Hal's leg, saw at the ready. 'Are you ready?'

'Don't I get anaesthetic?'

'Trust me, this won't hurt a bit.'

Hal screwed his eyes shut, clenched his fists and gritted his teeth. There was a gentle pressure on his shin, and he steeled himself for the bite of the saw. Instead, he felt rapid vibrations, and he realised Clunk was using some kind of self-healing surgical blade. The vibrations continued for several seconds, and then the pressure was gone.

'All done,' said Clunk. 'Let's go.'

'You might have to carry me.'

'There's no gravity, Mr Spacejock. You won't need your feet.'

'Yes, but . . .' Hal opened one eye, dreading what he might find. Then he opened the other eye, and breathed a sigh of relief. 'That's a nice clean cut. Very professional.'

Clunk was inspecting the barbed metal shard, which he'd sliced from the rest of the beam. 'Thank you. I always wanted to be a surgeon.' He flicked the shard towards the rear of the cavern and retrieved the memory module from the junk pile. 'Now, back to the *Volante.*'

❧

Hal was relieved to see Sandy in the main tunnel. He'd half-expected her to head for the *Volante* and try a few more override codes on his ship, but here she was, waiting patiently. Sure, she was hanging upside-down with her arms crossed, impatiently drumming her fingers on her sleeves, but at least she was there.

Clunk reconnected the safety line, and when they were ready he led the way to the surface. The door beneath the derrick was still open, and the three of them filed out. Hal could see the *Volante* across the asteroid's rocky surface, looming above them like a gleaming white moon. As they got closer he craned his neck to stare up at his ship, and then it dawned on him. He really was looking up at the *Volante* ... it had drifted away.

'Er ... Clunk?'

'It's okay, Mr Spacejock. The Navcom will bring her down again.'

Hal heard a buzz of static, followed by a series of cheeps, chirps and whistles.

'Don't forget you upped the security,' said Sandy. 'The Navcom can't hear you.'

'Great,' muttered Hal. 'We're running out of air and the ship's drifting away. Can things get any worse?'

Zing!

Hal jerked his head involuntarily. Something had just struck his helmet, scoring a line across the face plate.

Plip!

He looked down at his sleeve, where a pinhole was leaking air. His arm stung like crazy, and as he watched a tiny drop of blood squeezed out, before freezing into a sphere and drifting away.

Thud!

Something struck his backpack, and realisation dawned. 'They're shooting at us. Take cover!'

There was a mad scramble for the safety of the mine shaft, arms and legs flailing as they scrabbled for purchase on the rocky surface. There were puffs of dust all around as shots rained down, and Hal felt a searing pain down the side of his leg as another went home. He tried to shield Sandy, while Clunk tried to shield both of them. Eventually they got under cover.

'Kent Spearman, you're a dead man,' Hal snarled into his radio. 'How could you fire on a teenage girl, you louse?'

'It's not Mr Spearman,' said Clunk. 'And we're not under fire.'

'You could have fooled me!' snapped Hal. 'I was hit twice!'

'No, you misunderstand. It's not vengeful humans trying to kill us. It's mother nature.'

'What are you talking about?'

Clunk pointed to the scars on the door. 'Remember this, and the damage to the derrick?'

'Sure. You said the place had been shot up.'

'I now realise they were caused by micro-meteorites.'

'Why didn't we see any on the way in?'

'The forecast must have been scattered showers.'

Hal gave the robot a suspicious look, but Clunk's face was serious. 'How long will this show last?'

'Five seconds or five centuries.' Clunk spread his hands. 'There's no way to tell.'

'What about my ship? She's out there in this!'

'Mr Spacejock, the *Volante* was designed to navigate deep space. Her hull won't be troubled by chips of gravel.'

There was a gasp, and they both turned to look at Sandy. 'I'm sorry,' she said. 'I'm having trouble breathing.'

'It is a lot to take in,' said Clunk gravely.

Hal snorted. 'It's not your stunning revelations. We're running out of air!'

Clunk looked serious. 'In that case, there's only one solution. You wait here, and I shall venture out and fetch the ship.'

Hal looked out the door. The shower had intensified, and the ground boiled as thousands of micro-meteorites tore into it. The derrick was being eaten away as he watched, and shiny fragments mingled with the dust like confetti. 'Are you immune to these micro-thingies?'

'No.'

'You'll be torn apart in that lot.'

'I will take damage, but I've programmed my basic functions to continue . . . even if my brain is destroyed.'

'Clunk . . . '

'No arguments, Mr Spacejock. It was a pleasure working with you.'

Clunk put his hand out, and Hal took it in a firm grip. Then the hand was withdrawn, and Clunk braced himself. Outside, meteorites tore the ground, shredding the derrick and shattering the reinforced concrete.

'Are you sure about this?' said Hal.

'There's no alternative.'

'Yes there is,' said Sandy, her voice faint. 'You can use this door.'

Hal snorted. 'Going back into the mine won't help. We're out of air.'

'Not . . . what I meant.' Sandy gasped the words out. 'Take it off the . . . hinges. Use as . . . shield.'

'Clunk? Will it work?'

Clunk held up his middle finger.

'I guess that's a no.' Barely had Hal spoken when the robot's skin peeled back, revealing a flat-bladed screwdriver. Clunk crouched next to the door and had the hinges off in seconds. Out of the corner of his eye Hal saw Sandy's head drop. 'Make it quick, Clunk. She's all in.'

Clunk held the door over his head and dived out. He used the shield as a makeshift umbrella, warding off the meteorites as they pounded the heavy metal. The impacts drove him into the ground, but the robot staggered on: hunched over, knees bent, and barely visible through the swirling dust. Moments later the maelstrom swallowed him up completely.

Hal realised his own breathing was getting laboured. His tanks were larger than those in Sandy's lightweight pack, but he'd lost a lot of air when the metal shard snagged his leg. He put his arm around Sandy's shoulders and touched their helmets together. 'You'll be fine, kid,' he said, speaking directly into the helmet. 'Clunk's a champ. He can do anything.'

'Not . . . a . . . kid,' murmured Sandy.

◆

Hal opened his eyes. It was dark, his head was pounding and the air in his helmet tasted like sour milk. Fuzzy and barely conscious, his first thought was for Sandy. She was lying next to him, and with a horrible shock he realised her eyes were open. 'No you don't,' said Hal firmly. 'Clunk's going to save us! Come on, stay with me.'

Sandy squinted in the harsh light from his helmet. 'Why? Where are you going?'

'I, er ... ' As Hal's senses cleared he became aware of several facts. First, the floor was hard under his side, which meant gravity. Second, his helmet was open at the bottom, which meant air. And third, the lights on his helmet were not only illuminating Sandy, they were also shining on the interior of the *Volante*'s airlock. And finally, he could hear the ship's engines. 'We're safe?'

'Yes. Clunk said to rest here. He raised the oxygen content to help us recover.'

'Are you all right? Did you get hit?'

She shook her head. 'Not a scratch.'

Relieved, Hal glanced at the inner door and spotted Clunk peering anxiously through the porthole. The robot beamed and waved.

'Is the freight business always this exciting?' asked Sandy.

'Pfft. This is nothing.' Hal sat up, and immediately regretted it. His arm stung and his leg was aflame, but worst of all his head felt like a brand new universe ... one zeptosecond after the big bang. His brain was still inside his skull, but felt like it a hyperactive alien which could burst out at any moment.

The door opened with a crash and Clunk hurried in. 'Mr Spacejock! Miss Sandy! I'm so glad you're all right.'

Sandy raised a hand and Clunk hauled her up. Hal got up by himself, still groggy. 'What about that memory module? Was it any good?'

'The Navcom is parsing it now. Come and watch!'

Hal indicated his spacesuit. 'I need to get out of this thing first, and I'll need a first aid kit. I got one in the arm, and I thought that hurt until I took a meteorite in the knee. I swear it felt like an arrow.'

Clunk helped them with the spacesuits, wincing as he saw the dried blood on Hal's sleeve and trouser leg. Hal rolled his sleeve back and saw a deep graze near his elbow. His leg was worse, with a puncture wound just above his knee. 'It's still in there, isn't it?'

'Yes, but it's only a pinprick. It doesn't require urgent attention.'

Hal put his full weight on the leg, testing it. 'Stings a bit, but it won't slow me down.'

'Excellent. Then you must come and watch the data retrieval.' Clunk strode from the airlock, with Sandy following and Hal limping along behind. He led them to the console, where the main screen showed a single line of text:

Scanned: 94%

As they watched it changed to

Scanned: 95%

'Isn't it exciting?' said Clunk, barely able to keep the enthusiasm out of his voice.

'Totally wild,' muttered Hal. 'Any more of this and I'll need a stiff drink.'

Suddenly the screen changed, displaying a montage of old documents. 'There you are!' enthused Clunk. 'It's found something. Isn't it wonderful?'

'Amazing. Incredible.' Hal frowned. 'What am I looking at?'

'Purchase invoices for all six robots. Galactic Mining purchased us all from the same source.' Clunk pointed to an invoice. 'See? That's where we came from.'

Across the top of the docket was an official-looking header: Barwenna Customs and Quarantine, enforcement arm. Hal snorted at the sight. 'You were a customs officer? I should have known.'

'I probably made the coffee,' said Clunk mildly.

'What's that, another skill you've lost in the mists of time?'

'Never mind your insatiable appetite for hot drinks. Do you see the rest of it?'

Hal whistled. 'It says you served aboard a Battlecruiser. But I thought you were a pacifist!'

'Who knows what I did in my past lives?'

Hal looked at Clunk's warm yellow eyes and his friendly, squashy face. It was hard to picture the robot peering down a gun sight with murder in his electronic heart, but anything was possible with the right source code.

'What about the cruiser?' demanded Sandy. 'Decommissioned? Wrecked? Lost in space?'

Clunk checked the database. 'She's still in service. I'll set the course and secure clearance for a visit.'

Hal clapped him on the shoulder. 'Great work, Clunk!'

25

Two hours later Hal was less certain about their prospects. They'd arrived at the last-known position of the *Almara* but she was nowhere to be seen. They tried hailing her, but there was no reply. Either the Battlecruiser wasn't in range or the crew was ignoring them.

The *Volante* cruised on, widening the search, and Hal was about to suggest Clunk go and engrave burial instructions on a wall when Sandy pointed at the screen.

'Is that her?' she asked.

Hal squinted at the display, where a faint red dot had appeared at extreme range. 'It's either the Cruiser or a space pirate.'

'It's not a space pirate,' said Clunk.

'Really? Last time I saw a dot like that –'

'Was in a computer game, Mr Spacejock. If you recall, it also featured zombies and vampires.'

'Oh yeah, that's right.' Hal laughed. 'Who ever heard of space pirates, anyway? They're a myth!'

Clunk shook his head. 'They do exist, but in real life they mask ship IDs.'

'So that's the Battlecruiser then.' Hal looked closer. 'Any sign of Kent Spearman?'

'No. It's possible they're docked, but it's more likely they've already left.'

'We *have* to get ahead of them.'

'Indeed.' Clunk eyed him thoughtfully. 'Mr Spacejock, what would you say to a division of labour? What I mean is, why don't Miss Sandy and I obtain the required information while you maintain station?'

'Are you fobbing me off?'

'Indeed no! We've already seen two attempts at sabotage. Imagine if someone sneaks aboard the *Volante* while we're seeking information aboard the Battlecruiser? They might cut the *Volante* loose and strand us!'

'You're right, I'll stay here as backup.' Hal drove his fist into the palm of his hand. 'You can rely on me to negotiate with any sabotagers.'

'Saboteurs.'

'Them too. Now call up that cruiser and tell them what we want. We're in a hurry!'

❖

'Battlecruiser Almara, this is the *Volante*. We need to come aboard and –'

There was a hiss of static. *'I'm sorry, but our jump drives are charging. We're about to leave for the next system.'*

'But –'

'I'm sorry. Almara out.'

Clunk turned from the console, his expression serious. 'Mr Spacejock, they broke off communications.'

'You think?' Hal eyed the screen. 'Can we intercept them? Head them off somehow?'

'You want me to cut across the bows of a Battlecruiser?' Clunk blinked. 'It's possible there are faster ways to destroy the *Volante*, but I can't think of any.'

'All right, call them back. Not the same guy though. I want someone higher up.'

Clunk looked doubtful, but obeyed.

'*Almara,*' said a curt female voice. 'First Lieutenant Overmann speaking.'

'This is Captain Hal Spacejock, a fully qualified deputy of the intergalactic Peace Force.'

Clunk jammed his hand over the microphone. 'Are you insane?'

'Not at all. They love ranking in the military.'

'But you don't have a rank. You're not a real deputy!'

'They don't know that, do they?' Hal pushed Clunk's hand aside and continued. 'We need some information on a batch of robots sold to the Galactic Mining Company.'

'*What, again?*'

Hal's heart sank. 'Has someone else been there?'

'*Yep. You'll have to get the info from them.*'

Hal thought quickly. 'All right, never mind the data. We're also pursuing a vicious criminal and his desperate gang. The ringleader's name is Kent Spearman, and if you have any information –'

'*Kent Spearman of the* Tiger? *But . . . he's the one asking about Galactic Mining!*'

'No! Was he really?'

'*Sure! He just left five minutes ago.*'

'You'd better find out what he was doing aboard your ship.

We know he's been digging up old records for an identity scam, but that might be a front.'

'He did ask for records. I'll have them locked down immediately.'

'Before you do ...'

'Yes?'

'I have a forensic investigator on board.' Hal winked at Sandy. 'Can she come aboard to check for damage to your records?'

'Sorry, Captain Spacejock. We're leaving for the next system in minutes.'

'If you could just delay –'

'You don't know your Battlecruisers, son. It takes forty minutes to prep these babies, and there's no stopping the countdown.'

'How much time is left?'

There was a pause. *'Nine minutes, twenty seconds.'*

Hal covered the microphone and turned to Clunk. 'Well? Can we do this?'

'Impossible. Docking, quarantine procedures, locating a terminal ... we'll never make it.'

'Good stuff.' Hal moved his hand. '*Almara*? We'll be there in thirty seconds.'

'Affirmative.'

'Stand by for docking,' said Hal, cutting the connection.

'Mr Spacejock, we'll never do it!'

'Clunk, you have thirty seconds to dock with that cruiser. Get on with it!'

◆

Clunk was not happy. Twenty-nine seconds had elapsed since

Hal's order, and here he was, already hurrying along the docking tube to the Battlecruiser. Sandy ran alongside him, a sheaf of official-looking orders in one hand. She'd downloaded a batch of stories from a fan-fiction site, pasted them together and swapped some of the fictional names for 'Spearman', 'Cuff' and 'Fisher'. Unfortunately there were lots of paragraphs on wormholes and parasites, but Mr Spacejock was convinced the result would pass quick inspection. They could only hope the crew of the Battlecruiser didn't try to verify their identities.

'Welcome to the *Almara*,' said a voice, interrupting his train of thought.

Clunk stopped. The woman facing him was in her fifties, with grey-streaked hair and a rather severe expression. Her uniform sported an impressive row of campaign ribbons, and gold bands on her sleeve indicated a high-ranking officer. 'Major?' he asked, hazarding a guess.

'First Lieutenant Overmann.' The officer looked Sandy up and down in mild surprise. 'You're the forensic expert?'

'Miss West has proved herself in many pressure situations,' said Clunk. 'Why, with her multi-disciplinary education –'

'My apologies,' interrupted the officer. 'I didn't mean to question your credentials. Come, the terminal is this way.'

They followed Overmann down a corridor, moving quickly past rows of status screens. These blanked out at their approach, only to flicker into life as they passed by. 'Is there something wrong with your systems?' asked Clunk.

'Not at all. They blank out because you're not authorised to view them.' Overmann showed them into a cubicle. 'This is where Spearman was. Can you see what he was up to?'

Sandy took a seat and frowned at the prompt on the screen. 'Which operating system do you use?'

'How should I know?' Overmann glanced at her watch.

'You have less than seven minutes before we jump. Any more questions?'

'Not yet.' Sandy took out a hard copy of the docket from the Orbiter, and began entering the serial numbers.

'Good.' Overmann held up the sheaf of papers. 'I'll be back in a moment. I want to check your credentials.'

'Could you show me to another terminal?' said Clunk quickly. 'I'd like to upload everything we have on Kent Spearman and his associates. Just in case you run into them again, you understand.'

Overmann hesitated, then nodded. 'Follow me.'

◆

Hal was growing impatient aboard the *Volante*. He'd heard nothing from Clunk, and for all he knew both the robot and the girl had been charged and locked up, never to be seen again. He should have gone with them! Then a thought occurred to him. 'Navcom, what happens if the Battlecruiser jumps while we're still attached? Does it leave us behind?'

'Most of us.'

'Explain.'

'There are several incident reports covering similar situations, but evidence from the survivors was inconclusive.'

'Did you say ... survivors?'

'Yes. Those lucky souls who made it to the rescue pods before the total destruction of their ships.'

For the first time, Hal was truly aware of the vast bulk of the Battlecruiser looming over them. He hadn't really thought it through, but if something that large suddenly winked out of existence, anything nearby was bound to suffer from the effects. 'So how far do we have to be? What's the safe distance?'

'A few thousand metres would be good.'

'How long will that take?'

'Infinity. The main engines are powered down.'

Hal eyed the clock. Two minutes left. 'Okay, Navcom. Start main engines.'

'Are you sure?'

'I'm bloody certain. Get the things fired up and ready to go.'

'But Clunk ... Miss Sandy.'

'Can you contact them?'

'Negative.'

'Okay. If they're not in the docking tube with ten seconds to go, we leave. Understood?'

'Affirmative.'

Hal drummed his fingers on the console. The main engines rumbled in readiness. The clock ticked down. There was nothing he could do but wait.

◆

Clunk delayed Overmann as long as he could, asking questions about the Battlecruiser while he uploaded choice selections from Mr Spacejock's past interactions with Kent Spearman. If Overmann took a closer look at the printed 'orders' Sandy had mocked up they'd be sunk, but he also had to be careful with the data he shared. Mr Spacejock's rival had spent time in jail, but as far as he knew Kent Spearman was now leading a lawful life. He had no intention of framing an innocent man.

'And how much does it cost to service your engines?' he asked the lieutenant, trying to keep her talking as long as possible.

'How should I know? That's engineering.'

'What about your mission? Is it going well?'

'You'd have to ask the captain.'

'Tell me, do you have many weapons?'

Overmann's eyes narrowed. 'Any more questions like that and I'll turn you over to counter-intelligence for a little chat.'

Clunk raised his hands in apology. 'It's just curiosity.'

'Yeah, and you're the cat.' Overmann glanced at her watch. 'Two minutes left. You'd better collect your expert and leave.'

They returned to the alcove, where Sandy's screen was showing a picture of a smiling robot above a certificate. The award had a fancy border, a gold seal, and a flowery heading which read 'Top Employee Award'. Underneath, the description ran 'Most fines issued for contraband in the month of May'.

'I found a sales docket too,' said Sandy.

Overmann looked at the photo, then at Clunk. 'Close family?'

'A similar model.'

'What's this got to do with Kent Spearman?'

'We're building a case against him. I can't say any more.' Clunk snatched a hard copy and took Sandy by the hand. 'If you'll excuse us, we really must be going.'

They ran along the corridor, and were only halfway to the *Volante* when they heard a growling roar far below their feet.

'Thirty seconds,' shouted the lieutenant. 'If you're not inside the airlock in ten I can't let you go.'

'We're going, we're going!' shouted Clunk, putting on a spurt.

◆

Hal was hunched over the console, one hand gripping the throttle. The timer showed twenty seconds, and his knuckles whitened as it counted down. Where were they? Would they make it?

The console speaker crackled, startling him. 'Mr Spacejock, we're almost there. Don't leave!'

Hal smiled at the sound of Clunk's voice. Trust the robot to cut things so fine! 'No problem, Clunk. Abandoning you two would be . . . ' He reached for the right words. 'Hell, it would be inconceivable!'

There was no reply, and the timer continued to tick down. Fourteen. . . Thirteen. . .

Hal concentrated on the throttles. If he waited too long, the *Volante* would be destroyed. If he went too soon, Clunk and Sandy would be dumped into hard vacuum. They wouldn't have long to worry about it though, because the *Volante*'s engines would roast them to a crisp just before the Battlecruiser's jump drive reduced them to swirling molecules.

No, they had to be right inside the *Volante*'s airlock. And time had just run out.

Hal increased pressure on the throttles.

Eleven . . . Ten . . .

The impulse was travelling down his arm when there was a loud *Kerchack!*

'Was that the airlock?'

'Confirmed,' said the Navcom. 'The boarding tunnel is retracting and it's safe to –'

Hal didn't wait for the rest. He shoved the throttle forward and held on for dear life. The sheer force of acceleration was too much for the gravity generators, and Hal clung to the pilot's chair as his eyeballs tried to screw themselves into his brain. Through the vibrations he could just make out the numbers dancing on the screen.

Three ... Two ... One ...

The screen turned white, and Hal's vision split and blurred as the Battlecruiser jumped. Fortunately they were at extreme range, and the *Volante*'s engines powered on without missing a beat. 'Navcom, report!'

'We lost thirty millimetres from the starboard exhaust cone, but that's the only physical damage.'

Hal rubbed his forehead. His vision was returning to normal, although he had a splitting headache. As for the *Volante*, any closer to the hyperspace field and half the ship might have been sliced off, vanishing along with the departing Battlecruiser. Still, at least Clunk and Sandy were back with the data. Sandy had proved quite useful, and he was glad to have her aboard. And as for Clunk ... Hal smiled to himself. He'd never admit it, but the robot was indispensable.

Then he frowned. Why hadn't the others left the airlock? He glanced to his right, but the door was closed and the little porthole was dark. With a sick feeling he leapt up and charged across the flight deck. When he looked through the porthole he got a huge shock.

He was expecting one human and a robot, but instead there were *two* humans plus a robot ... and the robot wasn't Clunk!

26

Hal pulled the airlock open and saw Sandy lying near the outer door, dazed and holding her head. Nearby, Natasha Lucas was lying on the floor with her eyes shut and a large bruise forming on her forehead. The reporter was motionless, and Hal realised she'd been knocked unconscious when the ship accelerated away from the Battlecruiser.

As for the robot, that was inspecting a new dent on its shoulder. It noticed Hal and frowned. 'Where did *you* learn to fly, you ham-fisted wannabe?'

'Nice to see you too, Zee,' muttered Hal. He hurried over to Sandy and helped her up. 'Where's Clunk? What the hell happened?'

'We met these two and the robots played a little game.' Sandy shook her head. ''After you', 'no you first', 'no I insist' ...you get the idea. In the end one got through and the other didn't.'

'So we ended up with this bucket of bolts?'

'It's nice to be wanted,' snapped the robot.

'Thanks to you, Clunk's still aboard the Battlecruiser!'

Natasha groaned, and Hal helped her sit up. 'Take it easy. You've had a bit of a bump.'

'Where am I? What happened?'

'Good question,' muttered Hal. 'I thought you were sticking with Kent Spearman?'

'They dumped us both. Left us behind. We were still figuring out what to do when we heard you'd docked.'

'So you came to ruin my day. Wonderful.' Hal thought for a moment. They had two choices: chase after Clunk, or follow up the information Clunk got from the ... 'Damn it!'

'What?'

'Clunk ... he's the only one who knows where we're supposed to go next!'

'Don't worry, I got the info.' Sandy dug in her pocket and took out a crumpled sheet of paper. 'See?'

Hal eyed the 'Employee of the month' award. 'What's this Asset Removables thingy?'

'A leasing company. They rent equipment to other companies. Not just robots, either. Ships, computer hardware ... you name it.'

'Let's see if we can track them down.' Hal hurried back to the flight deck. 'Navcom, what do you have on Asset Removables?'

'They went bankrupt a decade ago. Garmit and Hash took most of their assets.'

'Oh, great,' groaned Hal. 'Of all the companies in the galaxy ...'

'You've heard of them?' demanded Natasha. 'Do you have any contacts there?'

'None that I want to meet.' Hal gave them a summary. 'I owed them a pile of money once, and they tried to repossess my ship. It was very messy.'

'Can we go see them?'

'No chance. They think I'm dead, and that's exactly how I want it.' Hal thought for a moment. 'Okay, here's what we'll do. We have to find a G&H office or one of their ships, sneak in and hack their computers, retrieve the data and leave without them seeing us.'

'You'll need a team of experts for that.'

'No, we need Clunk.' Hal paced the flight deck. 'We'll head back to Barwenna for fuel, then chase after the Battlecruiser and fetch Clunk. He can do the sneaking and hacking business, and then –'

There was a buzz from the console. 'That's not going to happen,' said the Navcom. 'If you inspect the viewscreen you'll discover an update on our fuel situation.'

Everyone looked. The update was displayed in friendly red letters: WE'RE OUT OF FUEL

'How is that possible?' demanded Hal. 'We had plenty left for this jaunt. Clunk said so!'

'That was before you hit the emergency boost. You remember, when we were fleeing total destruction in the Battlecruiser's hyperspace field.'

'Well that's it then.' Hal turned to the others. 'I don't know about you lot, but I don't have the cash for fuel.'

Sandy shook her head. Zee shrugged. They all looked at the reporter.

'How much are we talking about?' she asked.

Hal told her.

'Hell! What do you run this thing on ... printer ink?'

'Go on. You can put it on expenses.'

'I'm a freelancer!'

'Think of it as an investment. This article is going to make you a lot of money, isn't it?'

'Not that much.'

'So write a book: 'My life with the six finalists'.'

'Wow, catchy title. That's sure to sell up a storm.'

Hal pleaded with her. 'Come on! You don't want your novel to end on chapter 26, do you? And if any of us wins, we'll pay you back double. Right guys?'

Sandy and Zee nodded.

'All right, all right.'

Hal slapped Natasha on the shoulder, while Sandy allowed her a small nod of thanks.

'There you are, Navcom. Problem solved! Set course for Barwenna.'

'Mr Spacejock, that's not going to work.'

'Eh? Why not?'

'We can return to Barwenna, but landing requires more fuel than we're carrying.'

'The Orbiter, then. They must have fuel.'

'Only by special arrangement.'

'Are you saying we're stranded?'

'Not at all. We can dock with the Orbiter and wait for their supplies to arrive.'

'How long will that take?'

'Two days at last estimate.'

Hal frowned. 'Any passing ships we can tap?'

'Five small ones which wouldn't have enough fuel for your jetbike, and the other ... it's a Garmit and Hash corporate vessel on a team bonding cruise.'

'G&H, eh?' Hal looked thoughtful. 'We could ask them for fuel, and while they're filling up one of us could sneak over and hack their computers.'

'Deep space piracy?' said Natasha, with a snort. 'Don't they still hang people for that?'

'I'm already hung.' Hal realised everyone was looking at him, and he hastened to explain. 'I mean, I'm as good as hung

191

if we don't get any fuel. Clunk will never forgive me if I screw this up.'

'It won't work anyway,' said the Navcom. 'Their fuel is not compatible.'

'That's just great. Fantastic.'

'There is one other option,' said the Navcom. 'A local venue has fuel to spare, and –'

'Excellent! Program the course and hit the boosters.'

'But –'

'No buts. Get us there immediately.'

'You should know that –'

'Now!'

'Course set. Prepare for a micro-jump in three … two … '

Hal's vision split and blurred, and when it readjusted there was a white blob on the viewscreen. 'What's that?'

'It's a secret base. I found it by studying recent ship movements in the sector.'

The blob grew larger, resolving into half a dozen odd-shaped structures interconnected with boarding tubes. 'What sort of base is it?' asked Hal.

'It's a pirate base.'

Hal gaped. 'Are you insane?'

'They have fuel.'

Hal gestured at the screen. 'And missiles, and gunners, and dozens of pirates! These guys will board us, rip the *Volante* from our hands and then … ' He glanced at the others and realised he wasn't exactly boosting their morale.

'We'll have to arm ourselves,' said Sandy. 'You'd better break out the guns.'

'Guns?' Hal frowned. 'What guns?'

'Are you mad?' cried Natasha, her voice rising. 'Are you

saying you travel all over the galaxy in a brand new freighter ...completely unarmed?'

'Blame Clunk. He won't let me near any weaponry.'

The Navcom interrupted. 'According to Clunk, whatever the risk of kidnapping and violence at the hands of armed pirates, the risk of Mr Spacejock injuring himself and others with guns is far higher.'

'Yes, thanks for that,' muttered Hal.

'Why, there was this one time when Mr Spacejock –'

'Zip it, Navcom.'

'Archiving complete.'

'If I might interrupt?' said a voice behind them.

They all turned to see Zee fiddling with his chest panel, and after a loud 'click' it swung open. There was a whirr and a rack of blasters emerged, tilting and spreading until there was a fan of six weapons. His thighs opened to display two halves of a heavy blast rifle, which shot out on rods, spun ninety degrees and snapped together. Finally he reached behind himself, strained for a moment, then showed them a large grenade.

'Talk about sitting on a weapons cache,' remarked Hal, visibly impressed. 'What are you doing with that lot?'

'My owner was a gunrunner. I kept a few mementos after he was arrested.'

'May I?' said Hal, reaching for a blaster.

Zee drew back. 'Not if your Navcom's stories are accurate.'

'Great. You're as bad as Clunk.'

There was a snick as the rifle came apart, and a whirr of gears as the weaponry slid back into the original hiding places. The grenade went back with a muted 'plop'.

'Just don't sit down in a hurry,' remarked Hal. He glanced at the screen, now filled with a motley collection of ships. They were painted with a bewildering array of skulls, crossbones, graffiti tags and ... corporate logos?

'What's with the sponsorship?' demanded Hal. 'You'd think there'd be a backlash, advertising with immoral, bloodthirsty pariahs.'

'There was, so companies ditched their newspaper campaigns and switched to these guys. Incidentally, we're being hailed.'

Hal took a deep breath. Tension was high in the flight deck, and the upcoming negotiations would either bring them fuel ... or a fate worse than death. He eyed the others. He was putting them all in danger, and for what? A slim chance at a gigantic inheritance. How could he risk all their lives for an enormous pile of money? 'Okay, put them on,' he told the Navcom.

A man appeared on the screen, his face barely visible under the pirate trappings. Bandanna, eye patch, facial hair, broad scar, multiple earrings ... he was like something out of a low-budget movie.

'Hello,' said Hal, with a little wave. 'I was just wondering whether –'

'Oh-arr, me hearties! Be you here for the plunderin'?'

'Are we what?'

'Be you approachin' the Lost Den for the feast o' plenty?'

'I don't know what you're talking about,' said Hal.

'You bain't be the scurvy gods from ye good ship Garmit 'n' Hash?'

'Not bloody likely. This is the interstellar freighter *Volante.*'

'Be you insane?' demanded the man. 'Be you mad, approaching the lair of Roberts the Terrible? Be you –'

'Actually, we're just out of fuel,' said Hal.

'Out of fuel? That be your scurvy excuse? Spies say I. Spies, liars and thieves.'

'No, we really just –'

'Stand by to be boarded. Your money or your lives!'

'Now wait just a minute –'

The screen went dark, and the doom-laden silence was interrupted by Natasha's nervous laugh. 'That went well.'

Hal crossed his arms. 'I'm not just sitting around waiting for them. Navcom, stand by for an emergency jump.'

'Mr Spacejock, they have missiles and lasers locked onto the ship. Can I recommend an alternative?'

'What? Hyperspace out of here? Hit full power and dodge their fire? Cover the *Volante* in tinfoil and reflect their laser beams straight back at them?'

'No. Surrender.'

Hal made a rude noise, but it was just bravado. He knew the Navcom was right. 'Are they sending a ship to meet us?'

'No, they're instructing me to dock.'

'Drive-thru piracy. That's new.' Hal turned to Zee. 'Give me a couple of those guns, then take Sandy to the engine room. It's locked, but you'll be able to get through it in no time. Hide her in the generator alcove, then position yourself at the door and protect her with your life. Is that clear?'

Zee nodded. 'They won't get past me.' He passed Hal the guns, then shepherded Sandy towards the lift.

After they left, Hal turned to Natasha. 'I don't suppose you've had combat training?'

'I once wrote an article on schoolies.'

'Close enough,' said Hal, handing her a weapon.

'Docking now,' said the Navcom.

There was a metallic noise from the airlock.

'Boarding tunnel connected. Outer airlock opening.'

Hal tightened his grip on the gun. No matter what happened, his duty was to protect the others. It was his fault they'd been dragged into this disaster. Not for the first time he wished Clunk were there. The robot might be a wishy-washy gun-hating pacifist, but he made a useful shield in a pitched battle.

Hal heard a roar of voices, and the inner door began to open. He raised his gun in readiness, and alongside him Natasha did likewise.

'Safety!' she cried.

'Safety and honour!' yelled Hal. 'Death to the hoards of evil! You shall not –'

'No, not that,' Natasha waved her gun. 'Your safety is on!'

Hal was still fiddling with the catch when the door opened. A motley collection of pirates charged in, and Hal glanced up from his weapon to see a forest of cruel-looking swords coming towards him. At that moment he freed the safety, and the blaster promptly went off. The shot was deafening in the enclosed space, and the nearest sword was cut neatly in two.

The boarders skidded to a halt, and the leading pirate stared at his truncated weapon in disbelief. Then he rounded on Hal. 'You have real weapons? Are you out of your minds?'

◆

Hal, Natasha, Sandy and Zee were relaxing in comfortable armchairs. On the table in front of them was a pot of coffee and a plate of sandwiches. Nearby, a clean-cut man in his mid-twenties was talking into his commset. Andrew Roberts was sporting a large gold earring, and his bandanna was covered in fast food logos. The sword hanging from his belt was still smoking where Hal's lucky shot had cut it in two.

Roberts finished talking and turned his attention on them. 'The *Volante*, eh?'

'That's right,' said Hal. 'We're on a vital mission.'

'I see.' Roberts whipped off his bandanna and smoothed his hair. 'So how can I help you? Are you lost?'

'Like I said, we need fuel.'

'This is a corporate events facility, not a gas station. Try the Barwenna Orbiter.'

'They won't have any for days,' said Hal. 'Come on, we don't need much. Our credit is good.'

Roberts weighed him up. 'Okay, but on two conditions. We're supposed to be an outpost for bloodthirsty cut-throats, and if word gets out we've been refuelling passing freighters it'll destroy our cred on social media.'

'You can rely on us. Not a word to anyone.' Hal hesitated. 'What's the other condition?'

Roberts frowned. 'Twenty minutes from now we have to put on a show for one of our best customers. Thanks to your trigger-happy gunfire, two of my staff are under sedation and another three are suffering post-traumatic stress.'

'It was just a little misunderstanding. I wasn't trying to shoot anyone!'

Roberts raised his half-sword. 'I was there, remember? Anyway, as I was saying . . . they can't take part in proceedings, so I need replacements.'

'Sure. Fuel the *Volante* and we'll fetch them from Barwenna for you.'

'There's no time.' Roberts steepled his fingers. 'Anyway, that's not what I had in mind.'

'Oh, no. No chance. Forget it.'

'Garmit and Hash are my best clients. You put me into this situation, and it's –'

'Wait a minute. Garmit and Hash?'

'Sure. You heard of them?'

'You could say that.' Hal looked thoughtful. 'Did they charter a ship, or is it one of theirs?'

'Definitely theirs. Nothing but the best for this company.' Roberts eyed Hal across the desk. 'So, what do you say?'

27

The *Argon's* passengers were gathered in the observation deck, nervously facing the rear doors. Overhead, crystal clear viewing windows afforded a wide-angle view of space: a breathtaking vista of stars and distant galaxies. The crowd, dressed in evening wear, didn't care about the view of space or the breathtaking vista. No, they were all staring at the rear doors.

It was only moments since their cruise had been rudely interrupted by a blazing shot across the bows of their vessel. More shots had followed, some skimming the observation windows with multicoloured pyrotechnics and carefully orchestrated sound effects. If there were any scientists in the group, they'd yet to ask why laser beams and energy blasts were making sounds in hard vacuum.

The doors rattled, and someone in the crowd moaned.

'Folks, please don't panic,' said their pilot. 'These guys won't hurt you, I promise.'

There was a thud, a muttered curse, and then the doors swept open. A fearsome bunch of pirates poured in, shouting and waving their weapons. The four in the lead really stood out. One had a huge scar across his eye, a bushy black wig, two eye patches - one ridden up to his forehead - a big ginger beard and a set of false teeth that would have put a racehorse to shame. His gold-trimmed jacket shimmered in the light, and his oversized boots thundered on the decking. The apparition was gripping a silver-plated cutlass in each hand, and he swung them like an executioner on a piece rate.

Running alongside were two female pirates, one taller than the other. They were both wearing blood-red blouses and black trousers, and their white bandannas had a savage skull motif. They were brandishing wicked-looking daggers, and a pair of long beards completed their ensemble.

The fourth member of the leading group was a fierce-looking robot sporting a handlebar moustache and a brace of ancient pistols. He was twirling them around his fingers, faster and faster, until they blurred into spinning disks.

The pirate in the velvet jacket crossed his swords, and the marauding pack came to a halt. 'Oh-arr, me hearties!' intoned Captain Hal Longjock, as though he were reading from a shopping list. 'Bless my booties and, er, numb my rum. What 'ave we 'ere then? A sorrier bunch of sea-dogs I never seen!'

The pilot, who was in on the act, played up. 'Captain, I beg you, spare these souls!'

'What be sayin' you?' demanded Hal. 'I spare nothing! I mean nobody!'

'Oh please,' said someone in the crowd. 'My kid's a better pirate than you, and she's four.'

Hal eyed the heckler, a balding man with a glass of wine and a fistful of cheese. 'What be the matter, sorr?'

'I came to this thing last year and it was heaps better. You're crap. A total waste of space.'

Hal's knuckles whitened on the hilt, and he longed to show the mouthy yob just how bloodthirsty he could be. Unfortunately he had more important fish to fry, so he took a deep breath and skipped a few paragraphs. 'You folk are my prisoners, arrr, and you be invited into the lair of Hal the Horrible for a feast an' dancin'.'

'See? I told you he was a crap pirate. He can't even stick to the script!'

'I'll give you script,' muttered Hal, and before his fellow pirates could stop him he plunged into the crowd. He swung his sword with an almighty whoosh, and the heckler was left with half a wine glass and a much smaller piece of cheese. Hal thrust the second cutlass under the man's chin. 'Spoil the show for these people and you'll be the main course,' he muttered. 'Got it?'

The man nodded, carefully, and Hal lowered his sword. 'Right, me hearties. Time for the feast o' plenty!'

There was a cheer and the crowd poured out, shepherded by the rest of the pirate crew. When the dust settled only the pilot remained, together with the four pirates. After a nod from Hal, Natasha approached the man. 'I put a little something aside for you. Care to join me?'

The pilot didn't need convincing, and after he left it was just Hal, Zee and Sandy.

'Right,' said Hal, tossing the swords aside. 'That's enough of that nonsense. Let's find the ship's computer!'

◆

'Come on, get on with it.' Hal twirled his generous moustache. 'I'd never have agreed to this pantomime if I thought you couldn't crack a simple password.'

'It's not my fault!' protested Zee. 'They have multiple layers of encryption.'

'Clunk would have finished by now.'

'If he's so special, maybe you shouldn't have abandoned him.'

'If you don't hurry I'll abandon you too.'

'Oh arr,' muttered Zee. 'Make me walk the plank, will you?'

'Will you two give it a rest?' hissed Sandy. 'Someone will find us in a minute!'

Hal glanced around. They were in the *Argon's* flight deck, which consisted of a chair and a small control panel tucked away in a cramped nacelle. The ship was a pleasure cruiser, only good for local runs, which meant a basic navigation computer and very little in the way of security. Unfortunately the G&H company server was a tougher nut to crack.

'Come on!' muttered Hal. 'Surely you're in by now?'

Zee snorted. 'As the actress said to the –'

'Quit with the funnies and get cracking.'

The robot concentrated hard, then nodded. 'Test pilots.'

'What?'

'Asset Removables purchased six robots from an avionics firm. We tested control interfaces in sub-orbital vessels before they risked valuable human lives in the same ships.'

'Where? Which company?'

'Chris Test Dummies. They operated out of planet Greil, but shut their doors fifteen years ago.'

'Never mind. I'm sure we can trace them.'

'I can hear someone,' hissed Sandy, who was crouched in the doorway. 'We'd better leave!'

'You did a pretty good job, considering.'

They were back in Roberts' office, having removed their outlandish uniforms. Hal managed to pocket a gold earring, intending to clip it to his nose and give Clunk a surprise. He also grabbed a handful of sandwiches and drained three cups of coffee. According to his internal clock it was past midnight, and he needed the jolt to stay on his feet.

'I hear one of the guests played up?'

'He made like a big cheese, but I cut him down to size.'

'Well, Mr Spacejock. A deal's a deal. My staff are refuelling your ship, and if you'd care to authorise payment . . . '

Hal glanced at Natasha, who took out a card and touched it to the reader. She raised her eyebrows as a charge for 'Pirate Scum P/L' glowed on the back, but didn't comment. Once payment was complete, Roberts led them to the boarding tunnel, where the rest of the pirates had formed an honour guard with their swords raised high. They gave three hearty cheers as the visitors passed underneath, and Hal paused at the *Volante's* outer door to make a rousing speech. 'Thanks guys, it's been real. Catch you next time.'

Roberts shook hands, then put his arm around Hal's shoulders. 'Remember. Not a word about this operation to anyone.'

Hal tapped the side of his nose and followed the others into his ship. On the way he took a crumpled sandwich from his pocket and tucked in. When he reached the flight deck he gathered the others for a quick planning session.

'We've got a lead on this Chris Test company, but they closed down years ago. It's going to be tricky finding their records.'

Natasha yawned. 'What happened to them? Were they bought out?'

'No, they went bust.'

'What about the liquidators? They might have the records.'

'Good idea. I'll get onto it.' Hal turned to the console. 'Navcom, can you find the liquidators for Chris Test Dummies? I need you to put in a request for information.'

'The liquidators are Stuhr, Burlend and Wisk. Their offices are located in Greil City.'

'Can you search their records?'

'Negative. They will only share information in person.'

'Okay, hit the boost. We can be there in three or four hours, right?'

'Correct, but office hours are nine to five.'

'What time do they have now?'

'Greil City local time is two a.m. Would you like me to try again in the morning?'

'Sure. Make an appointment and tell them we'll be there at nine.' Hal looked at the others and realised they were all out on their feet. 'Look, why don't we grab a few hours rest? We'll head for Greil during the night, land in the morning and front these people first thing.'

Natasha yawned again, then nodded.

'You guys can take the lower deck. I'll kip here.' After the lift closed Hal glanced at Zee. 'You're very quiet.'

'I was reliving my life as a pirate. It was ... amusing.'

'Hey, you heard the guy. They're always chasing staff. When this is all over you could come back and sign up.'

'Me? Really?'

'Sure. I'll give you a lift out here myself.'

Zee smiled, and for a second his expression reminded Hal of Clunk. 'That's very good of you, Mr Spacejock.'

'You'd better get a charge. Clunk uses the cargo hold, but there are points all over the place.'

'Thank you. Rest assured I will refund the cost of my power usage, should I be lucky enough to inherit Baker's fortune.'

'Don't worry about it.'

The lift doors opened and closed, and Hal was finally alone. He took out a squashed sandwich and bit off a hunk. 'Navcom, any sign of the *Almara*?' he asked, through a mouthful.

'Negative.'

Hal sighed. Clunk was resourceful, and he'd be safe enough aboard a heavily-armed Battlecruiser. He just hoped the robot didn't do anything rash trying to get home. 'Okay Navcom, it's time to go. Set course for Greil.'

'Aye aye, Captain Longjock.'

28

Being rash wasn't in Clunk's nature, but as the night wore on he was certainly leaning towards inventive. Impetuous, even.

It was hours since the confused dash to the boarding tunnel, the surprise encounter with Zee and Natasha, and the despair as the airlock door sealed in his face. The sensible course of action would have been to report back to First Lieutenant Overmann, explain the problem and sit tight until he could leave the *Almara*. Somehow he'd have hitched a ride with a vessel bound for Barwenna, and there he'd have caught up with the *Volante* and Mr Spacejock.

Unfortunately, events conspired against him.

After the *Volante* sped away Clunk turned from the outer door and realised he was alone. Puzzled, he made his way up the passage towards the junction, hoping to find Overmann and explain the situation. Instead, he came face to face with a battered old robot. Short and grey, its outer shell was covered in scorch marks and badly-patched holes. Its eyes were wide and staring, and nervous energy had it dancing from one buckled foot to the other.

'Quick!' said the robot. 'They're after me! We have to hide!'

Clunk put a hand out and tried to soothe the robot with some well-chosen platitudes. Unfortunately, his speech was blocked. He frowned and tried again, but the words wouldn't come. He played back the last conversation he'd had with Mr Spacejock, and groaned. Inconceivable!

Red team. Target sighted in bay nine. Weapons free, I repeat weapons free.

Clunk stared at the overhead speaker. Weapons what?

The voices stopped, and seconds later there was a burst from an automatic pulse rifle.

Control, target is down. Repeat, target is down. Please advise.

Vectoring you now, Red Team. There was a pause. *Target two may be in the vicinity of airlock seventeen, deck two.*

The robot grabbed Clunk's arm. 'They're coming for us! Look!'

Clunk eyed the airlock doors, which were painted with a giant number 17. He opened his chest panel and took out a pencil stub, then wrote on his arm: 'What's going on? Are you running away?'

'Flee,' muttered the robot. 'Must flee.'

Despite the words it just stood on the spot, still hopping from foot to foot.

Control, confirm zone is hot?

Red team, zone is hot. All targets are shoot to kill. Repeat, shoot to kill.

Whoever they were, Clunk realised they were closing in. He decided to run first, ask questions later. He grabbed the robot's hand and hauled it bodily along the airlock corridor, dragging it clear off its feet in his hurry to get away. When they reached the T-junction he put his head out for a quick look … and nearly had it shot off. He saw the flash of an energy weapon and drew back just in time, wincing as the burst slammed into the wall right in front of his face.

Control, target sighted.

'Always dead,' said the robot. 'Over and over.'

Clunk glanced back down the tunnel. The walls were smooth, affording no hiding places. That only left the airlock. He ran to the controls and reached for the button.

'No! Not allowed!' exclaimed the little robot. 'Outside valid parameters! System abort!'

You're with me now, thought Clunk. There are no parameters. He pressed the button, and the inner doors slid open. He bundled the protesting robot inside, then sealed the inner doors. Through the porthole he saw armed troops at the top of the tunnel, scoping the doors through their sights.

Control, two targets sighted. Repeat, two targets sighted.

Negative, Red team. One drone in your sector. Over.

Control, I just saw two of them. Over.

You need your eyes tested, Red leader. There's only one.

I'll blast them both and bring the wreckage back to prove it.

Ten credits says you won't.

Make it fifty.

Clunk risked another look up the tunnel, where he saw a woman in body armour speaking forcibly into a commset. Her gun dangled by her side, forgotten, and he wondered whether there was time to open the door and charge the attackers.

One hundred credits, and I want the heads.

You're on, Control. Have my cash ready.

Clunk ducked as the woman raised her weapon. It was only a matter of time before the troops stormed the airlock, and while he might fight off one or two in the confined space, they'd only have to roll an EMP grenade in to finish him. He glanced at the small robot, but it was huddled in the corner and wouldn't be any use. Then his gaze shifted to the outer door, and to the control panel on the wall.

Crouched double, Clunk crossed the airlock and grabbed the

other robot's hand. Then, without hesitation, he opened the outer door. The air misted and thinned, and a red light came on overhead. Unfortunately he couldn't hear the speakers any more, but the startled face peering through the inner door's porthole spoke volumes. Clunk raised a hand in greeting, then back-flipped out of the airlock with the small robot in tow.

Clunk spent the best part of three hours drifting in space, sailing alongside the Battlecruiser with the robot drone by his side. The *Almara* tried to contact him by radio, but he didn't reply. A brief signal would betray him to the gunnery computers, and once they pinpointed him he'd be blasted into space dust.

It was another hour before a shuttle was launched from the cruiser. It powered away from the ship in a blaze of light, then turned sharply and headed directly for his position. Clunk braced himself for the withering laser barrage, and hoped the end would be quick. His only regret was that he hadn't said goodbye to Mr Spacejock.

Instead of blasting him, the shuttle kept coming, eventually stopping nearby. A door opened and Clunk saw a gun barrel pointing in his direction. So, they were going for the close-up shot, were they? He waved his arms to put them off but their aim was rock-steady, and before he could pull any other tricks they opened fire.

Splot!

Clunk felt the impact, and looked down to see a sticky blob attached to his thigh. There was a tug before he thought to cut the cable, and he tumbled head over heels towards the waiting ship. He considered pushing the drone robot away from him, but the skinny little droid was curled up in a ball and he'd only be delaying the inevitable.

Then he was aboard, and the airlock closed with a thud.

29

It was six a.m. by the ship's clock, and Hal was alone in the flight deck. He'd managed a brief nap in the pilot's chair, but he knew he wouldn't rest properly until Clunk was back. The Navcom was trying to pinpoint the Battlecruiser, although it was proving difficult because data on customs ships was restricted. 'Navcom, anything on the *Almara* yet?'

'Negative, but there is a news story you might find pertinent. A teenager is missing on Barwenna.'

'That's no good.' Hal frowned. 'But why is it pertinent?'

'Watch and learn.'

The screen cleared, and a photo flashed up. It showed a girl in school uniform, and Hal was stunned to recognise Sandy. 'Oh crap. What are they saying?'

'Authorities have further leads on missing schoolgirl, Sandy West. She was last seen yesterday morning, when she left the Hotel Grande in the company of this man.' The screen changed to show an artist's impression of the mystery man: overweight, balding and bug-eyed, he was leering out of the screen with an unpleasant drooling expression. Unfortunately the artist had just managed to capture enough of Hal's features to make it vaguely recognisable, in an over-the-top caricature fashion.

'It actually looks a bit like you,' said the Navcom.

'Thanks a bunch.'

'You can't argue with facial recognition software.'

'But –'

'Wait, there's more.'

'There was also a robot involved, an older model with the designation XG99. If you see either of these suspicious characters, or know of their whereabouts, please contact your local authorities immediately.'

'Oh, that's perfect.' Hal closed his eyes. On top of everything else, he was now chief suspect in a kidnapping.

◆

If there was one thing Hal was used to, it was unexpected dramas. Usually because he caused them. Unfortunately Clunk wasn't there to tidy up, which meant he'd have to use his own initiative. 'Navcom, get Sandy up here. She can explain to the authorities and we'll drop her off as soon as we land.'

Sandy looked apprehensive as she entered the flight deck, and she looked a lot worse after Hal played back the news bulletin. 'Care to explain?'

'It all started with my robot.'

'Don't blame that thing! They spend all their time keeping us out of trouble, not landing us in it.'

'I don't mean it was Daniel's fault.' Sandy took a deep breath. 'My parents had that robot before I was born. He was part of the family, and he looked after me from morning 'til night. One day, when I was five or six, I came home from school and he was gone. My dad told me we needed the money for bills, and they had to sell him.'

'It happens.'

'Yeah, well. A few years after that I got into the tool shed, and I found Dan standing in the corner, covered in a groundsheet. He hadn't left at all, he'd just broken down. My parents didn't have the money to fix him up, so they hid him away and spun me a story.' Sandy lowered her eyes. 'I used to sneak in there and talk to him. I promised we'd run away together one day.'

'Looks like you managed it.'

'I wasn't going to, but three days ago my parents told me they were splitting up. I–I got angry with both of them, and when I heard about this will business I decided to try my luck.' Sandy looked at Hal. 'You understand, don't you?'

'No wonder you didn't want to give Natasha an interview.'

'Yeah, photos in the media. Not the best way to keep a low profile.'

'Do you know how much trouble I'm in right now?' Hal gestured at the screen. 'They think I'm a kidnapper, and most Peace Force officers reach for their guns before their handcuffs.'

'I'm sorry, I didn't –'

'Don't apologise. I did far worse things at your age.' Hal thought for a minute. 'If we drop you off in the city, can you make it to the nearest Peace Force station?'

'You're kidding, aren't you? I'm not going anywhere.'

'You have to tell your folks –'

'Do I hell! There's a fortune at stake, and I'm not giving that up for the sake of my parents.' Sandy lowered her voice. 'They weren't thinking of me when they split up, were they?'

'These things happen,' said Hal gruffly. 'It's not your fault.'

'They've been arguing over me. Every night, on and on.'

'I'm sure they both care for you.'

'Oh yeah? They're each trying to dump me on the other! They don't want me!'

Hal shook his head. 'You must have heard wrong. People say things when they're angry, but they don't mean them.'

Sandy raised her chin. 'It doesn't matter. If I get my hands on this legacy I'm going to hire a ship to take me to the other end of the galaxy. I'll buy a bunch of schools and turn them into homes for unwanted kids. I'll hire pensioners to be their grandparents and everyone will be happy.'

Hal was silent. In hindsight, his own plans for the money seemed a touch selfish. A widescreen? New carpet? A drinks robot?

'If you take me back you're consigning thousands of kids to a life on the street. All those old people will be sad.'

Hal's eyes narrowed. 'You had me until then, kid.' He turned to the console. 'Navcom, send a bulletin in the name of Peace Force Deputy Hal Spacejock. Tell them I've found the missing girl and I'm bringing her in.'

'No, wait!' exclaimed Sandy. 'I'm sorry I exaggerated, but that really is my plan. I'll put it in writing if you like.'

Hal studied her face, trying to read the thoughts behind her brown eyes. She looked deadly serious, and he realised he'd misjudged her. 'All right, we'll hide you on board until this thing is settled, but you've got to dictate a message to your folks. The Navcom will hang onto it, and if I get arrested it should be enough to keep me out of prison.'

'It's a deal.' Sandy pointed to the screen, which was still showing her school photo. 'You can't tell Natasha about this. I don't trust the nosy ...'

'It's her job to ask questions. She's a reporter.'

'So she says.'

'What do you mean?'

'Have you seen her shoes? She's earning a mint somewhere, and it's not writing features.'

Hal shrugged. As far as he was concerned shoes came in two kinds: with heels and without. 'Some people save up for stuff.'

'I wouldn't share your life story, that's all I'm saying.'

At that moment the lift pinged, and Hal wiped Sandy's school photo off the screen. Fortunately it was Zee, not Natasha, and he was bouncing with energy after the lengthy charge.

'You have nice clean power aboard this ship. The waveform is remarkably square and consistent.'

'Good to hear it.'

Zee turned to Sandy. 'I hope you don't mind, but I worked on your robot.'

'Really?' Sandy's eyes shone. 'That's good of you.'

'It's a lot better, but I can't do much more without spares.'

'I don't suppose ...'

'What?'

'I was just thinking about those weapon attachments of yours –'

'No!' said Hal quickly.

The lift opened again and Natasha entered the flight deck. 'Morning all. What's doing?'

'We'll be landing in twenty minutes.' Hal turned to the console. 'Navcom, how's that appointment going?'

'Scheduled for nine a.m., as requested. I convinced their staff to bump a few others.'

'Well done.'

'You must be there on time, though. Miss this appointment and the next slot is two in the afternoon.'

— 30 —

The *Volante* set down without incident, and Hal led Natasha and Zee down the ramp to the car park. Sandy stayed on board, telling the others she had a headache. Hal said nothing. It was unlikely anyone on Greil would recognise her, but facial recognition cameras would store her image, as they did for everyone. If the Peace Force spread their net beyond Barwenna, Hal would be caught up in it.

As they crossed the landing field Hal kept an eye out for thugs in suits, but it seemed their intelligence didn't reach as far as this planet. No doubt they were still looking for him on Barwenna, but he'd just have to deal with that problem when it cropped up.

They reached the taxi rank, where two cabs were waiting for fares. The first drew away before they could stop it, and Hal saw a middle-aged man approaching the second. He put on a spurt and got there first, dragging the door open for the others.

'Hey, that was my cab!' protested the man.

'Medical emergency,' said Hal. 'Stand back! Infection risk!'

He slammed the doors and shouted at the driver. 'Take us to Stuhr, Burlend and Wisk. Double the fare if you make it quick!'

The cab took off, pressing him back in his seat. Hal recognised the narrow alleys around the pub, and his face tightened when he glimpsed the corner where Cuff had played out his little game. 'Faster,' he said. 'Triple the fare!'

The scenery blurred past, and they took corners like a racing car at full throttle. The engine roared on the straights and whined under braking, and it was only five minutes before they slid to a halt outside a modest office building.

Hal jumped out, leaving Natasha to pay the driver. He barged across the pavement and burst through the doors on the stroke of nine.

'Mr Spacejock? Through here, please. Mr Wisk is waiting for you.'

Hal followed the receptionist to an office, where he was shown to a comfortable chair. Zee came hurrying in, and Natasha arrived after a moment or two. The three of them sat there, whirring and panting, while the elderly man behind the desk studied them over his glasses. 'I take it you're after a quick wind-up?'

'No, he's battery powered,' said Hal.

Zee frowned. 'He's talking about our company.'

'What company?'

'The one you want to liquidate,' said Wisk.

'We don't want to liquidate anything. We're just after some old records.'

'I see.' The man reached for a timer and set it going. 'Which company?'

'Chris Test Dummies.'

'Ah yes, I remember it well. Nasty case. Lucrative for us, but rather unpleasant.'

Hal wasn't interested in the case. 'Do you know where the servers ended up?'

'Everything was auctioned off, and the proceeds were shared between the creditors.' The man smiled. 'After our cut, of course.'

'You mean it's all gone?'

'Of course.'

'What about stuff they couldn't sell? Paperwork, files, that kind of thing?'

'Dumped, usually.'

'Can you check?'

'It's your money.' Wisk studied his terminal. On the desk, his timer continued to tick. 'Chris Toast. Crass Tieste. Chris Test.'

'That's the one.'

Wisk nodded. 'It seems you're in luck. According to this, it was cheaper to store the junk than dump it.'

'Really?'

'Oh yes. Buy an old container, park it in some out-of-the-way corner of the spaceport and forget all about it. Much cheaper than paying by the kilo at the local tip.'

'Is that where it is? At the spaceport?' Hal leant across the desk. 'Do you know where?'

'I can give you the row, column and serial number.' Wisk touched a button, and a slip of paper shot out of his desk.

Hal reached for it, but it was pulled away.

'We'll just settle the account first.' Wisk stopped the timer and pressed another button. A much longer sheet spat out, and he slid it across the desk.

Hal took one look at the total and gulped. Then he slid it towards Natasha.

Natasha pressed her lips together, but paid up without arguing.

'A pleasure doing business with you,' said the elderly man. 'Do have a nice day.'

'I swear I'm in the wrong line of work,' muttered Hal.

⬥

They were back at the spaceport in minutes, where Hal got the cabbie to drive them to the shipping yard. They passed rows and rows of containers, towering stacks of them stretching as far as the eye could see. Hal glanced at the slip of paper and pointed further along the row.

The containers here were older, streaked with rust, and Hal wondered how many were crammed with the bones of failed companies. He remembered the container they'd shipped out the day before, the junk they'd found inside it, and he suddenly realised where Cuff had got it from. The spaceport must have been rubbing their hands with glee as they palmed the ancient container off on the *Volante*!

As they drew closer he realised they were approaching the spot where they'd parked his ship the day before.

'This is it,' said the cabbie.

Hal looked to his right. The wall of containers was perfectly even, except for a gap where one of the large boxes was missing. 'Wait here,' he told the driver, and jumped out of the cab. The area was deserted, not a soul to be seen, but Hal spotted a rough lean-to between the rows of containers. He ran over and hammered on the door.

'Yeah?' said a muffled voice. 'What is it?'

'I'm chasing paperwork. Urgent delivery.'

The door opened and a lanky robot peered out. 'Urgent? Around here?'

'The information inside it is vital,' said Hal.

'Share it, man. I'll get onto it.'

Hal shoved the liquidator's printout at him. 'We need that container. Where is it?'

The robot scanned the information, then smiled. 'Popular box, that one.'

'What do you mean?'

'I can tell you where it is, man. It's in space!'

'What!'

'Yep. Someone got here before you. Long gone, I'm afraid.'

'Kent Spearman!' breathed Hal. His rival had got there first. They were sunk!

'Kent who?' said the robot.

Hal put his hand up. 'About this tall, dead ugly, stupid little beard. Stinks of cologne.'

'You don't understand. I don't care who this Kent character is, I'm telling you I never heard of him.'

'You probably forgot.'

The robot regarded him steadily.

'Okay, maybe not.' Hal thought for a minute. 'Was it David Fisher? Older guy, maybe this high?'

'Nah. This was a really old dude. Cuff, that was his name.'

Hal groaned. Kent, Fisher or Cuff . . . it didn't really matter which. They were all working together. His only hope now was to catch up with the *Tiger*, head them off, get aboard, bust open the container and find the data. All without getting arrested for kidnap. 'How much of a head start did they have?'

'A couple of days.'

'That's impossible. You've made a mistake.'

Again the robot fixed him with a steady stare.

'All right, all right. But it's still impossible. We didn't know about the container until this morning!'

'Wait here and I'll get you the manifest.'

Hal glanced towards the taxi. He saw the others watching anxiously, so he gave them an encouraging smile.

'Here you are, man. Full details.'

Hal took the slip and scanned the dense lines of text. The container serial number ... check. Two days ago ... check. Shipped by ... Hal's eyes widened. No, it wasn't possible! Without a word, he handed the slip back to the robot.

'Did it help?'

Hal stumbled back to the cab. At his approach, the doors opened and Natasha and Zee climbed out. 'Well? What did you find?'

'We're sunk,' said Hal. 'There's no chance of getting those records. Zero.'

'Why? Where's the shipping container?'

Hal turned a haggard face on them. 'I incinerated it yesterday!'

⬦

During the short ride back to the *Volante*, Hal explained about Cuff and his fake shipment. 'We landed here a couple of days ago, and I went to the pub to pick up a cargo job. There were three people there, all desperate to get to Barwenna with their robots. I didn't realise it then, but they were all chasing this inheritance.' Hal took a breath. 'Clunk and I agreed we'd never fly another passenger, so I told them all no.'

'I thought you flew Cuff to Barwenna?' said Natasha.

'Yeah. He fooled us with a fake cargo job, and got the spaceport to load a random container full of junk. They were happy to get rid of it. Hell, they'd have stuffed a dozen into the hold, no questions asked. Then he pretended he'd been mugged, and after I rescued him he wangled his way aboard the ship.'

'And when you got to Barwenna?'

'Eventually we discovered the cargo job was a fake. Clunk thought the container might be stuffed full of weapons or drugs, so we busted it open. Instead it was just office furniture and paperwork.' Hal shrugged. 'When we took off yesterday I dumped the thing. It's burnt to cinders by now.'

There was a lengthy silence.

'You weren't to know,' said Zee finally. 'It's not your fault.'

Hal glanced at Natasha. 'I guess you've got your story. You should make a packet writing up this little comedy.'

The cab drew up in silence, and they all climbed out. Hal saw Sandy at the *Volante*'s airlock, and his stomach clenched. How was he going to explain this whole mess to her?

Ten minutes later Hal was sitting at the console, his feet up and a fresh cup of coffee by his elbow. The others were below, gathering their things. His plan was to drop them at the Barwenna spaceport, and then he'd set off to find Clunk.

The ships engines thrummed below decks, a soothing, familiar noise. Wills, shipping containers, fake pirates ... they could all join passengers on Hal's list of 'never agains', right below Peace Force officers and debt collectors.

Hal glanced at the main screen, where a digital readout was showing 2:31.

'Navcom, what's our ETA?'

'That combination traditionally represents two hours and thirty-one minutes.'

'What's the local time? Barwenna City, I mean.'

'Ten a.m.'

So, it was only two hours until the solicitors awarded the legacy, and thanks to him Sandy, Zee and Clunk were all out of the running. Hal drew a deep breath. Sandy had been understanding, but he'd sensed her bitter disappointment. Over the past twenty-four hours she'd really come alive, joining in the pirate role-play and contributing to their quest with gusto, but with the bad news she'd drawn back into her shell. Zee had been typical robot ...not shouting and screaming in anger, just letting Hal know by subtle signs. Forceful gestures, carefully chosen phrases ...Hal was used to those and more, thanks to Clunk. As for Natasha, she had no stake in the outcome but still managed to make Hal feel small and inadequate.

'If only I hadn't dumped that container,' muttered Hal.

'You did leave it a bit late,' said the Navcom.

'What do you mean?'

'You took too long ejecting it. Instead of burning up in a matter of hours it could orbit the planet for days.'

Hal stared at the console. 'Are you saying it might still be there?'

'Of course it's still there. I told you, you released it too late.'

'Can you find it again?'

The Navcom hesitated. 'Yes.'

'Can we get it back?'

'You want to retrieve a container from low orbit using a deep space freighter?'

'Yes.'

'It'll be tricky. The container may be tumbling end over end, and the atmosphere –'

'Yes or no, Navcom.'

'Yes, if Clunk were flying the ship. If you take the controls it's a big fat ...maybe.'

'Thanks for the vote of confidence.' Hal reached for the intercom, intending to share the news. Then he hesitated. Why get their hopes up? It was better to locate the container first. 'What's our ETA?'

On the screen, the clock ticked over to 2:26.

Hal gripped the flight stick, barely taking time to dash the sweat from his eyes. On screen, a shipping container was tumbling against a backdrop of clouds, oceans and land mass. Green cross hairs pursued it from one side of the screen to the other, and columns of text whizzed past too fast to read.

The container got closer and closer, and there was a *clanngg!* as it smashed against the hull. A welter of furniture and paper fragments sailed past, and the screen went dark.

'Would you like to try again?' asked the Navcom.

'Yeah, and this time keep it still.'

'I'm trying to simulate actual conditions.'

'Simulate them easier or I'll never get it.'

'Why don't you ask Zee for assistance?'

'What use is that? He doesn't know the first thing about flying a ship.'

The Navcom remained silent.

'Is it really going to be this hard?' asked Hal.

'The container will be moving at speed, and you imparted a spin when you released it from the cargo hold. The goal is to overtake it with the ship, open the hold, match the spin and slow down to draw the container inside.'

'And you can't use autopilot because ...'

'It was designed for take-off, navigation and landing, not sky hockey.'

'At least tell me where I'm going wrong.'

'So far, you've run into it every time you tried to overtake. You need to give it a bit more space.'

Hal gestured at the screen. 'How can I, when I don't know where the ship begins?'

'You could try third person point of view.'

'What am I, a console gamer?'

'Under the circumstances, perhaps you could swallow your pride.'

'Oh, all right. Give it a shot.'

The planet reappeared, with the container tumbling in the distance. At the bottom of the screen was a model of the *Volante*, her engines belching flames. Hal tried the stick and the ship rocked from side to side, closing on the container at a tremendous rate.

'Slow down!' cried the Navcom.

Hal eased back on the throttles, and the exhaust flames died. He zoomed past the container and threw out the anchors, then jinked to the side as it screamed past, narrowly missing the port engine. 'Why's it glowing?' he asked, eyeing the container.

'Re-entry. It's going to burn up in minutes.'

The container raced away, trailing a plume of smoke. Hal pushed the throttles forward to catch up, but this time he was ready and he eased back gently.

'Nicely done,' said the Navcom. On screen, the container was spinning through the air, just behind the ship. 'That'll shield it from the atmosphere.'

Hal wiped the sweat from his brow. 'Can we land like this?'

'Negative. At that speed it would level a city.' The Navcom hesitated. 'I'd hurry to the hold if I were you.'

'Why? I'm supposed to be chasing the container.'

'You already did.'

Reality dawned, and Hal looked closer. 'That's not a simulator, is it?'

'Not this time.'

'Why didn't you warn me?'

'Clunk told me you suffer from performance anxiety.'

'When Clunk comes back we're going to have words.' Hal leapt from the chair and ran for the lift, where he jammed his thumb on the second button. 'Keep it level, okay? I don't want to fall out.'

◆

Hal charged along the corridor to the hold, almost colliding with a stray robot on the way.

'What's the rush?' demanded Zee. 'Are we landing already?'

'Just picking up the trash,' called Hal, as he flew past. He yanked the inner door and hurried into the hold, where he grabbed a safety line with a hefty clip on each end. At the rear doors he activated the intercom. 'Navcom, how's the atmosphere?'

'Tense.'

Hal closed his eyes. 'I meant the air.'

'It's barely breathable. You'll have to work fast.'

Hal activated the controls, and there was a hiss as the doors parted. Air swirled by, and at the last second he remembered to clip on the safety line. The noise was intense with the doors open, even though the engines were throttled back for re-entry. It was hard to breathe too, and Hal was gasping in seconds. Then he spotted the container, and all thoughts of breathing were forgotten. It was just as he remembered it, rust-streaked and dented, only now half the paint had been stripped off and the corners were glowing cherry red. It was also spinning like a chicken on a turbocharged spit roast.

Hal studied it in concern. If he slowed the *Volante* and let it into the hold, the container would rip his ship apart from the inside out. Then he heard a buzz, faint in the thin air, and he saw the intercom flashing. 'What is it?'

'We're getting close to the ground,' said the Navcom. 'You really need to bring the container in.'

'I can't! It's spinning a damn sight faster than your simulation.'

'Then we'll have to leave it.'

Hal frowned. So near, yet so far! Then he felt a hand on his shoulder, and he almost fell out of the hold in surprise. It was Zee and the others, all staring at the container in amazement.

'What can we do to help?' shouted Zee.

'I can't bring it in. It's spinning too fast.'

Zee judged the gap. The container was heating up, and super-heated air was streaming off the *Volante*'s hull. 'What if I jump over there with a rope?'

'I wouldn't risk a crazy stunt like that. It'll fling you off like a bucking bronco.'

'It's the only chance!'

'You can't do it. Too risky.' Suddenly Hal stared. 'A crazy stunt!'

'So you said.'

'No, that's the answer!' Hal grabbed the intercom. 'Navcom, can you transfer flight controls down here?'

'Affirmative. Please note, your insurance policy doesn't cover a headlong dive into the planetary surface, and if you don't pull up soon –'

'Never mind the policy. Get on with it!'

The panel flew open and a joystick sprang out. Hal took it and waved the others towards the side of the hold. 'Clip on to something. Quick!'

Sandy and Natasha took the remaining safety lines and clipped on. Zee looked in vain for a spare, then grabbed hold of an upright with both hands. Once they were ready Hal gripped the stick, getting a feel for the smooth plastic. Then, without warning, he slammed it hard left.

The effect was immediate: side thrusters roared and the *Volante* performed an extended barrel roll, spinning faster and faster along her axis as she plunged towards the ground. From inside the hold it looked like the container's spin was slowing, until it was hovering just behind the ship, the right way up. The illusion worked until Hal focussed beyond the container, at which point he saw madly whirling stars. Hurriedly looking away, he eased back on the throttle and guided the container into the hold. He could feel the fierce heat radiating from the metal, and he prayed the contents weren't charred to a crisp.

When it was safely inside Zee sprang forward to fix the container down, while Hal closed the doors. The second the cargo clamps fired Hal got on the intercom again. 'Navcom, take control. Full emergency power, then auto-land at the Barwenna Spaceport!'

'Complying, Mr Spacejock.'

Hal breathed out. They'd done it. They'd really done it!

◆

The *Volante* was on final approach, and Hal and the others were up to their hips in the rubbish-filled container. It was baking hot and they were all running with sweat, but fortunately it hadn't reached critical temperature and the paperwork was still intact. Hal looted filing cabinets, desk drawers and old waste paper baskets, storming through the container like a child who'd lost their pocket money in a snowdrift. 'Didn't these people hear about the ebook revolution?' he muttered, surveying the massed boxes.

The others were more thorough, checking the files and papers Hal flung over his shoulder.

'Here!' shouted Sandy. With a triumphant grin she held up a handful of manila folders.

'What have you got?'

'Personnel records for all their robots.'

Hal took the files and flipped through. There were six photos, all identical, and each robot had a full history. He was about to check further when the ship lurched.

'Landing successful,' said the Navcom.

'What's the time?'

'Eleven forty-five.'

Hal opened the doors and they left via the cargo ramp. They were still running for Natasha's car when the ramp closed behind them, sealing the ship.

◆

Clunk sat on his bunk and stared at the wall. He'd been treated well, and his cell was suitably equipped with a nice rubber ball and a classic movie poster, but after a long night without contact his patience was finally running out. He'd tried communicating by radio, but the cell was covered by a jammer, and when he tapped Morse code messages on the water pipes the only response he got back was unprintable.

He'd whiled away the time by reprogramming his actuators, diverting extra power to his arms and fingers. The barred door to his cell was impressive, but it was designed for humans. Clunk calculated that by conserving his energy, then releasing it in a near-instantaneous burst through his reprogrammed arms, he could lever the door right off its hinges.

There was only one thing holding him back: Ripping the door off and escaping his cell was tantamount to declaring war on the Battlecruiser. Whatever trouble he was in now, it was nothing to the punishment they'd mete out if he were caught a second time. And thanks to Mr Spacejock, he couldn't even talk his way out of trouble.

Clunk checked the time. It was just after eleven, and the meeting was at twelve. It was too late to help Mr Spacejock and Sandy locate any missing information, but if by some miracle they'd found it by themselves . . . well, Clunk needed to be there before the deadline. And the only thing standing in his way was a cell door. That, plus hundreds of armed personnel, the Battlecruiser's automated defence system, and a long flight back to Barwenna.

Clunk came to a sudden decision. However slim the chance of escape, he couldn't afford to languish in the cell any longer. He stood up, swaying on his weakened legs. By contrast his arms felt like pile drivers, capable of punching a hole straight through the walls. He approached the door and took hold of the bars. Hidden motors groaned as they took up the strain, and Clunk's vision dimmed as tremendous amounts of power were diverted to his forearms. The strain was immense, and then he felt movement. For a split second he thought his arms had given way, but when he opened his eyes the door was loose in his hands. He'd done it!

There was a muted buzz and he spotted another door opening towards him. There was no time to hide, or replace his cell door, and he was still standing there with the evidence gripped in both hands when First Lieutenant Overmann walked in with a pair of armed guards.

◆

Natasha unlocked the car, and Hal was about to climb in when there was a deep BOOM directly overhead. He looked up, shading his eyes, and saw a gigantic ship materialising in the clouds. 'That's a Battlecruiser. I wonder what they want?'

'Do you think it's the *Almara*?' said Zee.

'How many Battlecruisers do customs have in this system?'

'That's classified information, but I believe it's more than zero and less than two.'

'That many?' Hal studied the huge ship. 'So it might not be the *Almara* at all.'

The others exchanged a glance.

'Can they land at the spaceport?' asked Hal.

'No, Battlecruisers are deep space only.'

'Mr Hal Spacejock,' said a rough voice. 'We meet again.'

Hal tore his gaze from the huge battleship and spotted the two well-dressed thugs. They grabbed Hal by the elbows, lifting him off his feet, and the blond one pushed his face up close. 'My boss wants to see you. He wants to pay you back for ruining his daughter's wedding.'

Hal closed his eyes. There was no escape this time.

'Ow!' shouted one of the men.

'Argh!' yelled the other.

They let go of Hal's arms, and he stared in amazement as the two thugs hopped around on one leg, each clasping their shins. There was no time to react ... before he could say anything Sandy and Natasha had bundled him into the car.

'What happened?' he demanded, as they roared away.

'We stamped on their feet,' remarked Natasha. She raised her hand and Sandy slapped it. 'More than a match for a pair of goons, am I right?'

'Deadly and dangerous,' muttered Hal. 'They didn't stand a chance.'

— 32 —

Hal ran up the steps at the solicitors, bundled the security guard out of the way and ran for the reception desk. 'Stop the clock. We're here!'

'Well, if it isn't Hal Spacejock,' said a laconic voice. 'Lost any passengers lately?'

Hal turned to see Kent Spearman's mocking face. Standing nearby were Cuff and Fisher. Behind them were their robots, two on their feet and Cuff's still lashed to the hotel trolley. 'And how are your treasured companions?' asked Hal. 'Thrown any out the airlock lately?'

Kent shrugged.

'Hey, that tactic on the Orbiter . . . tying up all the terminals. Was that all yours, or did these two chip in? And the Battlecruiser . . . '

Kent interrupted him. 'Did you get any info? Any proof showing where the robots came from?'

'Might have done,' said Hal warily. Then he noticed the glum expressions and a broad grin split his face. 'You didn't find anything, did you? All that huffing and puffing, cheating and lying, and the great Kent Spearman fell short. Again!'

'We found plenty of old records,' said Cuff. 'Alas, none were conclusive.'

Hal jerked his thumb towards the entrance. 'The door's that way, sunshine. Try not to cheat anyone on the way out.' He was about to turn away when his gaze fell on Cuff's robot. It was lying on the luggage trolley, immobile, but its blank eyes were staring right at him. Scoring points off Spearman and the others was one thing, but it wasn't their future he was playing with. On impulse, Hal opened the folder and pulled out three files. 'Here,' he said gruffly, shoving them into Kent's hands. 'You're back in the race.'

Kent stared at him, then looked down at the files. He looked stunned, and for once he was speechless.

'That's very noble of you,' said Cuff. 'If I win ...'

'If you win I want my fifty grand. Cash.'

'And if you win ...'

'Not much chance of that.' Hal glanced at the clock. It was five to twelve and Clunk was nowhere to be seen. He'd never make it now.

The receptionist took their signatures in a ledger, then announced them over the commset. A door opened and Mr Butt emerged from his office, dressed in a neat suit. 'Ladies, gentlemen ... robots. Please come in. It's time to settle Baker's legacy.'

◆

The boardroom was dominated by a huge wooden table, polished to a mirror shine. There were twelve places laid out along the sides, six with glasses of water and napkins, and six with recessed power sockets. Butt took his place at the head of the table and motioned the others to their seats. Zee sat alone, without a human alongside him. Hal glanced at Clunk's empty place and frowned. Then he realised someone was missing. Cuff, Spearman and Fisher were all there with their robots, sitting along the opposite side of the table like a living mugshot file. He'd spotted Zee already, and Sandy was sitting to his right, busy plugging her robot into the socket. But where was Natasha? The reporter had parked her car and followed them up the steps, but he didn't remember seeing her after –

'Before we begin, there's someone I need to introduce.' Butt nodded at the guards, who opened the doors to admit . . .

'Natasha!' exclaimed Hal.

The reporter ignored him, taking a seat alongside Butt. She took out her notebook and laid it on the desk. 'I have the report in full.'

'Excellent work,' said Butt. 'For now, perhaps just the summary?'

'Wait a minute.' Hal looked from one to the other. 'Natasha, do you work for this guy?'

'In a way.'

Butt explained. 'Ms Lucas is a private investigator. We employed her for background checks.'

Hal stared. 'What was all that crap about writing an article?'

'There's a lot of money at stake. We had to take every precaution.' Butt glanced at Natasha. 'I'm sorry for the interruption. Please proceed.'

'I interviewed five of the six candidates. The sixth, Sandy West, refused to answer any questions.'

'It was none of your business,' snapped Sandy.

Natasha ignored her, and frowned at her notepad. 'First, David Fisher. He makes a living buying and selling robots, cash in hand, and he obtained his robot by deceiving a Mrs Lily Turner.'

'I object!' shouted Fisher.

Butt frowned at him. 'Mr Fisher, this isn't a courtroom. Object all you like, but it won't make any difference.'

'I've had this robot for years!'

Natasha tapped on her notepad. 'That may be so, but you took the brain and half the components out of Mrs Turner's robot.'

'But –'

'If I might finish,' said Natasha. 'You played up a minor fault with her robot, offered substantially less than it was worth, and then paid an even smaller amount in cash. Suspicious of your motives, but afraid to confront you in person, Mrs Turner forged the signature on the receipt. Therefore, the brain and other parts of your robot still belong to her.'

'That tricky old trout,' growled Fisher.

'Not that it matters, since her robot is not the one we're looking for. It has no claim on the will.'

Fisher swore under his breath. Alongside him, his robot suppressed a smile.

'Next is Mr Cuff. He stole his robot from the science department at his local school, where he was employed as a part-time cleaner.'

'I did not!' exclaimed Cuff. 'They threw it out! I rescued it from the skip!'

'Not only did you steal it, you destroyed its speech circuits so it couldn't report you.'

'This is preposterous. This is a pack of lies. This ... '

'If you don't sit quietly I'll report you to the Peace Force. Your choice.'

Cuff leant across the polished table. 'You haven't heard the last of this!' he shouted, jabbing his finger at her. 'I'll sue you!'

'If you need a lawyer, the fees at Argisle and Butt are quite reasonable. In the meantime, your silence would be appreciated.' Natasha glanced at her notebook. 'Next we have Zee. Unfortunately you signed the initial paperwork in your own hand, whereas it was meant to be signed by your legal owner, Alan Dane.'

'I had to sign it myself,' said Zee. 'Mr Dane died two days ago.'

'Did he know you shopped him to the Peace Force? And deliberately led the competition to every one of his businesses and safe houses? And ... ordered his execution?'

'That's impossible. I'm programmed to obey! I would never harm Mr Dane, never! He took me in, he looked after me, he ... he cared for me!'

The robot sounded completely sincere, and his expression was distraught. Hal had no doubt he was telling the truth, and he was about to tell Natasha to lay off when she continued.

'What you don't realise is that you're programmed with split personalities, each totally separate from the other. I believe your activation keyword is ... Hyde.'

Zee's expression hardened, and a split second later he leapt up, kicking his chair back. There was a whine as his weapons deployed, but Natasha was ready for him. She calmly picked up a remote and zapped the robot right between the eyes. Zee froze, guns half erect, then toppled backwards to land with a resounding clang.

'It's his own fault,' explained Natasha. 'He paid someone to rebuild him like that. Incidentally, he wasn't Baker's robot either.' She glanced at the three remaining candidates: Hal,

Sandy and Kent Spearman. Her gaze settled on Sandy. 'Ah yes, the runaway.'

Sandy glared back.

'I don't have evidence of wrong-doing, but you're eliminated anyway.'

'What are you talking about?' demanded Sandy. 'Eliminated how?'

'Mr Butt, would you care to explain?'

'You're under eighteen, young lady.' Butt gazed at her over his glasses, as though studying a fascinating legal problem. 'When you signed the form it specifically requested approval from your parents or guardians, to be crossed out as applicable.'

'But –'

'It doesn't really matter,' said Natasha, with an impatient gesture. 'Your robot isn't the one.'

'I thought you were on my side,' muttered Sandy.

There was an uncomfortable silence, and she made to get up. Before she could leave, Hal put a hand on her arm. 'Don't you want to see how this turns out?'

'I–I guess.'

There were two left in the running: Hal and Kent. They exchanged a glance, both of them knowing the first person Natasha looked at would be eliminated.

Hal and Kent sat there, eyes locked in mortal combat. Then Hal saw an expression of joy cross Kent's face, and he realised it was all over. He glanced along the table to see Natasha eyeing him like a scientist studying a particularly virulent disease. 'Mr Hal Spacejock, freighter pilot. There are so many reasons why you should be eliminated I can't even begin to cover them.'

'It's not me you should be thinking of. Clunk's the one up for this inheritance. Why can't you examine his history?'

'Let's not kid ourselves. We all know where this money is really heading, and it won't be a robot's bank account.'

'I don't want anything to do with your bloody money,' snapped Hal. 'You've been sitting there tearing people apart, when all you had to do was point to a robot and say congratulations. Didn't your parents give you enough attention as a kid, or have you always wanted to host one of those crappy reality shows?'

Natasha was taken aback, and she looked to Butt for help. Unfortunately he'd just spotted something interesting on his notepad. 'It was important to deal with everyone in order,' said Natasha. 'We had to eliminate imposters until only the verified claimant remained.'

Kent Spearman laughed. 'Well, that's the best news I've had all day. When do you need my account details?'

'I haven't finished yet,' said Natasha. 'Mr Spacejock, you're unreliable and untrustworthy but you mean well. You helped the others where it would have been in your best interest to abandon them, and you acted in good faith.'

Hal's spirits rose. Was she switching things up? Was Spearman about to get a kick in the guts?

Ting!

Everyone turned to look at the clock. The hands were pointing straight up, and the delicate bell was marking twelve noon.

Ting!

Natasha smiled across the table. 'Mr Spacejock, according to your findings and our deliberations, Clunk is Baker's robot.'

Ting!

'Alas, the terms were quite clear.' Natasha raised one finger. 'When those chimes cease, he's no longer entitled to the inheritance.'

Ting!

'You have to give him more time!' protested Hal. 'He's only stuck aboard the *Almara* because you barged in front of him.'

Ting!

'I'm sorry, but the deadline is set in stone.'

Ting!

Hal felt rising anger, but what could he do? The Battlecruiser was orbiting the planet, and unless Clunk teleported down . . .

Ting!

Hal stared at the clock. Five more rings and all that money would slip through their fingers. How could he delay proceedings? What could he say?

Ting!

With four to go, Hal put his head in his hands. The situation was hopeless. They'd lost the lot.

Ting!

There was a distant whine, which became a roar, then an ear-shattering rumble. A shadow flitted across the windows, and then . . . *Craaaaash!* The end window exploded inwards and Hal caught a glimpse of a bronze missile, flames belching from its tail. The missile flattened a sideboard, sending the antique clock flying, then skidded the length of the room with a teeth-drilling squeal. Sparks and chairs flew until the missile crashed into the far wall, scattering plaster and bringing down a row of paintings. The clock spun round and round, then fell over backwards with a final 'ti-i-ing!'

When the dust and smoke cleared Hal saw the 'missile' was Clunk, with a rocket pack strapped to his back. His bronze skin was scorched and smoking from re-entry, and Hal realised he must have jumped straight out of the Battlecruiser. The robot gave him a fierce grin as he stepped away from the wall, and Hal couldn't help laughing as Clunk's big flat foot came down on the antique clock, crushing it flat.

Hal turned to Butt and Natasha, who were sitting in open-mouthed shock. 'I shouldn't worry about the repair bill,' he remarked. 'With all that cash to his name I reckon Clunk's good for it.'

33

It was several seconds before Butt recovered his composure. He frowned at Clunk, glared at Hal, then studied his paperwork. Meanwhile, Hal looked Clunk up and down. Something was different about him, and it wasn't the rocket pack. Then he realised what it was: Clunk had epaulettes at his shoulders, and there was a fresh serial number stencilled on his chest. 'What have you been up to?'

Clunk frowned and pointed to his mouth.

'You lost your voice? Never mind, we'll get it fixed.'

Clunk mimed a shape with the flat of his hand, circled it overhead, then gestured at his mouth.

'You want me to order a pizza?'

Now thoroughly animated, Clunk looked down at the table and saw the notepad. He grabbed it, scrawled with the pen and held it out.

'You want me to say the name of my ship?'

Clunk nodded enthusiastically.

'Why?'

There was a strangled groan, and Clunk scribbled again.

'You want me to say the name of my ship immediately, right now and without any hesitation whatsoever?' Hal frowned. 'I don't get it.'

'*Volante*,' said Sandy.

'I know that, and so does he!' protested Hal. Clunk advanced on him, and suddenly he remembered. At the hotel ... the speech suppression code ... the keywords! '*Volante*!' he said hurriedly.

Clunk stopped. 'Thank you, Mr Spacejock. It was a struggle, but you got there in the end.'

'It was nothing. And don't worry about the pizza, I'll order one later.' Hal gestured at the new serial number. 'So what's that about?'

'Pilot Officer Clunk at your service.' He saluted smartly. 'Seconded to the Battlecruiser *Almara*, chief test pilot for Green Flight Alpha.'

Hal blinked. 'How did that happen?'

'Actually, Green Flight only has one pilot. Me.' Clunk indicated the rocket pack. 'They had to create a new squadron before I could borrow this device.'

'That's a lot of favours. What did you do, save the ship from a black hole? Single-handedly defeat a rogue cruiser?'

Clunk gave him a brief recap. 'After you left, I was caught up in a training mission. I saved a drone from destruction by leaping from the ship. They sent a recovery vessel, and I spent the night in the brig.'

'Sounds like you put them through hell.'

'Not quite. Apparently it was the most challenging training exercise they've had for years. They're going to write it up and use it in future scenarios.'

'Do you get royalties?'

'Actually yes, but they kept my advance towards the cost of a new cell door. I broke out of confinement just as they were coming to release me.'

244

Butt cleared his throat. 'This is fascinating, but could we return to the subject at hand?'

'Oh yeah.' Hal patted Clunk on the shoulder. 'While you were off playing war games we managed to prove your history. You're Baker's robot, and you inherit the whole lot.'

'Really? That's a nice surprise.'

Butt frowned. 'That's not strictly accurate. There are still one or two conditions.'

'Oh, here we go,' muttered Hal. 'It's time for the fine print.'

◆

Butt pushed his chair back and stood, resting his hands on the polished wooden table. 'There are two matters to take care of before you inherit.'

Everyone turned to stare at him, and Hal frowned as he wondered what new hoop the old guy had come up with.

Butt continued. 'Before the inheritance is finalised we must verify your robot's brain is the original article.' There was a faint chime, and the doors swung open to admit a severe-looking woman in a white lab coat. Butt indicated Clunk, and the woman sat down and opened her briefcase. Out came a roll of tools, and she had the robot's skull open in no time. The woman withdrew a gadget from the case and connected it to Clunk's brain. Three seconds later there was a beep, and she frowned as she checked the screen.

'Well?' demanded Butt.

'It's a match.'

'Are you sure?'

'Definitely. This is the original brain.'

Kent Spearman snorted in disgust, while Hal breathed a sigh of relief.

'Very well. In that case, it's time for an announcement.' Butt smiled at Clunk. 'I'm pleased to tell you that Mr Baker would like a little word.'

Everyone turned towards the entrance, expecting the fabled businessman to burst in and announce the whole business had been an elaborate PR stunt. The doors remained closed, and instead a section of panelling slid aside to reveal a viewscreen. At that point Butt hesitated. 'Since this is for Clunk's ears, I would ask the rest of you to clear the room. My staff will provide you with coffee and sandwiches in the lobby.'

The others complied, grumbling under their breath. Hal went to follow, but Clunk stopped him. 'Anything Mr Baker has to say will affect the pair of us.'

'No problem.' After all, thought Hal, the coffee and sandwiches could wait.

Once the room was clear the screen flickered, and an elderly man appeared. He had short grey hair and a weathered face, but his most notable feature was his intense blue eyes. They crinkled around the edges as he smiled warmly at the camera, and then he began. 'My dear friend, I'm so glad you've been found. These past few years have been hard on me, and I often wondered what happened to you after we parted company.'

Hal glanced at Clunk, wondering what sort of emotions were rushing around his circuits. This old geezer must be like a long-lost parent to the robot, and he hoped the strain wouldn't be too much.

'You won't remember this,' continued Baker, 'but for three months you worked as a clerk in finance, overseeing stocks and bonds. Ahh those carefree days! The heady smell of finance, the whirr of the trading computers, the raw power of money.'

Hal glanced at Clunk to see how he was taking all this. Funny smells and odd whirring noises were daily occurrences where the robot was concerned, but he'd never shown much interest in finance.

'Then, that fateful day. How can I forget?' The old man's smile vanished, and his voice turned shrill. 'That was when you made your stupid, careless mistake. Instead of buying seventeen hundred shares in GMT, you purchased seventeen *million* shares in GMC ... ten minutes before the price crashed!'

Butt frowned. Clearly this wasn't in the script.

'You cost me one hundred and ninety two thousand, four hundred and eighty-six credits that afternoon!' shouted Baker. 'I was going to have you crushed. Ground up. Turned into road base! But no, my namby-pamby advisors convinced me to wipe your memory and flog you off. Well, my lead-brained friend, it's payback time. You're not laying any of your tin fingers on my legacy ... that's going to charity.' Baker's mouth twisted into a cruel smile. 'No, all you're getting are those seventeen million worthless shares you bought in my name. I hope you rust in robot hell!'

34

The screen went dark, and there was a shocked silence.

'What a prick,' said Hal at last. 'After all that messing about, the old bastard was just out for revenge?'

'So it seems.' Butt looked highly embarrassed, and busied himself by shuffling his paperwork. 'Unfortunately, this recording is legitimate, and despite the . . . the spirited delivery, Mr Baker did seem to know what he wanted. This recording overrides the terms of his will.'

'Bloody lunatic,' muttered Hal. 'What sort of person reaches out from beyond the grave like that?' Then he remembered Clunk, and he turned to the robot in concern. Clunk's expression was stony, unreadable, but his eyes spoke volumes. As he watched the reaction Hal desperately wished they'd never heard of Cuff or the stupid inheritance. 'Are you all right?'

Clunk shrugged. 'It could have been worse. Nobody died.'

Hal turned to the lawyer. 'What about these shares? Are they worth anything?'

'I'm afraid not. I believe the company is all but bankrupt, and has no prospects whatsoever.'

'GMC, right? Who is that anyway?'

'Galactic Mining Company.' Butt noticed Hal's start, and

he gave him a shrewd look. 'What is it? Have you heard something?'

'No, it's just one of the companies Baker sold his robots to.'

'I see.' Butt hesitated. 'I assume you'll be leaving Barwenna soon?'

'Why, is that a problem?'

'Not at all. I was going to make an appointment to transfer ownership of the shares, but we might as well do it now.'

'Will it cost anything?'

'A hundred credits.'

Hal reached into his pocket, but the solicitor stopped him. 'Under the circumstances, I think we'll do the honours. I'm just sorry Mr Baker ... '

'Yeah.'

Ten minutes later the paperwork was complete, and the secretary handed Clunk a nice colourful certificate proving his ownership of seventeen million shares in the Galactic Mining Company. A photographer took snaps of the happy beneficiary, and a tame reporter promised not to mention the fact the shares were worthless ... at least, not until they wrote a follow-up expos?.

They left the boardroom with Clunk still clutching his worthless shares, and Hal spotted the others in the reception area. Sandy hurried up to check out Clunk's certificate, while nearby David Fisher was arguing with the receptionist, trying to get the solicitors to pay for a cab ride home. Cuff was sitting by himself, lost in thought, and Kent Spearman had a flashy commset clamped to one ear. 'What, right now? That's great news! Top off the tanks, I'll be right there.'

Kent gave Hal a sympathetic wink. 'Bad luck with the whole worthless legacy business. That old boy was a real joker, eh?'

'Yeah. Hilarious.'

Kent gestured with the commset. 'Never mind, I landed on my feet again. I just picked up a fantastic cargo job.'

'Really?'

'Excellent pay, totally above board. It's a container of antique furniture parts for Evilon.'

'Evilon?' said Cuff suddenly. 'What a coincidence. That's exactly where I need to go!'

'Inconceivable!' said Hal quickly, before Clunk could intervene. 'I'm sure Spearman will give you a lift. I mean, he's already heading that way.'

Kent looked doubtful. 'Can you pay the fare?'

'Sure!' Cuff put his arm around Kent's shoulders, guiding him down the stairs to the waiting taxi. 'My uncle lives on Evilon and he's loaded. In fact, I'm his last remaining relative and it's only a matter of time before the inheritance is made out in my favour. If you can get me to ...'

The doors closed on the two of them, and Hal laughed aloud. Then Clunk tapped him on the shoulder, and he turned to see the robot's annoyed expression. 'Oh yeah. *Volante*.'

'I wish you'd stop doing that, Mr Spacejock.'

'I couldn't let you spoil the fun. Kent Spearman getting conned by that Cuff shyster? It's perfect!'

'Do you think anyone wants this?' asked Sandy.

Hal saw her inspecting Cuff's ruined robot, which was still lashed to the hotel trolley. 'Help yourself.'

'Not so fast,' said Clunk. 'Technically that robot belongs to Mr Cuff. You can't keep it without a receipt.'

'Yeah, but he just abandoned it. Plus it's wrecked.' Hal glanced at Sandy. 'What do you want it for, anyway?'

'I can use some of the parts to fix Daniel's cooling problem.'

Clunk nodded his approval. 'Your intentions are worthy but you still need –'

'Inconceivable,' said Hal. Clunk's mouth kept moving but no sounds came out, and while the robot was gesturing and slapping the side of his head, Hal grabbed a piece of paper from the reception desk and wrote on it. Then he scrawled his name across the bottom and handed it to Sandy. 'Cuff gave me the robot for his fare, so it's mine to dispose of. If anyone complains they can come and find me aboard the *Volante*.'

'–ing rude and inconsiderate,' finished Clunk with a rush.

'Thanks,' said Sandy, with a grin. She turned to Clunk. 'I really appreciate all the help. It was a blast.'

Clunk's angry expression relaxed into a friendly smile. 'It was my pleasure.'

'I'm really sorry about the will.'

'I've already forgotten about it,' said Clunk. 'Take care, young lady, and best of luck with your future.'

Sandy nodded, then turned to Hal. 'Thanks for looking after me. And, er, not handing me in.'

'No problem.' Hal hesitated. 'Will you be all right? Your parents, I mean?'

'I'll cope. It's only this year and then I can move out.'

'Call us when you're ready. We'll give you a lift anywhere you want. Any planet in the galaxy, free of charge.'

'Thanks,' said Sandy gratefully.

'Do you want some money for a cab?'

'No, I'll catch the bus. It's not far.'

They watched her leave, pushing the hotel trolley with Daniel sitting side-saddle on top of Cuff's faulty robot. Hal felt a surge of anger at Baker's mean-spirited revenge. The old buzzard had set out to punish Clunk for a petty error, but the fallout had hurt other people too. On the plus side, Kent Spearman had been sucked in, and Cuff was walking away without a bean to his name.

'Back to the *Volante*, Mr Spacejock?'

'Sure thing.' As they took the steps, Hal gestured at the share certificate. 'Let's see if we can find a frame for that thing on the way. We'll look back on it one day and ...'

He stopped as a gleaming black limousine drew up to the curb. The doors opened and two man-mountains in dark suits bounced out. 'Mr Hal Spacejock?' said one of them in a gruff voice. 'We've been looking for you. Get in.'

35

Hal and Clunk were pushed into the limo, where they floundered in the deep padded chairs. The doors slammed shut, and the heavy tint turned the interior into a darkened cave. One heavy sat either side of them, blocking the exits, and as the car drew away one of them froze Clunk with a remote.

Hal blinked in the darkness, and he made out a greying, smallish man with a silk neck tie and dark glasses. 'What have you done to my robot?'

'Don't worry, it's temporary.' The man spoke in a low voice. 'He'll recover.'

'If anything happens to him ... '

'Forget the damned robot. Do you know who I am?' The man didn't wait for an answer. 'You remember my daughter, right? Dressed in white, standing at the altar, wedding ruined by a practical joker with a thirst for acrobatics?'

Hal swallowed.

'Yes, thought so. She wants your head on a platter, did you know that?'

Hal felt his neck.

'You ruined her wedding and cost me a packet.'

'I-I'll pay you back. We have lots of shares!'

'I don't want your money.' The man adjusted his neck tie.

'You've been running from my men for two days now, but you must have known I'd catch up with you in the end. Big Vinnie always gets his man. Always!'

Hal eyed 'Big' Vinnie, and he was still wondering how the powerful man had earned the nickname when a briefcase landed in his lap.

'Open it.'

Hal hesitated. Was it a bomb? A noose? A blaster to shoot himself with?

'Come on. I don't have all day.'

The catches clicked open, the lid rose, and ... Hal whistled. The case was filled with credit tiles, neat stacks of them. Fifties, hundreds ... it was a fortune!

'That barrel roll of yours, best stunt you ever pulled.'

Hal blinked. 'I–I don't understand.'

'My daughter has lousy taste in men. Instead of marrying a loyal family man, she chose a yuppie. He votes, he volunteers in the community ... he even pays his taxes. I tried to buy the guy off and he laughed in my face.' Vinnie shook his head, clearly distressed. 'A guy like that around my family ... it would destroy us.'

Hal began to understand. 'So the wedding ... '

Vinnie laughed. 'They had a bust-up after you ruined the big day, and my little girl took up with my second cousin's youngest son. Result!' He nodded at the briefcase. 'My men have been trying to give you that for two days, but you kept giving them the slip.'

'But I thought ... '

'There's something else, too.' Vinnie handed him an envelope. 'A week for you at a five-star health resort. As much food as you can eat and seven days swimming with the fishies.'

'Eh?'

'Scuba diving. It's a beach resort.' The limo stopped. 'I believe this is you?'

Hal peered through the tinted windows and realised the limo had drawn up next to the *Volante's* passenger ramp. The doors opened and the heavies helped him out of the car. They stood Clunk alongside, and Vinnie unzapped him.

'Just one thing,' called Vinnie. 'If you ever need a job –'

'No passengers,' said Hal quickly. 'Just cargo.'

'As long as it's legal,' added Clunk.

Vinnie pulled a face. 'Never mind. See you around.'

The limo drove off, and they made their way up the ramp. Hal gripped the briefcase under his arm, hardly believing his luck. Never mind Baker and his poisonous legacy, he'd take cold hard cash any day!

◆

It was a week later, and Hal was returning to the *Volante* tanned, fit and healthy. He'd enjoyed seven days of five-star luxury, but towards the end he'd started to miss his ship, the Navcom and Clunk. Ten course meals and spa baths were all very well, but nothing beat hauling cargo through the vast reaches of space ... even if he was never sure where his next meal was coming from.

Clunk gave him a warm smile as he entered the flight deck. 'Welcome back, Mr Spacejock! Did you enjoy yourself?'

'Yeah, but it's good to be back. What's been happening around here?'

'I have three cargo jobs lined up, and I repainted the passenger cabins in a refreshing shade of green.'

Hal winced.

'Come on, I'll show you.'

Hal was about to refuse, but he decided to show a little enthusiasm. 'Green, eh? Let's have a look then.'

Inside the lift he was surprised to see a new control panel. It was polished brass, and the three matching buttons had the deck numbers carved into the surface. 'You've done more than just painting, I see.'

'Oh, just a little tweak here and there.' Clunk pressed the lowest button and the lift dropped smoothly. 'Close your eyes, Mr Spacejock.'

Hal complied. 'I'm guessing it's a very bright sort of green.'

'The brightest.'

'Never mind. We can always hand out sunglasses with every fare.'

The lift came to a halt and Hal heard the doors open. He almost looked, but stopped himself just in time. Clunk obviously wanted to give him the full eye-damaging effect, and who was he to spoil the robot's fun? The floor felt spongy underfoot, and he wondered whether Clunk had glued down extra layers of cardboard. Sound deadening perhaps, so they wouldn't hear passengers screaming to be let out.

Guided by the elbow, he took several steps towards the middle of the room. Then he was turned to one side and gently lowered into one of the ratty old armchairs. So much for his nice new flight suit. 'Can I look now?'

'Go ahead.'

Hal opened his eyes halfway, ready to shut them again at the first hint of damage. Instead, they opened wide by themselves. Directly in front of him, mounted on the wall, was the biggest viewscreen he'd ever seen. At his left elbow was an automated trolley with three cup holders and a touchscreen showing a giant list of tasty snacks. To his right was a remote with more controls than the *Volante*'s flight console.

Dazed, he turned his head to take in the rest of the lower deck. The tatty old passenger cabins were gone, and in their place was a polished wooden bar with half a dozen chrome stools. There was a fully-equipped gym, a sauna, a spa bath with a gravity net and ... in the far corner, behind a bank of safety shields ... the AutoChef.

'I turned the recreation room into additional passenger cabins,' said Clunk. 'I hope you don't mind.'

'I ... I don't mind at all,' said Hal. 'It's bloody amazing.'

'Thank you.'

'Was there anything left?'

'What do you mean?'

'That briefcase full of cash. You must have made a hell of a dent.'

'Oh, that. No, I didn't touch it.'

Hal blinked. 'Where did you get the money?'

'I sold those worthless shares.'

'You'll need to explain that one.'

'It's simple. The shares were worthless because the Galactic Mining Company had no future. However, once I returned the data we recovered from asteroid K-7X ... '

Hal frowned. 'The memory module?'

'Yes, it contained a complete backup of their survey data.'

'So Galactic Mining are back on their feet?'

'Absolutely. GMC are the fastest moving shares on the market.'

'How much did you get for them?'

Clunk hesitated. 'Let's just say it paid for the refit, and there was enough left over to fund a university scholarship for Miss Sandy.'

'Great thinking, Clunk. Hey, you did get something for yourself, didn't you?'

'Some tools, spare parts . . . I don't need much.'

'If you need any more you can use the cash in the briefcase.'

'Not quite. It was all counterfeit.'

Hal laughed and shook his head. Still, wasn't it a fabulous pad? Just wait until Kent Spearman saw it! He'd turn a brighter shade of green than Clunk's imaginary paint job. 'Oh, before I forget . . . ' Hal dug in his pocket and took out a small gift-wrapped parcel. 'Here. I got this.'

'For me?' Clunk tore the wrapping to reveal a small tin of toffee. 'That's . . . thoughtful. I shall treasure this delicacy forever.'

'No, you dummy. Look inside.'

Clunk took the lid off, removed a wad of cotton wool and stared at the gleaming gold badge. It was engraved with the Spacer's Guild logo, and underneath was the legend 'First Class Pilot'. 'I can't possibly wear this. I'm only second class!'

'You've never been second class, my friend.'

'You don't understand. This can't be mine. I'm not qualified!'

'Sure you are.' Hal winked. 'I asked Sandy to hack in and boost your rank, and she found out you were eligible anyway. You just needed to fill out a few forms, that's all.'

'Inconceivable!' said Clunk.

Hal mimed trying to speak, and they both laughed.

'I do have one regret,' said Hal.

'What's that?'

'It's a real shame we couldn't get our revenge on Baker. That stunt he pulled with the will was evil.'

'Yes . . . about that. I found out Baker Corporation is hosting a dinner party next week. They're wining and dining dozens of top politicians, hoping to score a major contract. As it happens, we've been hired to deliver the food.'

'Really? After that mess with the wedding?'

'Yes indeed.' Clunk looked thoughtful. 'I think you should handle the landing. A series of barrel-rolls would do the trick nicely, don't you agree?'

Epilogue

◆

Private eye pens bestseller!

Natasha 'Lookie' Lucas, Barwenna's very own private investigator, recently released her first book to wild acclaim. Titled 'My Life with the Six Finalists' it's an insider's blow-by-blow account of the race for Baker's Legacy, complete with steamy passion, rich double-crosses . . . and vampires. When questioned about the book's accuracy, Ms Lucas admitted there were minor embellishments for dramatic effect. A twelve-movie deal is currently under negotiation, with several heartthrobs in the running for the plum role of Hal 'Grand Fang' Spacejock.

In other news, it's seven days since Baker's Legacy was settled but the great robot exodus shows no sign of letting up. Spaceport traffic is at an all-time-high as hundreds of our treasured mechanical companions depart on chartered flights. When asked where they were going, the secretive robots would only tell this reporter they were 'seeking a better future'. Rumours abound that a derelict, polluted planet recently changed hands for a suitcase full of cash, but we've been unable to verify this story.

Finally today, 'Big Sally' – daughter of waste disposal king-pin 'Big Vinnie' – announced her engagement to John 'Bulldog' Lockup, a decorated Peace Force captain famed for his crusade against organised crime. Big Vinnie declined to comment.

If you enjoyed this book, please leave a brief review at your online bookseller of choice. Thanks!

About the Author

Simon Haynes was born in England and grew up in Spain. His family moved to Australia when he was 16.

In addition to novels, Simon writes computer software. In fact, he writes computer software to help him write novels faster, which leaves him more time to improve his writing software. And write novels faster. (www.spacejock.com/yWriter.html)

Simon's goal is to write fifteen novels before someone takes his keyboard away.

Update 2018: goal achieved and I still have my keyboard!

New goal: write thirty novels.

Simon's website is spacejock.com.au

Stay in touch!

Author's newsletter:
spacejock.com.au/ML.html

facebook.com/halspacejock
twitter.com/spacejock

Acknowledgements

To Pauline Nolet, and to Jo and Tricia
thanks for the awesome help and support!

To Ian, Mike, Hugh and Fahim
Well spotted!

The Hal Spacejock series by Simon Haynes

1. A ROBOT NAMED CLUNK

Deep in debt and with his life on the line, Hal takes on a dodgy cargo job ... and an equally dodgy co-pilot.

2. SECOND COURSE

When Hal finds an alien teleporter network he does the sensible thing and pushes Clunk the robot in first.

3. JUST DESSERTS

Gun-crazed mercenaries have Hal in their sights, and a secret agent is pulling the strings. One wrong step and three planets go to war!

4. NO FREE LUNCH

Everyone thinks Peace Force trainee Harriet Walsh is paranoid and deluded, but Hal stands at her side. That would be the handcuffs.

5. BAKER'S DOUGH

When you stand to inherit a fortune, good body-guards are essential. If you're really desperate, call Hal and Clunk. Baker's Dough features intense rivalry, sublime double-crosses and more greed than a free buffet.

6. SAFE ART

Valuable artworks and a tight deadline ... you'd be mad to hire Hal for that one, but who said the art world was sane?

7. BIG BANG

A house clearance job sounds like easy money, but rising floodwaters, an unstable land-scape and a surprise find are going to make life very difficult for Hal and Clunk.

8. DOUBLE TROUBLE

Hal Spacejock dons a flash suit, hypershades and a curly earpiece for a stint as a secret agent, while a pair of Clunk's most rusted friends invite him to a 'unique business opportunity'.

9. MAX DAMAGE

Hal and Clunk answer a distress call, and they discover a fellow pilot stranded deep inside an asteroid field. Clunk is busy at the controls so Hal dons a spacesuit and sets off on a heroic rescue mission.

10. Cold Boots

Coming 2019

Ebook and Trade Paperback

The Secret War Series
Set in the Hal Spacejock universe

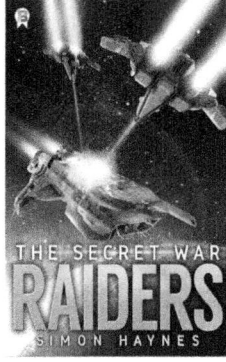

Everyone is touched by the war, and Sam Willet is no exception.

Sam wants to train as a fighter pilot, but instead she's assigned to Tactical Operations.

It's vital work, but it's still a desk job, far from the front line.

Then, terrible news: Sam's older brother is killed in combat.

Sam is given leave to attend his memorial service, but she's barely boarded the transport when the enemy launches a surprise attack, striking far behind friendly lines as they try to take the entire sector.

Desperately short of pilots, the Commander asks Sam to step up.

Now, at last, she has the chance to prove herself.

But will that chance end in death... or glory?

Ebook and Trade Paperback

The Harriet Walsh series

Harriet's boss is a huge robot with failing batteries, the patrol car is driving her up the wall and her first big case will probably kill her.

So why did she join the Peace Force?

When an intergalactic crime-fighting organisation offers Harriet Walsh a job, she's convinced it's a mistake. She dislikes puzzles, has never read a detective mystery, and hates wearing uniforms. It makes no sense ... why would the Peace Force choose her?

Who cares? Harriet needs the money, and as long as they keep paying her, she's happy to go along with the training.

She'd better dig out some of those detective mysteries though, because she's about to embark on her first real mission ...

The Peace Force has a new recruit, and she's driving everyone crazy.

From disobeying orders to handling unauthorised cases, nothing is off-limits. Worse, Harriet Walsh is forced to team up with the newbie, because the recruit's shady past has just caught up with her.

Meanwhile, a dignitary wants to complain about rogue officers working out of the station. She insists on meeting the station's commanding officer ... and they don't have one.

All up, it's another typical day in the Peace Force!

Dismolle is supposed to be a peaceful retirement planet. So what's with all the gunfire?

A criminal gang has moved into Chirless, planet Dismolle's second major city. Elderly residents are fed up with all the loud music, noisy cars and late night parties, not to mention the hold-ups, muggings and the occasional gunfight.

There's no Peace Force in Chirless, so they call on Harriet Walsh of the Dismolle City branch for help. That puts Harriet right in the firing line, and now she's supposed to round up an entire gang with only her training pistol and a few old allies as backup.

And her allies aren't just old, they're positively ancient!

Ebook and Trade Paperback

The Hal Junior Series
Set in the Hal Spacejock universe

Spot the crossover characters, references and in-jokes!

Hal Junior lives aboard a futuristic space station. His mum is chief scientist, his dad cleans air filters and his best mate is Stephen 'Stinky' Binn. As for Hal ... he's a bit of a trouble magnet. He means well, but his wild schemes and crazy plans never turn out as expected!

Hal Junior: The Secret Signal features mayhem and laughs, daring and intrigue ... plus a home-made space cannon!

200 pages, illustrated, ISBN 978-1-877034-07-7

"A thoroughly enjoyable read for 10-year-olds and adults alike"
The West Australian

'I've heard of food going off
                ... but this is ridiculous!'

Space Station Oberon is expecting an important visitor, and everyone is on their best behaviour. Even Hal Junior is doing his best to stay out of trouble!

From multi-coloured smoke bombs to exploding space rations, Hal Junior proves ... *trouble is what he's best at!*

200 pages, illustrated, ISBN 978-1-877034-25-1

Imagine a whole week of fishing, swimming, sleeping in tents and running wild!
Unfortunately, the boys crash land in the middle of a forest, and there's little chance of rescue. Is this the end of the camping trip ... or the start of a thrilling new adventure?

200 pages, illustrated, ISBN 978-1-877034-24-4

Space Station Oberon is on high alert, because a comet is about to whizz past the nearby planet of Gyris. All the scientists are preparing for the exciting event, and all the kids are planning on watching.

All the kids except Hal Junior, who's been given detention...

165 pages, illustrated, ISBN 978-1-877034-38-1

Ebook and Trade Paperback

New from Simon Haynes
The Robot vs Dragons series

"Laugh after laugh, dark in places but the humour punches through. One of the best books I've read in 2018 so far. Amazing, 5"*

Welcome to the Old Kingdom!

It's a wonderful time to visit! There's lots to do and plenty to see!

What are you waiting for? Dive into the Old Kingdom right now!

Clunk, an elderly robot, does exactly that. He's just plunged into the sea off the coast of the Old Kingdom, and if he knew what was coming next he'd sit down on the ocean floor and wait for rescue.

Dragged from the ocean, coughing up seaweed, salty water and stray pieces of jellyfish, he's taken to the nearby city of Chatter's Reach, where he's given a sword and told to fight the Queen's Champion, Sur Loyne.

As if that wasn't bad enough, the Old Kingdom still thinks the wheel is a pretty nifty idea, and Clunk's chances of finding spare parts - or his missing memory modules - are nil.

Still, Clunk is an optimist, and it's not long before he's embarking on a quest to find his way home.

Unfortunately it's going to be a very tough ask, given the lack of charging points in the medieval kingdom...

Ebook and Trade Paperback

Printed in Great Britain
by Amazon

18748053R00161